"Superbly splenailicious! No living author reinvents the English language with such conniving wit as John Vorhaus. It's time to put everything else on hold—the new Radar Hoverlander novel has arrived."

—Stephen Jay Schwartz
L.A. Times bestselling author of *Boulevard* and *Beat*

Praise for the Radar Hoverlander Novels

"Grand entertainment ... No caper-novel fan should miss this one."
—*Booklist*

"Pleasantly preposterous…what Radar (and Vorhaus) understand is that every emotional attachment can be exploited for the sake of a scam ... A lighthearted caper with psychological insight."
—*Kirkus Reviews*

"I loved this comic caper with its twisty pretzel plot, clever invented language, and an attitude that's Carl Hiaasen channeling Dane Cook."
—*Milwaukee Journal Sentinel*

"Vorhaus keeps things moving briskly, and Elmore Leonard and Carl Hiaasen fans should be pleased."
—*Publishers Weekly*

Also by John Vorhaus

NONFICTION

The Comic Toolbox: How to Be Funny Even If You're Not

Creativity Rules! A Writer's Workbook

The Pro Poker Playbook

Killer Poker: Strategy and Tactics for Winning Poker Play

Killer Poker Online

The Killer Poker Hold'em Handbook

Poker Night

The Strip Poker Kit

Killer Poker Online/2

Killer Poker No Limit!

Killer Poker Shorthanded (with Tony Guerrera)

Decide to Play Great Poker (with Annie Duke)

Decide to Play Drunk Poker

The Little Book of Sitcom

How to Write Good

FICTION

Under the Gun

The California Roll

The Albuquerque Turkey

World Series of Murder

Lucy in the Sky

The Texas Twist

A Radar Hoverlander Novel

by John Vorhaus

PROSPECT
·PARK·
BOOKS

Library of Congress Cataloging in Publication Data
on file with the Library of Congress

For reference only:
Vorhaus, John, 1955–
The Texas twist / John Vorhaus
ISBN 978-1-938849-07-7
1. Novelists—Fiction. 2. Crime—Fiction. 3. Texas—Fiction
I. Title

 Published by
Prospect Park Books
www.prospectparkbooks.com

Distributed by
Consortium Book Sales & Distribution
www.cbsd.com

Design by Amy Inouye/Future Studio
Printed in the United States of America

Table of Contents

Olivier de Havilland

A cold wind fell across the face of the west; a scratchy wet towel of a wind that poured down the front range of the Rockies, gathered speed across the prairie, and blasted into Manhattan, Kansas, slamming it sidewise across the north-south artery of Seth Child Road. Rain mixed with sleet rattled the January skeletons of the poplars dotting Kansas State University and thrummed against the casement window of a basement space in a weathered red brick building on the ragged eastern fringe of campus. Inside the lab, a goggle-eyed man in a lab coat with a slight hitch in his giddyup moved frantically—corybantically—from his computer keyboard to his laser array, cold storage units, and test bench equipment. The scientist (well, he looked like a scientist) paused to glance at his watch. He peered out the window, then back at his watch. He looked nervous. He looked nervous even though no one was looking. That's how good he was, how deep he got into his thing.

He glanced once more at his watch.

They were late.

Back on Seth Child, a boxy black pickup truck roared north. It was a new Song Staccato that, as the driver described it, "handled like an auditorium." He drove aggressively, power-merging with nary a thought to potential collisions and hitting hit holes in the traffic flow like a running back running scared. At Dickens Avenue he slewed savagely into the right-turn lane, fishtailed in the wet, hopped a chunk of corner curb, jammed onto Dickens, and barreled toward campus. A woman in the back seat moaned softly, fighting down her gorge. She caught the driver glancing at her in the rearview mirror. He may have seen her distress, but his eyes showed no mercy and he continued to drive as though hounds of hell had caught the scent of Pup-Peroni in his pants. *Damn it, Mirplo,* she thought, *learn to freaking drive.* Then she reminded herself that he wasn't Vic Mirplo just now. He was Nick Eintritt, private-equity consultant and angel investor.

And maniac driver.

Why couldn't he leave that out of his docket? wondered Allie Quinn, using common grifter slang for the package of name, personality, backstory, attributes, business cards, websites, phantom friends, bogus bona fides, and ad hoc bafflegab that comprised a con artist's adopted identity. (Allie's own current docket identified her conclusively—albeit fully fictively—as Fabrice Traynor, BSc, MBA, PhD, notionally in from Princeton, and here to lend her expertise to the task of vetting the invention they were about to see.) According to Nick, Nick was in business development, specializing in alternative-energy investments. Mostly ag-based, of course—biofuel—here in the nation's breadbasket, but every now and then something special came along.

Something for special customers.

Today's special customer, one Sterling Holton, sat in the shotgun seat, himself not terribly enthralled with Nick's driving. Holton was an adult child of prairie privilege with a tycoon scion's trust fund and a chip on his shoulder you could see from space. He hated his father—"that asshole entrepreneur"—and desperately wanted to beat the old man at his own game. Get there first for once. For once be the one to score the big score. He looked down at the electric blue clamshell case he'd borrowed from Nick to hold his money.

This might be that once.

Holton didn't know, though the two gifted grifters in his company did, that it was his hate, not his money, that made him such a productive lead. Hate caused errors in judgment. Big ones, like bringing cash to a product demo. Nick had amplified those errors by applying deft pressure (it's called rushing the mark), presenting this deal as a hush so hush you couldn't even pass papers, and with so limited a time to act that Sterling had rashly resolved, *I'll show you, Dad! I'll show you who's the genius investor!*

The Staccato bombed on, its onboard navigation system guiding Nick (when you were on the job, you always went by your docket name) through a hashtag of campus access roads to his destination. He seemed not to be paying much attention, for he always took the indicated turn at the last possible second, heaving his passengers back and forth, two unhappy corks bobbing on the sea of the Staccato's spongy suspension.

Fabrice had never been motion sick before but had no trouble recognizing the state. She pushed her cinnamon shag hair off her forehead, letting the sweat there cool. Then she threw up, just a little, in her mouth. At last Nick sprayed the truck into a gravelly parking spot outside the red brick building. He jumped out and stood reveling in the rain; having grown up in the desert southwest, he was still knocked out by the novelty of winter. Holton climbed down from the Chinese behemoth, using the clamshell case as an umbrella. Fabrice staggered out as well, thankful for the feel of solid earth beneath her feet and hopeful that it would settle her stomach.

Nick walked over to the others and drew them in close, conspiratorial. "Now look," he said, "this guy's a little twitchy, right? Off the charts brilliant, but totally paranoid. So be cool with him. He's taken a lot of heat for his ideas, as you can imagine, and he won't naturally believe that you trust him."

"What makes you think we do?" asked Allie as Fabrice, her adopted voice sounding like honey spiked with bees.

"You've seen the prospectus," said Nick. "You've seen the computer models."

"I once saw a monkey play Mozart. Doesn't mean I'm sending it to Juilliard."

Nick put his hand on her shoulder. Holton noticed her muscles clench at his touch. *No love lost there,* he thought—as he was intended to. "Look, Fabrice," said Nick, "I don't blame you for hiring yourself out to my client. Everybody needs an expert. I've got no problem with that. But sometimes the real deal is just simply the real deal. So give Dr. de Havilland the benefit of the doubt, okay? He's a pretty amazing guy."

"We'll see," said Fabrice.

"Yes," said Nick earnestly, "you will." He led them around to the back of the building. Fabrice lagged behind, and Nick used the opportunity to tell Sterling softly, "I told you to get your own consultant, and okay you got the best, but, sheesh, what a ball buster, huh?"

"Is she seeing anyone?"

Nick skipped a beat—a stumble that probably only another con artist would notice—and said, "You know, I don't know." But he did. He knew very well.

They reached the blank face of an emergency exit door. Nick tugged at the door and it came open. With a nod to the patch of duct tape covering the latch, he said, "We're expected." Just inside, a flight of galvanized steel stairs led down into a dimly lit corridor dotted with dented filing cabinets and old broken office chairs. Allie's high heels ticked along the cracked and peeling linoleum floor as she and the others walked the length of the building, past unmarked and unnumbered frosted-glass doors. This was the Christiania of KSU, an academic free state where the school's scientific minds could hack around on projects of their choosing, unfunded but also unburdened by invasive oversight. KSU had no illusions about itself. It was a practical institution and turned out a decent engineer, but it didn't have the resources or brainpower for world-class science, and anything on that order springing forth from Manhattan would be a fluke—hence this facility, officially known as the Incubator, in which de Havilland, whose credentials identified him as an adjunct lecturer, had claimed lab space according to the time-honored system for doing so: he just moved in. Behind closed doors he investigated the superconducting properties of amorphous metals and ran arcane experiments in Zwicky box contraptions that generated streams of data—though what that data represented, no one but the admittedly eccentric Dr. de Havilland could say. Were you to ask him, he would merely note that while mankind's capacity to gather groundbreaking data was increasing exponentially, its ability to interpret such data continued to just plod along.

It was before de Havilland's office door that Nick, Fabrice, and Sterling now stood.

Nick rapped softly on the frosted glass. There was silence from the other side, then a distracted mumble, the sound of unevenly shuffling feet, and the rasp of a sliding dead-bolt. De Havilland opened the door. He looked at Nick for a long moment, as if struggling to place him. Then he muttered, "Eintritt. Good, good." Leaving the door open, he turned his back on them and limped back to his lab bench. To Holton's eyes he seemed homuncular, so hunched over and self-absorbed—just how you'd expect an obsessed scientist to look. Fabrice knew that he stood up straighter than that.

Once they were inside, de Havilland looked balefully at the open door and shot Nick an imperative glare. Nick closed it, first glancing outside to make sure they were alone. Holton was impressed with the air of secrecy. It sent a shiver through him. De Havilland, meanwhile, lost himself in calibrating an apparatus comprising three triangulating lasers aimed at a glass-walled cube that measured about ten inches square. He ignored Nick's *ahems* for as long as he could, then said impatiently, "Very well, very well, step over here."

Nick ushered the others to the lab bench and introduced them to the scientist, who only reluctantly shook hands with

Holton, then wiped his hand briskly on his white lab coat, as
if it carried plague. Fabrice he ignored altogether. Said Nick,
"Fabrice, Sterling, I give you Dr. Olivier de Havilland."

Holton couldn't help himself. He practically snorted,
"Not really?"

De Havilland looked at him blankly and said, "What?"

Holton spread his hands. "Like Olivia?"

De Havilland considered this for a moment, seemed to
comprehend nothing of note, and turned his attention to
Nick. "You explained about the money?"

"I did."

De Havilland turned back to Holton. "Let me see it."
Holton went to put the clamshell case on the lab bench, and
de Havilland practically swatted it to the floor. "Not there,
you idiot. These lasers are precisely tuned. The slightest
bump or jar and the whole process breaks down." This drew
a thin *harrumph* from Fabrice, and de Havilland seemed to
notice her for the first time. He asked of no one in particular,
"Who is this bonbon?"

"Fabrice Traynor," she said, visibly bristling at the bonbon tag. "I'm here to validate your findings." She took a scur-
rilous beat and continued, "If such a thing is possible."

De Havilland became irate. "You know what?" he said,
"Get out. All of you. Just leave. There will be no demonstra-
tion today."

Nick glowered at Fabrice. "Come on, Doc," he pleaded.
"We drove all the way from Tulsa." He shot a nod at the
clamshell case. "And we did bring the money."

De Havilland considered this. He templed his fingers at
his lips and said, "The money. Yes. It always comes down to

Mammon. Well, let's see it." He gestured Holton to a scarred steel desk. There Sterling set down his case and opened it to reveal a loose pile of stacked and bundled hundreds. De Havilland thumbed through it approvingly, then shut the lid with a snap. "There was a time, you know, when scientists had patrons. Da Vinci and the Medicis, Galileo and the Catholic Church."

"The church didn't sponsor Galileo," sniped Fabrice. "They persecuted him. They tried him for heresy. Get your facts straight at least, geez." She turned to Holton. "Sterling, we have a credibility issue here."

Nick placated with his hands. "Let's just watch the demo, okay?" He turned to de Havilland. "Stick to science, Doc," he said. "Leave history to the histrionics."

They stared at each other for a second. Holton looked on, manifestly vested in having the doctor relent. They *had* driven all the way from Tulsa, and he had no mind to make the drive twice, not with Eintritt at the wheel. Besides, this was exciting, all this investigation and discovery, just the sort of hole-in-the-wall gold mine that his father would disdain. The fact that it all looked so slapdash gave it a kind of low-rent authenticity. Clearly this de Havilland wasn't going out of his way to impress. That said something. It telegraphed integrity.

Exactly as it was designed to do.

De Havilland moved back to the lab bench. His fingers danced over the keys of a battered laptop as he initiated a start-up sequence that had the lasers humming and glowing. He opened a freestanding freezer and a white cloud fell out, pooling on the floor until it dissipated. "That's just a cooling agent," said de Havilland. "It won't hurt you." He grabbed a pair of industrial forceps, reached into the freezer and extracted a small slab of metal, about the size of a deck of cards. "This, though; this would." He swung it casually past them so that Holton, at least, flinched and backed away. Fabrice stood her ground, her narrow eyes soaking up the detail of the smoking ingot and its vapor trail of dry ice.

"Superconducting metal?" she asked.

"Of course," said de Havilland. "And it would zap you like a downed power line." He placed the artifact inside the glass box. To Holton's surprise, it floated there.

Holton looked at his consultant. "How—?"

"It's voltaic," she said tiredly. "Electromagnets hold it in place." She whistled a few bars from *The Magic Flute.*

"What are you whistling?" demanded de Havilland.

"Nothing," she said. "Just a little Mozart."

De Havilland returned to his laptop and punched another sequence of strokes. The laser lights turned blue—cobalt blue, like the clamshell case that still lay on the doctor's desk—and the air took on the crackly expectancy of a summer night before a storm. "You'll smell a little ozone," said de Havilland. "It can't be helped. If I had some decent funding I could conduct this operation in a proper vacuum, where it belongs. As things are, we lose…" he paused to calculate "… eleven percent efficiency."

Again Fabrice emitted an audible scoff. Nick glanced at her sidelong. He turned to de Havilland. "Why don't you tell us how the whole thing works, Doc?" Nick tapped his own temple. "Keep it simple for us slow kids in back."

"Very well." He said to Fabrice, "Bonbon, try to keep up."

"Please don't call me bonbon."

"Would you prefer…" he paused to let the word roll out, "tart?" Fabrice seethed, but said nothing. De Havilland gestured to the lasers. "These," he said, "are light-emission heaters. They excite the target alloy sequentially. Both the alloy and the sequence are my proprietary formulas. Essentially what I'm doing is sculpting amorphous metal on a molecular level, creating a shaped electrical imbalance." Two keystrokes. The lasers dropped down to a deeper hum, almost a thrum. "What we have now," said de Havilland with a sudden and unexpected gloss of pride, "is a supersaturated energy source. Think of the potential stored here as water behind a dam. Once something breaks the dam, all that power comes pouring out."

"More than the lasers put in?" asked Fabrice, well, tartly.

"And what," asked de Havilland, not at all appreciating her tone, "would be the point of building a closed energy system if it weren't net plus?" He turned to Holton. "Do you pay her a lot? You're not getting good value."

"He's getting great value," Fabrice said, "and I'll tell you why. Because you slipped 'closed energy system' by us like it's an assumption that doesn't need testing. If the system's not closed, if it's drawing energy from elsewhere—"

"—then it's a so-called 'perpetual motion machine' and I am a charlatan, is that it?"

"You said it, not me."

"Look here—" He was perhaps on the point of uttering "bonbon," but as he saw Fabrice actually ball her fist, he refrained. "—madam, you are free to inspect this lab, the apparatus, isolate any part of the process you wish. You won't find an outside energy source because there is none. I know you won't be satisfied until you snoop around, so please, be my guest."

Fabrice sniffed. She circled the lab bench, closely examining all its components. Dropping to her knees, she checked underneath, looking for, but apparently not finding, hidden electrical leads. She cast a jaundiced eye on the cooling units, the lasers, and, finally, the glass cube. "There's energy coming in here, of course," she mused, "to power the electromagnets. But even accounting for that...." Her voice trailed off. She took a beat, then suddenly demanded, "What breaks the dam?"

De Havilland shot her a smug smile. "I thought you'd never ask." He crossed to a tiny, burnished aluminum box. "Think of this as an atomic autoclave," he said. "It sterilizes atoms."

"What does that mean?" asked Holton, enthralled.

"It halts the orbits of electrons." De Havilland opened the box and withdrew a vial full of translucent goo. "So when this gets in contact with that," he pointed to the ingot, "all these electrons," indicating the vial once more, "they're set free. They go in there and go nuts, according to the template laid out by the lasers. So that's a shaped charge, and you understand about shaped charges from atomic bombs, where if the explosives aren't aimed correctly at the plutonium, the whole thing won't go boom." He walked them back to the glass box, tilted the vial, and let a dribble of goo slide down. "You have to go slow," he said with a wink, "otherwise, boom. But if you do it right..." A dash of goo hit the cold metal block. It sizzled and disappeared, and the lights in the lab grew noticeably brighter. "…one of these will power a house." He looked at Holton. "With your investment I can build dozens, prove the concept, move to manufacturing, and get us both very, very rich." He hesitated, then with great effort and forced bonhomie, extended his hand. "So what do you say, 'partner'? Shall we do business?"

Holton ran his tongue over his dry lips.

Said Fabrice, "Are you kidding me?"

Nick strode quickly to her side and whispered harshly, "Don't queer this."

But she brushed him aside. "Come on, Sterling, this is ten ways wrong. I shouldn't even have to explain it. Let's go."

She steered Holton toward the door. De Havilland moved to block her. "You're standing in the way of science," he growled.

"Yeah, and commerce," added Nick. He backed away slowly until he reached the desk.

"All I'm standing in the way of," said Fabrice, "is bullshit. 'Too much juice go boom,' for Pete's sake. Step aside. We're leaving." She tried to push past de Havilland, but he chested her, and that fully flipped her anger switch. "Fine," she said, abruptly plucking the vial from his hand. "Let's find out how *much* juice go boom." She strode to the metal mass and held the vial out over it.

"Don't!" cried de Havilland. "It's toxic!"

But it was too late. Fabrice dumped the full vial on the core. A gout of flame shot straight up amid a billowing cloud of gray-green smoke. "Get out!" shouted de Havilland. He scrambled for a fire extinguisher. Holton suddenly remembered his cash and turned back for it. Anticipating this natural move, Nick was waiting for him, and from across the room flipped Holton the case.

Well, *a* case.

De Havilland spewed foam onto the blaze, but the smoke just billowed higher. "Oh, that's not good," croaked the scientist. He suddenly coughed and collapsed to the floor, clawing frantically at his throat. "Run, you idiots! Run!" Holton gawked. Nick grabbed Holton, threw open the door, and dragged him from the office. Fabrice ran after them, and the three sprinted back through the basement, up the stairs, and out into the damp January afternoon. Holton's heart raced.

"Let's go!" shouted Nick, beeping his truck open as he ran.

Fabrice, though, paused and looked back at the building. "Serves the bastard right," she muttered grimly. Just then she saw a figure sprinting out the front door of the building with no sign of a limp at all. "Son of a bitch! Nick!"

Nick looked up to see de Havilland jump into a sports car and speed off. He got in the Staccato and fired it up. Fabrice pushed past Holton, and the case came flying out of his hands. "Wait here!" she ordered. "Call the police!"

Holton tried to tell her that the case had slid under the truck, but she was already in the cab. Nick stomped on the gas. Holton watched, gobsmacked, as the thundering Chinese hardware shot away.

Then he looked down. Turns out those clamshell cases aren't that strong after all. Nor, after all, do stacks of filleted paperback books look much like Big Bens once you get them out into the light.

And behind the wheel of the sports car, Olivier de Havilland—otherwise known as Radar Hoverlander—looked not much the worse for all the colored water vapor he'd inhaled. He glanced at the clamshell twin he'd thrown onto the seat beside him. All those hundreds.

All those pretty, heavy hundreds.

The Zizzles

When Sarah told them about it later, she said that it happened like this....

On the steps of a medical center in downtown Austin, a young mother named Sarah Crandall stood crying, her frizzy brown hair hanging limp along her cheeks as the tears streamed down. Her son, ten-year-old Jonah, reached for her hand. He wanted to comfort her so badly, but when he touched her, the pain came: electric shocks at his fingertips, followed by searing pins and needles over the back of his hand, up his arm, and across his chest, then sharp darts straight into his heart. In this little battle between love and pain, pain won. Jonah pulled his hand back, ashamed. Sarah looked down and suffered for her son. She knew the word for what he was experiencing, *dysesthesia*, but she couldn't imagine his anguish, his sense of touch so brutally hijacked and bent to his torment in agonizing patches of skin fire or the razor-blade rasp of even the softest cloth against his skin.

How do you live in a world where soft doesn't exist? Where hugs don't exist? How is that fair to a ten-year-old?

But the zizzles, as Jonah called them, wasn't the word on Sarah's mind. The new one was the one she carried out of the medical center: *prions*.

Now, at last, she knew the enemy's name.

Folded protein, she thought. *What's a folded protein? What does it look like? A taco? A towel? Why is a misfolded one bad?* She couldn't wrap her unschooled mind around the science—a baffling maze of amyloids, fibrils, and spongiform encephalopathy—but she easily understood prions as tiny PAC-MANs munching countless infinitesimal holes in Jonah's brain. The image was inadequate, but it didn't matter. The holes were killing her son. What else did anyone need to know? She reached down to rub his head, but refrained. Lately even that had become intolerable to him. The doctors said it would get worse. Then, worse still, it would stop. That's when they'd know. That's when the brain would lose its war.

She fought to stop her tears. *Can the waterworks, sister,* she told herself. *Be strong for your son.* She pulled herself together, straightening up, wiping her eyes, and smoothing the pleats of her yellow blouse. As she pushed her hair off her face, she looked back up at the medical center behind her, all soaring steel and grand glass panels. So much science in there, so little help.

That's what they mean by incurable.

"Come on, buddy boy," she said as brightly as she could manage, "let's go home."

They started down the steps of the plaza. Jonah took them two at a time. He seemed to have recovered his mood.

Dysesthesia ebbed and flowed, Sarah knew, and thank God for the ebbs. Though lately it seemed to be flowing higher, faster. Were the holes getting that much bigger? Were the prions that hungry? She fought back the thought—*No waterworks!*—as she called out to her son, "Be careful, Jonah, those steps are steep. You don't want to trip and—" she caught herself. *What? Hit his head?* The idea was almost funny, considering everything. She smiled in spite of herself.

Sarah noticed a man at the bottom of the stairs. She saw immediately how sad he seemed, and how used to the sadness he looked.

But he brightened when he saw Jonah come clumping down the steps, taking the last five of them in a giant leap. "Stuck the landing!" cried the man when Jonah touched down. This amused Sarah, until he added, "Good job, Jonah!"

She raced to the bottom of the stairs and demanded, "How did you know my son's name?"

"Well, I must have just heard you use it…." he said. Sarah felt foolish for a moment, until he added with a shy smile, "Sarah Crandall."

"Wait, you know my name? No one said that."

"I know. I'll explain in a moment." He offered his hand. "I'm Adam Ames." She shook it because that's the polite thing to do.

Ames turned to Jonah. "I'm not gonna shake your hand, little man. I know how much that would hurt." Sarah gasped. Ames turned back to her and looked her in the eye. She saw the sadness return. "What does he call it?" Ames asked.

"Wh-what?"

"His condition. Has he given it a name?"

"The…zizzles."

Ames nodded his empathy. "Zizzles. That makes sense. Mine called it the creepy-crawlies."

"Yours?"

"My Dylan. That was at first. Later he just—" Ames cut himself off. "I'm getting ahead of myself," he said. "Can I buy you a cup of coffee?" A nod to Jonah. "Some juice?"

His Dylan? "Will you tell me how you know me?"

"Of course," said the handsome and somehow innately charming man. "I want to tell you." He touched the back of her hand with his palm. "Believe me, it's worth sitting down for. We'll just go across the street."

Sarah looked at Jonah. "What do you say, buddy? Want some juice?"

Jonah seemed to give the question more consideration than it deserved, as if his brain were slow to process his thoughts. "I like juice," he said at last. "Juice is good."

They went to a Java Man opposite the medical center. Sarah and Jonah waited at a patio table while Adam got drinks. As he walked back toward them with two Latte Sapiens and a Caveberry Supreme, Sarah gave him the quick once-over. She judged him to be perhaps thirty years old. Some muscles. No gut. Sandy blond hair in an un-self-conscious Super Cuts cut. Smooth face, strong chin. Straight teeth. Good vibe. Vibe was important to Sarah.

She thought his vibe was okay.

He caught her staring at him and again essayed his shy smile. "Are you checking me out?" he asked indulgently, like they were old friends who had already been through everything together. Sarah thought it was a strange way of being, yet somehow comfortable—and comforting. "It's all right," Ames assured her. "I'd check me out, too. Who wouldn't? Some total stranger seems to know your name? That's worth checking out for sure."

"Yes," said Sarah. "Please, let's start with that."

"Of course." Ames sat down. He toyed with the lid of his cup. It took him a while to speak. He seemed nervous, unsure of where or how to begin. "I have a friend, a nurse," he said at last. "She told me about you. About your son and his…situation."

Jonah disappeared into the soothing music of his iPod, which he usually did when grownups started to talk. The last thing he needed was more doctory gab. Sarah regarded Ames with the appropriate circumspection of a mother looking after her child's interest. "This nurse," she asked, "she told you we had an appointment today?"

Ames nodded. "So I loitered out there to meet you, to see how it went."

"Why is that of interest to you?"

"My son had what yours has."

"I thought he might from what you said. I'm so sorry."

"And I'm sorry for you." His eyes rose to the façade of the medical complex across the street. "I know how hopeless those offices are. All bad news and no real answers. When I heard about your son, I just had to reach out."

"Well, I appreciate your sympathy."

Adam fixed her with a firm gaze. "I'm not here to offer sympathy, Sarah. I'm here to offer hope."

"I could use some hope."

"I know you could." He sighed to the depth of his soul. "I could've used some, too." With that he told his story.

He said he'd been a divorced dad with sole custody, doing his best, getting along, raising a decent son. There were women in the picture again at last, one he even thought he might marry. Then, two years ago, it all came unspooled. It started with small complaints: phantom rashes, tingling fingers, clothing that chafed. The doctors thought Dylan had an allergy. It wasn't an allergy. It grew to thrashing nights when even his bed sheets burred his skin and cheated his sleep. They thought it was psychosomatic. It wasn't psychosomatic. It was a neurodegenerative brain disease. Not Creutzfeldt-Jakob or mad cow, but closer to them than to measles. And rarer. So much rarer. Adam uttered a name, Karn's Syndrome, and Sarah shuddered. The very mention of it made her blood run cold. She could see that it had the same effect on him, and although it was misery that connected them, she drew odd solace at being in the company of, at least, someone who knew how she felt.

"Do you live here in Texas?" she asked.

"New England," he said. "But I've been all over the world with this."

"What do you mean?"

"When they told me Dylan had Karn's, I thought, 'Okay, let's give him drugs. Let's get this over with.' But you know as well as anybody that there are no drugs, no 'over with.'" Sarah nodded. "I thought that was impossible. I thought modern medicine studied everything, cured everything. I thought there must be some way to fix it." Again he brought his eyes to hers, and this time she saw fierceness there. "And you know what? There could be, if someone would just damn look. But Karn's is too rare. There's no money in curing it. Have you heard what they call it?" Sarah shook her head. "An orphan disease. I find that ironic, don't you?"

Sarah said nothing, but her heart went out to Ames. She spontaneously reached out and patted his hand.

"We got six months," said Adam quietly. "I don't count the last two. By then he was on machines, and—" Sarah blanched. "Oh, I'm so sorry," he said. "I didn't mean—" She thought he was going to cry. It wouldn't have been unmanly, just rue for the pain he'd provoked, pain they both could well understand. There was an awkward pause, which he finally filled with, "Of course my lady friend left. I don't blame her. What I was going through, she didn't need to be burdened with that." Sarah found that attitude admirably compassionate. She hadn't been nearly so charitable toward Jonah's absentee dad, who in all of this had proven as useful as a chocolate teapot.

"Plus, I wasn't at my best," Adam continued. "I was angry."

"Angry?"

"At medicine. God. Angry at me. I was vile. No fun to be around."

Sarah sighed. "I can relate."

His voice softened. It almost caressed her. "I really wish you couldn't," he said. "Anyway, in the end I was just drained, you know? Numb. I might have stayed that way forever. I wanted to. But then I got a phone call." He scratched his left eyebrow. "This was about a month after the funeral. It was a Swiss pathologist. He'd been trying to get in touch with me. He'd heard about Dylan and had a promising therapy he wanted to try. But of course he was too late.

"A thing you'll learn about me," said Adam, "I'm like a dog with a bone sometimes. Stubborn. When you call a boy untreatable, when you condemn him like that…no. No, that I can't accept. I understood that Dylan was gone, but I had to know if he could've been saved. I can't explain it. I just had to know. So I went to see this man. And I learned the truth about orphan drugs."

"Which is what?" asked Sarah.

"Okay, in civilized places, let's say here, Europe, a few other spots, sometimes there actually is help for orphans. Radically reduced testing-pool parameters." He saw that he almost lost her on that one, so he backed up a bit. "With most diseases, when they do clinical trials, there's lots of subjects to test on. But with Karn's…we're not statistically significant. So how do you test? Well, you test fewer people and hope for the best. You also fast-track approval for some of these drugs, and give the developers extended patents or market monopolies, incentive to do the research. But here's the thing. Only big pharma scores. They're in bed with the FDA or its overseas counterparts. The little guy never has a chance, especially if the little guy is studying something as rare as Karn's.

"Sarah, you don't know me. I'm just a guy you met on the street. But I'm one in a million who knows what you're going through, and I know something you don't: This doctor's therapy would've worked. I'm sure of it. I've seen his studies." He squeezed her hand urgently. "I've seen his subjects."

"Subjects?"

"Chimps. Bonobos. He gives them Karn's, then he cures them."

"How?"

Adam laughed self-consciously. "You're asking me? I'm not a scientist. To me, Karn's was this acid dissolving my baby's brain."

"I see it as PAC-MAN."

He smiled wanly. "Prions. Misfolded proteins. What's that?"

"I know, huh?"

"But this man, this Dr. Gauch, he's found some way to fold them back."

"You mean—?"

"That's right, Sarah. A cure. And when I found that out, well, I just had to find someone, anyone, I could help. I had to make Dylan's death be not in vain."

"And your nurse friend?"

"I have a lot of 'friends' like that," he admitted. "People on the lookout for, well, for people like you." He ran his fingers through his hair, a gesture that seemed to sum up all his struggles. "I'm not a rich man. Caring for Dylan really spent me down. But I've put a fair amount of money into this, into tracking folks down. I've come to understand that it's my mission. I'm here to help you, Sarah."

He embraced her with his eyes and she felt her heart melt. "Sarah," he said, "your son doesn't have to die."

3

Magic Bullet

This money is a problem."

"What do you mean?"

Radar looked down at the stacks of cash in the blue case on the coffee table. It wasn't an overwhelming take, but on top of all the other money they'd made recently.… "We might have too much."

This comment surprised both his girlfriend, Allie Quinn, who stood with her arm around his waist, and his best friend, Vic Mirplo, sprawled on the rented leather couch in the Austin apartment they now shared. They both knew what kind of a roll they'd been on, a roll that had begun with the Albuquerque Turkey, an elegant performance-art fraud they had helped Radar's dad perpetrate against a Las Vegas hard guy named Wolfredian. It had netted them substantial fresh green and ended with Vic faking his own death, which he had found fun.

They weren't surprised to find themselves well bankrolled, just that Radar should find it a problem somehow.

Mirplo asked, "Too much money, Radar? How does that work?"

Of course they couldn't remain in Vegas after they'd buttoned up the mark—finished the con in con-speak—so they smudged their identity trails and resurfaced here in a low-rise condominium complex in Austin's lakeside Doke neighborhood, from which beige base they had spent the end of the old year and the start of the new quite successfully prospecting America's heartland for unprotected pockets of liquidity like Sterling Holton's. Their dockets these days were one-offs, purpose-built for each snuke, or scam. Some relationships, however, naturally recurred. The fake fury generated by Allie and Radar, for example, always worked a treat to put marks on the wobble, especially the ones who thought they might have a shot with her. Allie was a fading fan of the play. She hated arguing with Radar, even in the world of make-believe. After all they'd been through, from the crosses and double-crosses that first forged their bond through the tests they'd faced as two lifelong dissemblers struggling to build a bridge of honesty between them, they had arrived at last at a certain casual intimacy. *We two are one,* thought Allie, and any grifter's script that moved them off their unity seemed strange to her, even undesirable now. *Especially now,* thought Allie with a secret smile. But if that was Radar's problem, too, she couldn't quite see the connection. So she waited for him to finish speaking his mind. That's one thing she loved about him: He always spoke his mind.

"It just sits there," said Radar. "It's starting to weigh us down."

"I am so not tracking your target," said Vic. Of the three, he was the least experienced in the art of the con. No rookie for sure, but he'd been the worst sort of grunt-level grifter, unschooled and unskilled, till Radar came along and raised him up from the short cons and street gags that had been his clownishly unproductive stock in trade. While Vic had grown quite a lot in the years of their association—he'd had plenty of headroom in that area—he remained intensely loyal to his friend, and admired the devious dodges and elegantly executed scripts that Radar cooked up.

"I'm just thinking, we're plenty well rolled now. There's not much point in more of the same. After a while, the money just piles up."

"Which is exactly what it wants to do," said Mirplo. "Money loves company. It likes nothing better than to pile up around other money." He thought for a moment, then added, "But, hey, look, if you've got a debt wish, I'll be happy to make yours ameliorate."

"I'm not sure that word means what you think it means," said Allie, who was well used to Vic's verbal assaults on the English language. These were often synapse accidents, but equally often intentional linguistic mangles that Vic treated as twisted points of pride.

"Sure it does," said Vic. "Vanish or disappear, like Amelia Earhart."

Allie chuckled. When she buried her knuckle into Radar's shoulder blade, he leaked an *aah* at the sweet pain she produced. "What's really up, bub?" she asked.

"How many perpetual motion machines can we invent?" he replied. "Do it long enough, we just become hacks."

"Yeah," said Vic. "Rich hacks." He shook his head with exaggerated sadness. "Lamentable."

"What do you want to do instead?" asked Allie. "Something bigger?"

"I don't know," said Radar. "Bigger…different.…" The thought settled on him like a cloud, but he shook it off, for Radar Hoverlander did not dwell in clouds. He dealt in logic, practical aspects, cool analyses of best paths. Balance was a strength of his game. It's what made him a top grifter and the three of them a top team. But there was so much more to him than that. His talents, like his interests, ran off in all directions, from reading lips (in several languages) to rebuilding engines, from free climbing to BASE jumping to that ancient mariner's art of knot tying, macramé. He could pitch a tent in the dark, land a plane in a pinch, and, if he had a decent manual to work from, probably perform surgery. A polymath, they'd called him as a kid, and they imagined that he didn't know what that meant. "Whatever," he said. "I'll think of something."

For a week now Allie had been looking for a certain opening, and when she saw this one, she took it. "I know something you can think about."

"Oh," said Vic, affecting a bored tone, "I already know this."

Allie's eyes went wide. "You do?"

"My driving never made you sick before. You got the flu?"

"No."

"Eat some bad clams?"

"No."

"Then…" Vic got up from the couch, throwing a whole-body shrug at Allie. "Tell 'im."

"Tell me what?"

Allie clasped her hands around Radar's neck. "I'm knocked up, lover. What do you think about that?"

A grin split Radar's face. "I think that's great, amazing!" He kissed her hard. Utterly without affectation, he said, "I am going to be the best dad ever."

"And there you go, Radar," said Mirplo. "All the more reason to keep up your game."

"Nope. All the more reason to do something better. Be an example for the kid."

"It's the goodness virus is what it is," said Vic. "I always knew you had it in you." He jabbed an accusing finger. "You've shown flashes."

"Vic, trust me: My morality is as frankly self-interested as ever."

"Whatever you say…Daddy."

Just then a dog ambled into the room, and this would be Boy, Radar and Allie's unlovely but deeply loving big pooch of mixed provenance. Last year, using nothing more than sleight-of-mind and the power of persuasion, Radar had rescued Boy from the hands of a tweaking, violent meth head. This may have been an outbreak of the goodness virus Vic named, for grifters, peripatetic by nature, generally avoid the canine encumbrance, but in this case Radar embraced it. He loved his ragged old hound, missing ear and all. Behind Boy came Emily, a feisty toy spaniel playfully hectoring his back legs, an assault she seemed to have been at long enough to prompt Boy's strategic advance into the room with the people in it; perhaps Emily would attack a lap instead.

"When's Em going home?" asked Radar. "She's driving Boy crazy."

"Sarah said they'd be back by now. Maybe the appointment ran late."

"And how is it exactly that we became the neighborhood dog sitters?" asked Vic.

"Emily's cute," said Allie. "Boy likes her."

"Boy wants to stomp her," said Radar. "She won't let him nap."

"Well, there you go. She's keeping him fit."

The doorbell rang. Vic flipped down the lid on the clamshell case and slid it under the couch. Allie kissed Radar's cheek. "You're taking this pretty calmly, big guy. You know it's gonna put you through changes."

"Change is good," said Radar. "Change is growth." He turned to Vic and stage-whispered, "Don't worry, I'll freak out later."

Allie opened the door for Sarah and her son and immediately noticed the sparkle in her neighbor's eyes. "Well, you look happy, Sarah. Good news from the docs?"

"No," said Sarah, "same news from the docs." Then she added explosively, "But Allie, I found a cure!"

"What?"

"I mean, not me, I didn't find it, but this fellow did, this man I met."

As she blurted the detailed tale of Adam Ames, Radar and Vic were soon exchanging looks. Allie intercepted these and said sternly, "It doesn't have to be that."

"It's that," said Radar.

"It doesn't have to be," she repeated, though with less conviction. To Sarah she said, "You'd better come in." She got Jonah a snack and settled him down with the dogs—dog fur still soothed him. He disappeared back into his music as Radar led Sarah to the couch.

It turns out there really is such a thing as snake oil. It's a homeopathic cure, made from Chinese water snakes and traditionally used to relieve pain because Chinese water snake fat is just dripping with—here comes the big word—eico-apentaenoic acid, which may or may not, you know, relieve pain. Nineteenth-century railroad coolies brought it to the Old West, where it met modern commerce and morphed into what we now know it to be: patent medicine; placebo-effect drugs pimped by fictive testimonials.

Snake oil. It's the first thing you see on display in the Quackery Hall of Fame.

One thing, though: With snake oil, at least there's a product. Radar surmised that this Ames was selling nothing to Sarah but Sarah's own hope. According to the script for this snuke, she would soon be touched up for front money, and if she proved promising, they would settle in and just milk her. They? Of course they. You don't run this scam on your own. There was Adam's nurse friend for starters, plus other friends like her, bird dogs ensconced in medical suites far and wide. These could be honest people even, except that they took cash to steer potential victims Ames's way. Eventually, if needed, there would be the Swiss pathologist, armed with ironclad proof of a cure just a few tantalizing dollars away. It was a pretty straightforward snuke, one of many designed to strip-mine a desperate and vulnerable mother. In scam circles it was called the Magic Bullet.

A shiver ran through Radar. *Have I done things like that? I have done things like that.*

Radar studied Sarah. She'd moved into the complex a few months ago, shortly after they had. She was relentlessly peppy, despite her son's condition, and always had a cheery greeting when they met in the elevator or laundry room, or in the parking lot beside the building. Then their pets became playmates—whether Boy liked it or not—and she became a fixture among them. Radar had been leery at first, for it was ever his policy to hold citizens at arm's length. But Sarah and Allie had a relaxing, chatty gal-pal friendship of a type Radar had never known Allie to have before, and for that alone he was willing to make room for Sarah in their lives. For his part, Radar found Sarah's fluffy nature soothing, like dog fur in its way.

Now she's facing a Magic Bullet, and how do you break that bad news? "This Adam Ames," he began, "don't you think it's a pretty big coincidence that his son had your son's same rare disease?"

"But he explained that," said Sarah. "He's been looking for people like me."

"He's always looking for people like you," said Radar. "He knows how desperate you are."

"I don't understand."

Vic cut bluntly to the chase. "Sister, he's a con artist. He doesn't have a cure. He'll let you believe he does, and make you pay for your belief. Has he asked you for money?"

"No."

"He will."

Sarah's mouth formed a small o as the allegation sank in. "But that's horrible," she said. "Who would do a thing like that?"

"It doesn't matter," said Radar a bit too quickly. "The important thing is to cut him off right away. Don't initiate contact. If he contacts you, tell him you've lost interest. You can't let him get his hooks in."

"But what if he really does have a cure?"

"He doesn't."

"How do you know?"

"We…" said Allie, "we know people like this."

"You *associate*?" With a word, Sarah conveyed her shocked contempt.

"Hey, now," said Vic, but with a look from Radar he put his affront back in his pocket.

"Sarah, I'm sorry," said Allie. "He's selling smoke."

"But what if he's not? I can't leave this stone unturned. I can't leave any."

"Sarah…." Allie reached out a hand.

Sarah practically slapped it away. "No. No, I have to know."

"You'll just be wasting your money."

"So? I'd spend every cent I had to save Jonah. Wouldn't you if it were your son?"

Radar and Allie exchanged looks. For the first time in their lives, such a question was not rhetorical. Nevertheless, "That's the attitude they want," said Radar. "It's what they feed on."

"Feed on? You make him sound like a vulture."

"He is."

"No, he's not. I *know* he's not. I looked him in the eye."

"So he's a skilled vulture," said Vic.

Tears welled up in Sarah's pale blue eyes. "I don't understand why you want to hurt me like this."

"Honey," said Allie, "we're not trying to hurt you."

Sarah angrily rose to her feet and brought Jonah out of his iPod. "Come on, Jonah, let's go."

Radar knew that this friendship hung in the balance. Under other circumstances, he'd have cut ties without a single backward glance. But this was different. If they didn't act, she'd be hurt, badly hurt, not in just her wallet but her soul.

Is it the goodness virus?

What the hell, she's a friend.

Radar said suddenly, "We'll meet him."

Sarah sniffed. "What?"

"If he contacts you again. We'll be your well-meaning friends. The skeptics, you know? If he's in the game, he'll expect skeptics and have a script for them."

"Script?"

"A set of steps to get your money."

"And you'll recognize this...script?" Radar nodded. Said Sarah, "What kind of people are you?"

Allie said, "Not the kind you think."

Sarah sagged. "An hour ago I was so happy." Allie crossed to her and held her in an embrace. Sarah pulled back and looked in her eyes. "Is there any chance you're wrong?"

"There's always a chance," said Allie.

"That's all I need," said Sarah. "All I need is a chance."

4

Mirplovian Logic

Quick in, quick out," said Radar. "We get next to this guy, move him off Sarah, move on with our lives."

Radar, Vic, and Allie had gone out to a nearby Rudi's Eatateria for a skull session and some awesome chili pot pie. Under the table, Radar's hand kept creeping up Allie's leg. It couldn't help itself, that hand. It felt giddy. "What's our script?" asked Allie, not so much ignoring his hand as refusing to dignify it with a response.

"Just like I said. Skeptical friends. Our Sarah blew in all bubbly; we just want to make sure the bubbles are justified."

"This Adam Ames," said Mirplo, "shouldn't we Google him first?"

"Already have," said Radar. "He returns exactly as Sarah saw him. Citizen, widowed father...."

"Wait, widowed?" asked Allie. "Sarah said he was divorced."

"Maybe she misremembered," said Radar.

"True," intoned Vic. "Witness memory is crap, this we know." He cocked his head at his own thought, then pulled from his hip pocket a small Hello Kitty notebook and a pen, and laboriously inscribed, *Witness memory is crap, this we know.*

"What are you doing?" asked Radar.

"Starting my book."

"You're writing a book?" asked Allie. "About what?"

"This. Us. Life on the razzle. How grifters roll."

"It's a memoir?"

"Maybe. Maybe a how-to. Maybe a novel. I haven't made up my mind."

"Uh-huh. And when did you decide to write this book?" asked Allie.

"Just now," said Vic. "When I said that aphormism about witnesses. I thought, 'That's good. Someone should write that down.' So I did."

"And the notebook?" asked Radar.

"Oh, I started carrying it."

"What for?"

"In case I decide to write a book. Come on, Radar, keep up." Radar didn't keep up; he gave up. At a certain point, Mirplovian logic becomes so circular that there's no sense in following it. You're much better off just staying in one place and waiting for it to swing back around. He and Allie exchanged the looks of indulgent parents as, unbidden, Radar's hand went scurrying back up Allie's thigh. That was one happy hand. Fatherhood, it seemed to be saying, would suit it fine. Allie was happy with the happy hand, but she wondered how it would feel when the giddy wore off. The truth is revealed under pressure, Allie knew, and this would be a new kind of pressure for the man she loved, a man whose own childhood—dead mom, disconnected dad—left lots to be desired in the department of love. Not that hers didn't—all those foster homes, all those mauling foster fathers—so it was new ground for them both. It didn't feel like shaky ground right now, but of course that could change.

"So maybe that's a hole in his docket," said Radar, returning his brain's, if not his hand's, attention to the apparent inconsistency in Adam's story, "and maybe we can dig there. But whatever we find, we don't make a big deal about it. We just help Sarah disengage. If this guy's on the snuke that's fine, his affair. We just want him to snuke elsewhere. He doesn't need to know anything about us." Radar indicated Vic's notebook. "He can read about us later when we're a bestseller."

"Anyway," said Allie, "widowed or divorced, how does he present to the world?"

Radar woke up his tablet computer, the latest generation Grape with its distinctive purple synthetic rubber frame and ergonomic teardrop form. He started off by showing them Adam's handmade website, a static offering of financial services, evidently created many years ago and barely updated since. Next came a Facebook page, a tribute to the departed Dylan with hopes of heaven and statements of Adam's dream to give back. Surfing on, Radar pointed out a couple of online medical-discussion forums where Adam's name had popped up; someone wondered if Ames was on the level, a question to which no one had replied. The website didn't strike Allie or Vic as particularly fishy, but that didn't mean much. It could easily have been an artifact of an earlier snuke, or for that matter something recently created and anchored to an heirloom URL in order to backpredict a credible narrative. All three of them could do that sort of work before breakfast. As for the tribute to the son, there was nothing in the language that definitively linked Dylan's tale to any particular hospital or medical institution. To the casual eye, it seemed to be the heartfelt and intimate grief of a bereaved dad, long on emotion and therefore plausibly short on detail. To a more jaundiced eye (of which this particular table seated six), it conveniently blocked any tangible avenue for further investigation. And the discussion boards? Either dead ends or misleads designed to look like dead ends. You couldn't tell. These days, any decent grifter could create a solid, internally consistent online reality. It meant nothing and proved nothing, any more than a bogus badge proved you were a cop.

After they'd run through all the links, Mirplo went back and lingered over the Facebook page, with its slide-show display of photos of Dylan. He furrowed his brow in concentration, and Radar feared he might birth another aphormism, but instead he said, "Interesting thing about these photos, they're all park shots." He pointed out how all the pictures in the slide show showed Dylan skateboarding or rollerblading, kicking a soccer ball, or just hanging out, all at fall foliage time, presumably somewhere in New England, which Ames had told Sarah was home. Vic zoomed the display to maximum resolution, whereupon the grainy quality of the images became evident.

"Telephoto," said Radar.

"That's how I see it," said Vic.

"But a good job," added Allie. "You could easily mistake

them for natural close-ups." She winked at Vic. "Unless you had a suspicious mind." Mirplo graced her comment with a minimal nod of his head, as if she had bestowed upon him great praise. As with his knack for barbarous malaprops, Vic had a gift for missing meaning—or perhaps he just convened reality at a location more to his liking.

"The boy's wearing different outfits," noted Radar.

"Shots taken on different days," postulated Vic. "Ames photo-stalks for a week, maybe, builds up a decent portfolio of snaps."

"That's going the extra mile," said Allie.

"You'd have to," said Radar. "You can't filch pictures like this from Flickr, not when people like us can do reverse-lookup match searches on your images. You'd have to use originals, nothing that could be tracked."

"It's still not dispositive," said Allie. "Maybe he just liked shooting telephoto of his son."

"And maybe my great-grandfather invented PEZ candy," said Radar. "In fact, I'm sure he did. I inherited a piece of the patent. Want to buy out my share?"

She smacked him for teasing her, which quickly led to some tickly monkey business and kissy-face, whereupon Mirplo declared, "Bored," and buried himself in Radar's Grape.

Radar suddenly pulled back from Allie and said, "Triton!"

"Excuse me?"

"For a name. Boy or girl, doesn't matter. Cool either way."

"Too soon," said Allie, kissing his nose. "Way too soon."

"Triton Hoverlander," said Mirplo, reaching for his notebook. "I'd better write that down."

5

We Smell a Rat

You *called* him?"

"You said you wanted to meet him," said Sarah.

Radar leaned against the door frame of his flat, regarding Sarah, who stood before him in the taut jeans and tight sweater that comprised her standard winter outfit. He didn't quite know what to make of this. "No, I said if he contacts *you*." Radar had assumed Sarah would understand that her default move was to take no action, but he looked into her guileless eyes and realized that this wasn't the case. *Spell everything out,* he told himself. *With this one you have to spell it all out.* Radar sighed. "Come on in," he said. "Where's Jonah?"

"Fishing."

"I'm sorry?"

Sarah self-consciously mimed donning a helmet, and Radar understood her to mean the new class of virtual-reality video game controllers, the ones where you do everything with your eyes. A glimpse here, a blink there, and, apparently, you've landed a bass. "I can't get him off it," she said. "I know it's not good for him, but when he's there, he's not.…" She rubbed her arm in a way that conveyed her grasp of the agony her son's own skin brought him. "He's better when he's distracted."

Radar nodded. He took her into the kitchen and sat opposite her at the long, narrow farmwood breakfast table that had come with the place. "Okay," he said, "tell me what you told him. Don't leave anything out."

He must have sounded brusque, for Sarah suddenly, defensively, asked, "Where's Allie?"

"Hot yoga. A last going-away sweat before she gives it up for the duration."

"Duration?"

"Of the pregnancy. She'll be taking, I don't know, cold yoga instead."

"Pregnancy?" Sarah's wide blue eyes poked soft holes in the air.

"Oh, God, she didn't tell you? I would've thought—"

Sarah's arms shot across the table to wrap around his neck and she dragged them both half to their feet. "Oh, Radar, that's wonderful!" She hugged him as hard as their awkward embrace allowed, and mashed her cheek against his. Then she withdrew, but not before, Radar had to think, nuzzling for a beat. "Well," she said sternly, "I'll have words with Allie later. The things a friend has to hear from her friend's boyfriend. Are you going to make an honest woman out of her?"

"That might be harder than it looks," said Radar, deflecting the question, as he did most personal ones, with a joke. Sarah, though, didn't quite get it. She laughed self-consciously, cued more by his tone than his words.

"Well, congratulations either way," she said as she sat back down. She clasped her hands and placed them on the table. "Okay, what I told Mr. Ames...Adam. I told him that you were like me: excited to know there was hope for Jonah." She lowered her eyes, "Only maybe not so inclined as me to believe. I just asked him to have a word with you, tell you what he told me and answer all your questions. He was completely agreeable. He offered to meet right away. Surely that's not the sort of thing a scoundrel would do."

Radar asked, "Did he think it was odd, having the neighbors look in?"

"Not particularly. I told him we were friends. I confessed I'm not very good with money, which is true, and that you're really good with numbers, which is probably true, huh?"

"Probably."

"I did tell one little lie."

"What's that?"

She spun her answer into a timorous question. "That you helped me rent my condo?"

"Helped how?"

"With the paperwork." She paused, then added, "And the security deposit."

"What? Why?"

"Well, to give you say-so. Didn't you want that? I thought you would want that. So that if we smell a rat, then you can be the one to tell him no thanks."

"Oh, man. Oh, Sarah." Radar pinched the bridge of his nose with his thumb and first finger.

"What? What did I do wrong?"

Christ, thought Radar, *where to begin? With overselling the goods? Building unnecessary backstory? Abdicating authority. And binding me to you with debt. Hell, that alone would wave a red flag.* Said Radar, "Unfortunately, you told him we smell a rat."

"No. I said it's only fair to include you in my decisions."

"He won't take it that way. He'll see right through it." Radar reflected for a moment, then added, "Which actually might not be so bad. Now that he knows you're backstopped, maybe he'll bail, go after softer marks. Maybe he'll just never set up a meeting."

"Oh, but he already did."

"What?"

"Tomorrow at noon, at the Hyatt downtown. Honestly, Radar, maybe you're just too suspicious. I mean, if he were a con man, would he be staying at the Hyatt?" Radar couldn't begin to answer. Where did she think con men stayed? In tents? She continued. "Radar, listen to me: I told him we were friends. Are we friends?"

"Of course."

"Then as my friend, I have to ask you a favor: Keep an open mind. If you're right about Adam, then okay, he was just a straw I had to grasp. But if you're wrong...if this is real...Radar, I can't afford to not know." She braced him with her soulful blue eyes, conveying all her vulnerability and need. "Will you meet him?"

Radar nodded. What else could he do? "I'll meet him."

Sarah rose from the table, came around to his side and gave him a proper hug. "Oh, Radar, thank you so much!"

She lingered there with her arms around him. "You know, I know I'm no genius or anything, but you have to admit I'm at least a little bit smart."

"How so?"

"Well, I picked you for a friend, didn't I?" She pecked his cheek and, as with the nuzzle, held the kiss a beat too long.

6

You'd Think It's a Scram

Radar Hoverlander had a saying, which Vic Mirplo had perhaps recorded in Hello Kitty by now: "Make the latest possible decision based on the best available information." You don't win in the grift, Radar knew, with sloppy, untested assumptions, even when the play seemed obvious, as this one did. You find things out. You keep an open mind (whether Sarah asks you to or not). The internet evidence was inconclusive, but one would expect that. So he'd just have to look this Ames in the eye and take his true measure. That said, he had to admit that he expected to find what he expected to find: a paltry grifter on the make. It might be some creative variation of that, but it certainly wouldn't be a miracle cure. In the narrow world of Radar's cool logic, miracles did not exist. He figured to size up Ames, confirm his suspicions, and then make him see he was drilling a dry hole.

Which Mirplo didn't quite get. "Why not just put the

fear on the guy?" asked Vic as he barreled the big Song Staccato down Lake Austin Boulevard toward downtown. "Lean on him. Make him melt. I'll do it if you like."

"I don't want to confront him," said Radar. "I just want to ease him down the road. Besides, thug docket?" He theatrically eyed Vic's sticklike build. "You really think you could pull that off?"

"Oh, very nice," said Vic. "Very supportive." He mimed writing in his notebook. "*Radar disrespected me as muscle. I swore I would have my revenge.*"

"Dark," said Radar. "Brooding. I like it." They drove on until they reached the north end of the 1st Street Bridge, where Radar got out. As a matter of standard grift hygiene, Radar arrived at most meetings on foot, for why expose your vehicle, its contents, or its license plate to potentially prying eyes?

He thought about Mirplo as he headed over the bridge. When they'd met, Vic had been a bottom feeder, selling bogus tickets or even public parking places to unsuspecting tourists at concerts and sporting events in Los Angeles. Radar liked to think that he'd taught Vic a thing or two, imparted some wisdom, but mostly he'd just watched him evolve. Gone was the scared street mook from the days of the California Roll, their plot to rob China one penny-skim at a time. Gone too was the pretentious artist manqué of the Albuquerque Turkey. Now he was just Mirplo, a man who was, in Vic's own words, "uniquely one of a kind."

The 1st Street Bridge crossed one of the world's few bodies of water that's both a river and a lake: a dammed segment of the Colorado River, here known as Lady Bird

Lake. At the far end of the bridge Radar dropped down a flight of steps and made his way along a well-groomed path to the Hyatt's lakefront grounds. There he hopped a fence, skirted the swimming pool, and found a rear entrance to the hotel. Thus he came upon the lobby from behind and stood in the shadow of a service corridor, watching Adam Ames. The latter sat near the reception desk in one of two buckety, burnt-orange leather chairs. He had a slender leather briefcase by his side, and occupied his time with a copy of the *Austin American-Statesman*, glancing up just often enough to keep tabs on lobby traffic. To Radar, Ames seemed intense, engaged, maybe a tad apprehensive, but this told Radar nothing: Either Ames was who he was, or else he knew better than to act otherwise just because probably no one was watching. This disappointed Radar, for he had expected, and half hoped, to catch a fellow grifter with his guard down. After a few moments' quiet observation, Radar retreated back through the hotel, retraced his steps past the pool, and entered the hotel through the main front entrance.

Sarah must have described Radar's appearance—his wiry frame, boyish round face, and unruly mop of brown hair—for Ames seemed to recognize him at once. He stood with a self-conscious smile and extended his hand as Radar approached. They introduced themselves and made a bit of small talk, and then Adam said, "If you're wondering, it's miles."

"Miles?"

"Airline miles. How I'm able to stay here." Ames's wave indicated the Hyatt, its pink marble and ash concierge desk, and the entrance to the Marker 10 expense-account restaurant. "I used to travel a lot, racked up a ton of miles. Finally have something useful to spend them on. Do you want to sit down?" Ames started to sit, then paused, waiting for Radar to take the lead, as if he were not quite sure what was the proper protocol here.

Radar, reading Ames's agitation, asked, "Mr. Ames, am I making you nervous?"

"Adam. Of course you are. I…from the way Sarah talked about you, I was half expecting a hit man."

"Not seriously."

"Well, I didn't *really* think so, but still.…" Ames took a breath. "I gather you think I'm some sort of flimflammer. I've never…no one's ever thought of me like that before. I'm having some trouble dealing with it."

"Then let's slow down," said Radar. "Are you okay here in the lobby or would you rather we talked in your room?" He asked the question just to see how Ames would react, for con artists had a long tradition of burnishing their scams with appropriately swanky surroundings. It was well within the realm of possibility that this lobby was no more than Adam's office, and that he was no more overnighting at the Hyatt than Radar.

But Ames's reaction was unremarkable. "No, this is fine," he said, settling back into his chair. "They haven't made up my room yet." Which, again, told Radar nothing: It was either preplanned bafflegab or a genuine response. Adam gestured Radar into the opposite chair, then picked up his briefcase and set it on the low glass coffee table between them. "So, 'Radar,'" he said, "that's an unusual name."

"I get that a lot."

"As in O'Reilly?"

"As in airborne threat detector, but I get that a lot, too."

"So what would you name your own kids? Sonar? Loran?" Ames smiled weakly as he essayed the joke, but the fact that Radar had been talking baby names, joke names, with Vic and Allie somehow brought Adam's comment to him at an odd angle and temporarily locked his reaction. It was a tiny stumble on Radar's part and had the effect of leaving Ames floating, momentarily, in a conversational void. After an awkward pause, Ames carried on. "Well, anyway," he said, "I guess I have some explaining to do." He opened the briefcase. "Now, I have some reports here, lab findings...." Ames rummaged inside and withdrew a binder-clipped sheaf. "It's not much. I don't...I'm not great at presentations. You'll get the gist of what Dr. Gauch is driving at. It's pretty straightforward. I really can't add anything to it."

"I'll take a look at it, Adam, and if I see anything that looks like it'll work for Sarah, we'll be in touch. But that's how I want to leave things today, okay? We'll be in touch with you."

"Uh-huh. When?"

"I'm not sure you understand."

"No, I understand, I understand." Ames leaned back in the round leather chair, frowning. "Guilty until proven innocent." He interlaced his fingers behind his head. "Wow," he said. He fell into silence. To Radar it almost seemed as though he was having a conversation with himself. Finally he spoke. "There's something I learned with Dylan," said Ames. "Something about acceptance. You face a situation, you say, 'I can resist this or I can embrace it.' I don't mean that I wanted Dylan to die, but I had to participate in his death as an ally, not an adversary. That I was with my son, really *with* him, while he shed the agony of his broken brain and left this life, well, it's made lots of things easier for me since. I think it saved my sanity." Ames took a breath. "So now here we are. I'm trying to help Sarah, and I guess you are, too, in your way. If you have a role to play in this, her sentinel or whatever, then I can either resist that or embrace it. I choose to embrace it, and if I have to climb a mountain of your skepticism to do so, so be it. So let's start again. Just tell me what I have to do to prove myself to you."

"I'm sorry," said Radar. "I've seen situations like this before."

"Are you a doctor?"

"No."

"Then what do you mean you've seen situations like this before. This is a medical situation."

"It's also financial."

Ames asked plaintively, "Am I asking for money? Have I asked anyone for money?"

"Will you?"

"Well, not me, but the clinic. They have to keep the research going. As I told Sarah, they get no support from official channels."

"I see." Radar rifled through the documentation he'd been given. Nothing immediately jumped out at him as bogus, but he doubted it would stand up to close scrutiny. "Very well," he said, standing up. "I'll give these papers all the consideration they deserve."

Ames leapt to his feet. "Listen, I appreciate that you

think you're looking out for Sarah and Jonah, but remember one thing: *It's not your son who's dying.*" He raised his voice. "For someone looking out for their interest, I think you're overlooking the possibility that this might actually save his fucking life!" He looked around, self-conscious at his language, then engaged Radar with pleading eyes. "Radar, I don't know what makes you such a suspicious person, and I don't know why Sarah gave you the say-so in this, but at least ask me some questions. At least make me feel like you heard me out. The way things are," Ames pointed to the printouts, "that might as well be toilet paper. It is in your eyes. And I don't understand why you're so prejudiced against me. You don't even know me. If you don't mind my saying so, you're really a closed-minded guy." That point resonated with Radar, who realized that he was, despite policy, letting himself be guided by untested assumptions. Could he really say, based on what he had seen so far, that the guy was a fake? No, he could not. So he sat back down and gave Ames a chance to tell his tale.

Adam did a comprehensive job, outlining his hunt for breakthrough research on Karn's and, having apparently found it, his equally fervent search for someone in need. Radar heard nothing in the narrative that lifted it above the level of a yarn, yet nothing that manifestly unraveled it, either. It had the ring of, if not truth, verisimilitude; Ames sounded like a normal person recounting normal events—if you bought the central premise that the tragic death of a son could turn a man's life into a crusade, and the secondary premise that a cure for Karn's was out there, undiscovered or at least unexploited by the medical community at large.

Radar could neither buy these premises nor reject them outright. So he shot a couple of questions.

"Sarah says you're divorced."

"Well, yes. And widowed."

"Excuse me?"

"My wife died during the separation."

"I see." Well, that answered that. Or not. "How? Karn's?"

"No," said Ames. "Karn's is not hereditary, just an unhappy accident. The wiring in your brain goes bad."

"Good thing it's rare."

"I wish it weren't. Then maybe there'd have been a cure for Dylan."

"Yes, as you told Sarah. Why did you meet her on the street? Why didn't you—"

"What? Email? Text? IM?" Ames looked Radar square in the eye. "What would you do with such correspondence?"

"Trash it."

"Trash it. Right. Because you'd think it's a scram."

"Scram?"

"You know, a con."

"Scam," corrected Radar.

"Scam, of course. I'm new to this language. I'm…new to the whole idea. I thought if I showed up here, flew to Austin, made the trip, that would make me seem more legitimate somehow. Show my commitment. Now I see that it just shows my, I hate to say, naïveté. Radar, can I ask you a question?" Radar said nothing, just waited for Ames to continue. "If I were who you…I'm trying to think of the right way to put this…someone who you legitimately had to keep out of Sarah's life, what kind of man would I be? I don't mean the question rhetorically. Who did you fear you would meet?"

"You really want to know?"

"Yes."

"Some people prey on weakness. I don't like them preying on my friends. Which brings us back to..." Radar stood to go, "don't call us, we'll call you."

Which, he well knew, they would not.

7

His Pollyanna Docket

When the short winter days were mild, Radar, Vic, and Allie would sit out on their balcony to read or work or just mark the sun's march across Lake Austin and over the far hills of Laguna Loma. From here, five floors up in their shoreline condo complex, they could see downriver to the Tom Miller Dam and upriver to nothing in particular. Today they occupied themselves with the paperwork of Adam Ames, looking for what Vic dubbed the smoking gun of hooey. To this point, it remained unfound.

The documents came across as a hasty potpourri of available information, just the sort of found artifacts an earnest, honest-Abe Ames would pull together to mollify the suspicious friend Radar purported to be. There were photocopied research reports, laboratory data sheets with timelines showing Karn's in remission, and a couple of web-press fluff jobs: happy journalism about prospects for a cure to this heartbreaking disease. Regarding the latter, Radar had planted enough faux news stories in his time to know how easily it was done. For that matter, these could be legitimate articles about legitimate wins against Karn's, and yet be completely unconnected to Ames, apart from the fact that they had passed through his printer.

Ames also provided the mission statement and available financials for the Gauch Institute. The mission statement was a standard medical reacharound about the betterment of mankind, but the financial information gave Radar pause, for it was the practice in scams of this sort to skimp on that, yet here was a deep drill into the clinic's funding sources, research budget, and revenue projections. Radar handed the report to Vic, who skimmed it and passed it on to Allie.

"What do you think?" asked Radar.

"Those are some lily-white numbers," said Allie.

Vic's fingers danced across the surface of his Rabota, the sexy new Russian tablet computer that everyone seemed to want but only able navigators of the international gray market (such as Vic) could get their hands on. He found and opened the Gauch Institute's own annual report. "And they match the Institute's," he said.

"Why is he selling the financials so hard?" asked Radar.

"Because he can," said Allie. "Because they're there." She added, referencing her own tablet, a next-generation Geoid, "Just like the medicine is there. Radar, this all looks square."

"So it's a piggyback play," said Radar. "Ames goes fake middleman between Sarah and them. Leverages their authenticity."

"Or," said Allie, "he's exactly who he says he is."

Radar braked. He looked at Allie. "You don't mean that."

"Why not?" she asked. She waved her hand at the documentation. "Show me anything here that really proves otherwise."

"All this could be faked," said Radar dismissively. "Besides, 'scram' instead of 'scam'? That business about the miles? The lengths he went to to meet her? The guy is way overselling his Pollyanna docket."

"You don't know that. You only feel that."

"Allie, we've seen this play before. Hell, we've *run* this play before."

"What Radar's saying," said Vic, "is if it barks like a duck, it's a duck."

"Ducks don't—" Allie didn't bother. She merely repeated to Radar, "You don't know that."

"It's the Samaritan gag, straight out of the playbook. And now that we know it's a piggyback, we can challenge him to liaise with the Institute. When he can't do it, we win."

"We win? A mother's hope for her son is destroyed, and we win?"

"That's not what I mean and you know it. Apart from the money, apart from getting scammed, Sarah needs to focus on Jonah right now."

"Don't you think that's her choice?" Allie wasn't sure Radar was wrong, but it irked her how Radar was sure he was right. "At minimum, she could put herself on the Institute's map, make Jonah a candidate for treatment."

"That's fine if she wants to do that," said Radar. "Only not through Ames. He'll dead-end her money and she *won't* get on the Institute's map."

Allie grabbed the big water bottle she now felt compelled

to carry with her everywhere and downed a significant chug. She felt herself becoming frustrated with Radar. Was it hormones already? The thought made her cheek twitch. Morning sickness. Ridiculous thirst. Food cravings next, she supposed.

Allie admired and appreciated Radar's bright and shiny reaction to her pregnancy, for it was unguarded, and in a Hoverlander, unguarded moments are rare. She felt she could trust that Radar wanted a kid, but here in her fifth week, ambivalence was Allie's middle name. Not about the body stuff. That she could handle. But Allie, as a damaged child of damaged parents, with further damage inflicted by all those fosters, feared she'd be a damaged parent, too. She looked at Radar and knew she could count on some of his courage to carry her. *This is a good man,* she thought. *Against all odds, a good man.*

When they first met, Allie thought Radar was damaged, too. He had to be, or why would he be attracted to someone damaged like her? By now, though, she had met Radar's long-lost father, the roguish Woody Hoverlander, himself a con artist of the first water, and she understood that her link with Radar was the game, not the pain. He had been trained in the grift, raised in it from birth, prodigiously talented and soon great at it, but he never got a chance to show off for the person who mattered most. Through her he had filled a long unrequited need. So she drew comfort from his comfort and accepted his acceptance of her. That he showed off for her made her something of a surrogate, and she accepted that, too.

She just worried that he was showing off now.

"Radar," she said, "I don't get you. We've done diligence. You met the guy. So he acts too innocent. So he misuses a word." She shot a look at Vic. "Like that never happens around here." She leafed through the documents. "I don't see anything here that barks like a duck, Radar, and if you're honest, I think you'll agree. We've done our job. We can let Sarah handle this now."

"End-around Ames direct to the Institute?"

"If that's what she chooses. But Radar: *She* chooses."

"No. She's not that smart. She'll screw it up."

Something in Radar's voice shot through Allie to a place deep inside her, for she detected his sense of protectiveness, a protectiveness she'd have sworn he reserved only for her, or possibly for Mirplo at certain particularly clueless points in his past. She said, "Radar, do I have to quote you to you?"

"What do you mean?"

"'There's two kinds of problems in this world, my problem and not my problem.'"

"She's right, Radar," said Vic. "I've heard you say that."

"We can tell Sarah what we've found—and what we haven't found. We can suggest a course of action. Anything beyond that is making not our problem our problem. I don't understand why you'd want to do that."

"And I don't understand how you can be so cold. Sarah's in trouble. This Ames is bad news."

She pointed to the papers. "You can't prove it with this. Radar, she's my friend, too, and I don't want to see her hurt any more than you do. But you can't trash the guy and dash her hopes just because you've got a hunch—"

"It's more than a—"

"It's a hunch! And if you sell it as more than that, you're not telling the truth, and you're not doing a service to a friend."

"I see your point," he said at last. "But I'm not done digging."

"That's up to you," said Allie coldly. "The rest is up to her."

Vic glanced back and forth between Allie and Radar. He hated it when mom and dad fought.

Later that night, after Allie had gone to bed, Radar found Vic sitting at the kitchen table, messing with his Rabota, and said, "Let's have a closer look at those pictures of Dylan. If we knew where that park was, we'd know Adam's home base."

"Maybe."

"Likely. Look, if you're right that he photo-stalked some stranger's kid, it would have to be someone familiar, someplace familiar."

"Where he could exploit a routine, like?"

"Exactly."

"Like where the kid plays after school."

"Like a park." Radar tapped open his Grape and navigated to the Dylan Ames tribute page. "This park."

"You know what?" said Vic. "Let's have a closer look at those pictures."

"Excellent idea."

Vic navigated his tablet to the same page. They clicked through the pictures, scanning for location clues in the backgrounds. Most were leafy frustrations of featureless green, but one showed Dylan grinding a rail in a skate park, with a sign behind that read, *Town Ordinance 3.14, No*

Skating After Dark. Radar called it to Vic's attention.

"What?" asked Vic, staring blankly at the photo.

"What what? All we need is to find the town with this ordinance and we're home and dry."

"How will we ever…?" Vic started, then stopped. "Race you?"

"Go!"

And off they sped through a slew of government databases, PDFs of regulations in parks-department manuals, and microfiched municipal statute books. Their fingers hopped and danced across their tablets in a ballet of hacking and cracking that each had internalized through the practice of long years. God, was it getting to be long years already? Well, yeah. They were both pushing thirty and, as Vic would put it, no springing chickens. Through long practice, then, of wielding the internet to find marks, hide tracks, or support short stories, they'd become adept at ferreting information and habituated to the lines of logic (yes, logic, even for Mirplo) that would guide them through their search. Still, *Town Ordinance 3.14,* that was a bit of a needle in a bytestack.

It took Vic ninety seconds.

Radar got there first.

"Here we go," he said. "Athol, Massachusetts. 'Town Ordinance 3.14: There will be no use of skateboards, roller skates, rollerblades, bicycles, or any other human-powered conveyance for any purpose other than point-to-point transportation between the hours of sunset and sunrise.'"

Vic meanwhile had already located Athol, a town of ten thousand people some two hours' drive west of Boston. He studied a map of the place. "Skate park might be closed for the winter," he said, "but there's a pond right there. If it's frozen there'll be hockey. Let's see." He accessed a keyhole satellite that offered earth views as current as the last orbital pass. It wasn't strictly legal for Vic to visit, but nobody seemed to have minded so far, or anyway caught on. "It's frozen," he said. "Infrared says sixteen inches."

"Plenty enough for hockey. Zoom in."

"Zooming." A moment later, Vic said, "Yep, they've cleared a rink."

"Then I guess it's worth a visit," said Radar. "You want to check it out?"

"Austin to Boston, baby." He gave his friend a mischievous smile. "Speaking of babies, what are we calling yours today?"

"Oh, I stopped doing that. Can't be obsessing over names for the next nine months." Mirplo just stared until Radar relented. "Coyote."

"Coyote Hoverlander. Not in a million years will Allie go for that."

"You're probably right."

"But you're cool with this, aren't you?"

"What?"

"This. You know, daddyness."

"Yeah, you know what? I think I am. It'll be fun. Daddyness. Raise the kid in the business."

"Thought you were tired of money."

"Not that business." He tapped his temple. "The thinking business. I'm looking forward to tuning that tool."

"Oh, now I get it. You've discovered your immortality. Gonna train you up a new model Hoverlander, better than the original."

Radar said sternly, "Athol, Vic."

Vic left the next morning. Late that afternoon, Sarah ran into Radar in the hall between their apartments and asked about the meeting with Ames. When he told her the jury was still out, she smiled and hugged herself. It made Radar feel strange to see a hope so misplaced, yet so fervent. He wished he could be wrong. He wouldn't bet that he was.

I bomb out to Athol (writes Vic Mirplo) in a rented Song Salsa, a ridiculous kiddy compact that fights my every effort to squeeze performance out of her malnourished four-banger, rubber band steering and little red wagon wheels. A Mirplo doesn't belong in a car like this. A Mirplo belongs in a candy flake Caddy, 1959, convertible, with fins that cause local atmospheric disturbance when they pass.

But the last one just left the lot, so I'm stuck with this.

Beneath leaden winter skies, Athol is brown, the color of a brown goat. I easily find my way to the park. I don't need directions; a Mirplo knows his way around. A crust of ice crunches beneath my feet as I cross the park to the shore of Silver Lake. There I see the ad hoc hockey rink, its perimeter defined by heaped walls of plowed or ploughed snow. Kids sit on the snowbanks, about two teams' worth, lacing up their skates. My timing couldn't be better, like my timing always is. I shift my leather duffel to my left shoulder, looking cool, and bestow myself upon them.

"Mirplo," I announce.

"That supposed to mean something?" asks one of the boys. From the look of him, I guess his name is Tommy.

"Just want you to remember it," say I. "Case I get famous."

Tommy slides back and forth on his blades. It's about a foot down to the ice from where I stand, but his face is level with mine. Even accounting for skates, this is a big galoot. That's good. I like my galoots big. "What would get you famous for?" he asks.

I look him dead in the eye and say, "I'm writing a book." I whip out a printout of Adam Ames's picture and shove it in his face. "You seen this mug?"

"Mug?" asks Tommy's buddy, who I judge to be Wayne.

"Face. Appearance. Physiognomy." I speak slowly and clearly, as if to infants. "Do you know this jamoke?"

"Why? Is the book about him?"

I square my jaw. "The book," I say, "is about punks who ask too many questions."

Tommy and Wayne exchange looks. And then they laugh. "Okay," says Wayne, looking around, "where's the hidden camera?"

But my jaw is still set. "No camera," I say, then ask again, "Do you know the guy?"

"If we did we wouldn't tell you."

"Figured as much." I nod toward the near net. "How about a shootout?" I drop the duffel and kick it open. A pair of skates falls out. Black leather bruisers. Even my skates look tough. The other kids stir, thinking, *This could get good.* Of course it could. With a Mirplo it always gets good. Let's see what these Massachusetts Athols are made of. "Here's the deal," say I, "ten shots on goal. I make more than half, you spill all beans. If not, you keep my skates."

"What would I want with your dog-ass skates?"

"I keep my dough in there." I grin, slit-eyed. "And ten to one on a Mr. Franklin says you can't half shut me down."

Tommy skates backward in a lazy weave. "I'm a pretty good goalie," says he.

"I'm a pretty good shot," say I.

"Then let's get it on."

On it is gotten. Borrowing some local lumber from a gaunt, angular chick named Valerie I assume, I lace up and glide out on the frozen plane. It's bumpy. Kids need a Zambezi. Zamboni? An ice resurfacer. I stretch my calves and they feel good. Then I do a few quick sprints up and down the ice and I can tell that they're impressed with my speed. Can a Mirplo skate? Of course a Mirplo can skate. Well, since last night.

I've always been a quick learner.

Someone chucks me a puck and I make it dance on the ice, flicking the stick like a snake's tongue. Tommy takes his position in the crease. The others gather round, all going "Woot, woot!" for Tommy. All except Valerie. She looks at me with doe eyes.

Chicks get crushes so easy.

I make my first run at the net, and send the shot wide on purpose, just to check his tendencies, and yep, he goes left. So next I come right, and he easily stops that shot, anticipating that I'd try for his off side. So now he thinks he's got me figured out, only guess what? Now I'm riding the levels between what I know and what he thinks he knows, and it's child's play to get him leaning the wrong way. Which he does, over and over, as I rack up the goals. I shoot him a couple of cupcakes, so he can look good in front of the girls, but the conclusion is foregone. I beat him with brains, like you do.

We skate back to our gear, and I can see the admiration on Tommy's face. He appreciates this moment as a life lesson in humility. Very likely he will be transformed, as people often are when they meet me. "First things first," say I. "You owe me ten bucks."

"What?"

"Ten to one on the Benjamin, remember?" I open my hand flat. "Cough up." Tommy coughs up a crumpled sawbuck. Best ten dollars he ever spent. "Now, tell me about the guy."

Tommy sifts through his memory for the trenchant details. I can tell he's starting to like me. Well why not? Who doesn't like a Mirplo? "Yeah, he came around last fall, asked if he could take some pictures. He offered good money. He could've been a perve. Could've been a...." Tommy gropes for the phrase.

I help him find it. "Photo hobbyist?"

Tommy nods. "Either way, he paid."

"And bought us beer," pipes up Wayne.

Figures. Scum like that would naturally abet underage drinking. "Well, no beer from this quarter," I aver, "but let me ask you this: He live around here?"

They all shake their heads. But then Valerie says, "I know what he drives."

Bingo!

"A Song Signature."

Mentally my jaw drops. A *Signature*? Those bad boys push 600 horses and go from zero to too fast too quick. Of course, they cost more than the house you grew up in and rock the mileage of a backhoe loader, but they sure are pretty: low white wedges you simply can't ignore. And every one is autographed like a lithograph. Signature, man, that's a rare breed.

Be on the lookout for that.

I get ready to split. "All right, kids, that's rock 'n' roll. Be cool, stay in school." I toss my duffel over my shoulder and hump it on out of there. Not before giving Valerie my skates. Something to snuggle with at night.

As I walk away, I hear someone mutter, "That's a cool guy."

Of course I'm cool. I'm a Mirplo.

And cool is how I roll.

8

The Gun Smoketh

They sat around the kitchen table, eating baba ghanoush on pita chips, something Allie had never been fond of before, but now, suddenly, couldn't resist. Vic had just gotten back and was raving about New England clam chowder, and to Allie that sounded good, too. *With about half a bottle of Tabasco sauce, mmm.* Mirplo told them he'd tracked down Ames through his car. It hadn't been hard. "They don't exactly drape the landscape," said Vic. "I asked a few car fans around town. They were happy to tell me about it. They'd never met a real Formula One driver before."

Allie smiled. "So now you're a Formula One driver?"

"According to me I am."

"Vic, why do you do that?" asked Radar.

"What, oversolve the problem? Same reason you do, dude. That's where the fun is. Besides," he tapped his noggin, "you're the one saying to keep the tool sharp. If you always have a story to tell, you'll never be short a story. We writers know that."

Radar shook his head. "The amazing Vic Mirplo."

"Many people say so." He turned back to Allie. "The guy's got a McMansion in Orange, the next town over from Athol. The Signature, meanwhile, is frequently seen at the Orange Municipal Airport, for our hero also owns a plane, or leases it. Plus a boat. And a couple other cars. Museum-quality stuff, they say."

"Did you check out his place?" asked Radar.

"Of course," said Vic. "This ain't my first chicken dance."

"And?" asked Allie.

"He's put a lot of money into it."

"New money?"

"Nope. Been at it since he moved in. Got solar. Got sauna. Raluca likes it."

"Raluca?" asked Allie.

"The girlfriend. Says he's lived there three years. It's mad stylish inside. Artwork up the wazoon. That's the word she used, wazoon. She's not exactly strong on English. And apparently in Romania they don't see a lot of direct-to-door marketing."

"What'd you sell her, Vic?"

"Nice little rug shampooer. It'll last 'er a lifetime. Well, it would if it ever arrived."

"In any case," said Radar, "that sounds like stable money. So now we can hypothesize that he's been running games for a while, pluck-and-ducks, with a specialty in medical mischief. He finds his Sarahs, flies out to meet them, fleeces them, and recycles the proceeds into new toys." Radar turned to Allie, "But it isn't dispositive, is it?"

"Nope," said Allie. "Just because he splashes money around doesn't make the gain ill-gotten. Sorry, boys, I still don't see a smoking gun."

"Never fear," said Vic, tapping his Rabota, "I've got that, too."

As it turned out, one of Mirplo's new race fans had a sister-in-law with cancer. From out of nowhere, Ames had become her new best friend, supporting her in her time of need, and soon producing exciting reports of cures out of Mexico. "She wrote him a lot of checks," said Vic. "I have copies. Plus emails. The gun smoketh."

Allie and Radar reviewed the evidence on Vic's tablet. When they were done, Allie said, "We'd better show Sarah."

That evening they brought Sarah in and laid it out for her, chapter and verse. It was not a happy moment, no sense of triumph in unmasking a rascal. She sat on their couch, her hands clasped tight in her lap. Boy lay at her feet, not moving, seemingly in tune to the potent portent of the moment. Or perhaps he napped. "So then he's rich?" They nodded. "He told me he wasn't." Sarah looked at the images of the cancelled checks and shook her head sadly. "Of course it isn't true. How could it be true? I don't deserve that kind of luck." Just when it looked like she was about to start leaking tears, a renegade thought made her face brighten. "Unless he has the cancer cure, too, though, right? He could have both."

"He doesn't have either," said Allie gently. "Sarah, he doesn't even have a son."

"What?"

"Dylan isn't real. He made him up."

"No," Sarah protested. "No, that's too much."

Radar nodded to Vic, who had tracked down the boy through his skate pals and now showed Sarah a shot of him holding yesterday's paper.

Sarah blinked. "He's alive?"

"He's somebody else. Someone else's son."

Sarah fell silent, processing all the evidence before her. "Yes," she said at last. "Yes, I see he is." She squared her shoulders. "Well, that's it, then. I'm going to the police." The others said nothing, but their stone faces told her plenty. "What, I can't even do that?"

"It would be better if you didn't," said Rader. "Most likely it goes nowhere. This sort of case rarely does. But it could stir a certain hornet's nest. With Ames, I mean. Guys like him, you don't want them mad at you."

"Why not? What could he do to me?"

Radar mentally surveyed the many ways a man in Adam's line of work could wreak havoc on Sarah's life, just for spite. He could rape her credit rating, of course; that would be easy. Do back-office nastiness to her medical insurance. Sell her identity on the black market. Sic other swindlers on her. Put her on terrorist watch lists. Get her arrested. Radar didn't bother sharing these scenarios. Instead he said, "Don't worry about that. Just make a clean break and send him on his way. Once he knows it's no sale with you, he'll move on."

"They do that? These…con people?"

"Sure they do," said Vic. "The ol' shade 'n' fade. There's always other fish to freeze."

She looked bewildered. "What is he talking about?"

"Few people know," said Radar.

"He means marks, honey," said Allie. "Potential victims.

Look, just don't have contact with Adam. Let him pass out of your life."

"Of course," said Sarah. "I mean, if I can't have him arrested. But it doesn't seem fair. It seems like he should be punished."

"A lot of people in this world go unpunished," said Radar. "With some it's best just to give them a wide berth."

"What about you?" Sarah joked dimly. "Should I give you guys a wide berth?"

An awkward silence ensued. "I don't know what you mean," said Radar levelly.

"I'm sorry," said Sarah, covering her mouth, "I apologize. What a thing to say. It's just...."

"It's just that you can't help noticing how much we know about his world."

"No, no, it's none of my business," Sarah said, flustered. "And just rude. To accuse you guys of being...bad people, and after all you've done to help me." She stood up abruptly and dusted her hands theatrically. "Well," she said, "no more Adam Ames. No more foolish dreams. Again, I'm sorry for...."

"It's not important," said Radar. "Don't worry about it. But don't have this moment with Ames, understand? Whatever he proposes, decline politely and say goodbye. Con artists don't like being unmasked. It hurts their pride, and then they can lash out. Keep what you know to yourself."

Sarah nodded her understanding and departed, but she left an odd, unpleasant mood in the room. Well, it happens from time to time. You rub up against a genuine innocent and see the dark side of your business model. Every grifter goes through it. You either harden your heart or find another line of work. Vic shook off the moment by sitting down to record a bent, Mirplovian version of current events, right down to the fish to freeze.

Radar cleared his disposition by downloading baby books, which made Allie chuckle indulgently. "You're gonna obsess all over this, aren't you?" she said.

"Why not?" said Radar. "I plan to be a thorough dad."

"Thorough?"

"Thorough. Comprehensive. The whole package. Cognitive play. Changing diapers. Two a.m. feedings...."

"I think that might be my department."

"And I'll be right there with you, babe. Sleep-deprived right along with you. They're gonna say, 'That Radar Hoverlander, he's almost a mother.'"

"They say that now," muttered Vic.

"Radar, let's not go overboard."

"Fine, fine, have it your way. I'll be an aloof and distant dad. Little Pandemonium will hardly even know me."

"Pandemonium?"

"Only if it's a boy. Pandemonium is no name for a girl." His eyes went to a faraway place. "Although, Panda...." He paused. "Panda Hoverlander?"

"I don't think so." Allie turned to Vic. "Have you been writing these down?"

Vic nodded. "So far I like Madrigal and Flintlock."

"Oh, I *so* hope we have twins."

A few days later, Radar reported back on his reading and informed Allie that she was probably far enough along to expect to start getting cranky.

"Cranky? Why?"

"It's genetic. Your DNA tells your hormones to make

you disagreeable as a test of your mate's loyalty. If he bails, you're not so far along that you can't land another one, but if he puts up with you at your worst, then you know you've got a keeper."

"Radar, do you know the phrase 'critical thinking'?"

"Of course."

"Apply it to your reading."

"I'm just saying, if you become irritable I will totally understand."

"Go for a run," snapped Allie.

"See? This is it!" crowed Radar. "This is the irritable!"

"Go for a run," she repeated, and Radar suddenly got it that he should go for a run.

He crossed the Colorado River below the Tom Miller Dam and followed the Redbud Trail all the way out to Washington Hollow. The day wasn't too cold, probably not much below fifty degrees, but the wind had some bite to it, and it buffeted Radar when he ran into it or across it as he wove his way through the West Hills, past the water treatment plant and the widely scattered ranch houses with their pools tarped over for the winter. Whenever Radar ran, he tried to empty his mind. He did this by focusing strictly on the visual, absorbing the passing landscape like cinematography. Today, though, he couldn't get clear of the thought of himself tarred with Ames's same brush. Radar always thought that, despite his avaricious aims, crossing paths with him wasn't the worst thing that could happen to a mark. At least he was good entertainment. Seen through Sarah's eyes, though, he knew he was no different from Adam; no different, really, from any Spanish Prisoner practitioner or three-card monte man. During his entire life on the razzle he had built nothing, created nothing, helped no one. That's why the money bugged him, he realized. There was no design behind it, no mission. It was only meant to be gotten and spent, and he no longer felt completely comfortable with that. Not with the baby coming. Role models are supposed to, you know, model roles.

Radar finished his run, walking the last quarter-mile to cool down. As he neared the condo complex, he saw Sarah's car roll into its assigned space in the long, low parking shed that protected residents' vehicles from the brutal Texas summer sun. He wondered if Ames had approached her again and whether she'd had any difficulty disengaging from him.

Well, some.

For the driver's door opened and Adam Ames stepped out. When Ames saw Radar, his face creased into a big grin, and he immediately strode over. "Radar!" he said with frank enthusiasm, "How the heck are you?" He extended his hand, and Radar shook it quite quizzically. "I'm so glad I ran into you, I really wanted to thank you."

Radar refrained from asking what for, for in a situation like this, where you're absolutely spun sideways by the unexpected, it's best to act as if the unexpected is expected, at least until the spinning stops. The fact of Ames's presence told him that, obviously, Sarah hadn't given him the heave-ho, though right now who could say why? Maybe she just cowered out. Some people hate confrontation like a cat hates baths—you just can't drag 'em to it.

"Listen, as long as you're here," continued Ames, "would you mind giving me a hand?" He popped open the trunk of the car and Radar was surprised to find it filled with groceries.

"Save me a trip?"

"Sure," said Rader. He could see spaghetti, bread, fresh vegetables, red wine, all the fixings for dinner. This told him that, far from getting sent on his way, Ames had actually drawn himself closer. Sarah had lent him her car; apparently they would dine. Radar and Adam grabbed a couple of bags each and headed into the building.

Ames humped his load with a completely casual air. If he was at all self-conscious about being with the skeptical Mr. Hoverlander, he didn't let on. The reason for this became clear when he said, "I have to say I was surprised."

"Surprised by what?"

"Getting your thumbs up. When I saw you at the Hyatt you made it pretty clear that you didn't believe me. But Sarah said you came around."

"Did she?"

"Look, I know you still have your doubts, but you'll see. Dr. Gauch is going to come through."

Radar gave a nod to the groceries. "And in the meantime?"

"Well, I can't stay at the Hyatt forever."

"Run out of miles?"

"Hmm?"

"The miles you were using to pay for the room."

"Oh. Yeah." They reached the elevator. Ames stabbed the call button with a free pinkie.

"So you're staying here?"

"Till I can find an efficiency."

"Or Jonah gets cured. What is he, on some sort of recipient list?"

"Something like that."

"Something rare as Karn's, it wouldn't be that long a list."

"I don't know exactly how it works. You probably know as much about it now as I do. Sarah says you're a studier."

"A studier."

"You studied me pretty hard, didn't you? You know, I respect the work you did. You're a true friend to Sarah. She appreciates your support. And now I do, too."

Radar wanted to say, *Dude, I've seen your house,* but Ames was on script, and when a grifter's on script, you don't overtly move him off it without consequence. Radar wasn't ready to make that play. First he wanted to hear Sarah's side.

So he said nothing, which is often an eloquence.

When Sarah opened the door and saw Radar, her face skipped a beat, but she covered with small talk as she led them into the kitchen to set down the groceries. Radar asked after Jonah. She said he was sleeping a lot this week. She asked if he wanted some wine, but Radar begged off and said he had to get going.

Sarah followed him out into the hall, pulling the door half closed behind her. "Radar," she said, "I want to thank you for everything you did. Look, I...I know you don't trust Adam. But I thought it over and I thought about it from Jonah's point of view. Doesn't he deserve hope? Even if I have to pay for it?" Radar started to speak, but she cut him off. "So I told Adam that you approved but didn't want to be involved. Radar, you needn't trouble yourself over us anymore."

"You've got it covered, then?"

Sarah smiled shyly. "Covered, yes. Adam is good company. Under the circumstances, I think I'm entitled to good company." Sarah suddenly kissed Radar, briefly but with purpose. "Since the company I really want is taken." She winked, then turned and went back inside.

Radar returned to his flat, showered, then reviewed for the others that surreal piece of theater. He didn't omit the kiss, but felt nervous as hell putting it out there. When he was done, Vic said dismissively, "Well, he's her problem now."

"Agreed," said Allie. "We don't even need to have this discussion."

"Guys, he's a schmo," said Radar. "We can't leave her in his clutches."

"'Schmo,' Radar?" asked Allie. "'Clutches?' Since when do we talk like that?"

"Don't forget that she kissed him," chirped Mirplo. "Women's lips are a powerful force that can only be used for good or for evil."

"Yes, thank you for that contribution," said Radar. He looked at Allie. "There's only one pair of lips I want and you know that." He kissed her for a moment to prove it.

"Be that as it may," said Allie when they unclinched, "she made her choice. Women do that. I'll have to thank her for choosing an available man."

"You don't know him. You haven't even met him."

"I'm sure he's formidable. But like Vic said, he's her problem now." His face was still set. "Radar, come on. You know I'm right."

"Of course you are." He shut his eyes and opened them. In the blink of those eyes, Radar dropped Sarah once and for all from his to-do list.

But she didn't stay off it for long.

9

True Believer

Winter had found Austin again, and its icy rain found Radar and Vic huddled over hot Neanderspressos at the nearest Java Man, which was four hundred yards nearer than the next nearest one—the damn things were everywhere. "So," asked Vic, "any more stupid baby names?"

Radar thought about not answering, but ultimately confessed, "Lysander."

"Lysander Hoverlander? They're not getting better."

"They're not meant to. Self-indulgence is its own reward."

Allie stepped in out of the wet. Her cheeks were red from the raw weather, but that didn't explain the sparkle in her eyes. "Guess what?" she said as she shed her slicker and slid in beside Radar. "I just met Adam Ames."

"Really?" asked Radar. "Where?"

"At our place. Sarah brought him over. I think she was showing him off. She was like, 'You've got a boyfriend, now

I've got a boyfriend, too.' "

"And Ames?" asked Radar. "What did you think of him?"

"Well, it's like you said, he's totally locked onto his script, heavily invested in getting Jonah cured. Radar, it's absurd on the face of it."

"Thank you! That's what I've been saying."

"Hey, get this: They don't even have to go to Switzerland."

"What, Gauch is making a house call?"

"Not even. He's sending the serum FedEx."

"Oh, now it's a serum," said Vic.

"Yup. Very exciting. A breakthrough. Hundred percent proven on monkeys."

"And Sarah's buying that?"

"She's leading it. She couldn't be more psyched."

Radar sighed. "Some people are hopeless. Now I just feel sorry for her."

"Any guess on the get?" asked Vic, using grifter slang for the sum a mark might pay.

"I don't have to guess. I know. Twenty grand."

"What, they just gave that number up? You asked, they answered?"

"Who asked? Sarah almost begged to say: how it's gonna cost so much but be so worth it."

Radar said, "Allie, this feels like a cartoon. Are you sure you had the right read?"

Allie cocked her head to one side and grinned, and for the first time Radar saw what they call the pregnancy glow. It made his heart rise like a helium snowflake. "Please," she said. "To paraphrase our dear Mirplo, I have danced with the chickens many times. Besides, I know him."

"Who? Ames?"

"Uh-huh. We met years ago in the upper Midwest. Minneapolis or Madison. Madison, I think."

"Wow, that's an outside chance," said Vic.

"Not really. We were running the same game. Herbal supplements. We were in and out of the same health food stores all day. He was a hippie back then. Big, bushy beard. Dreadlocks. Tie-dye shirt. Not long on showers, as I recall. In fact he stank. Took the whole shaggy chic thing way too far. Passionate about his product line, though. Chi balancers. Dream enhancers. I thought he was a true believer."

"What were you selling?" asked Radar.

"Oh, libido blends for the ladies."

"But mostly franchise fees."

"You know how these things work. The product never nets like the network nets."

"Was he good?" asked Mirplo.

"I don't know," said Allie. "We really just crossed paths."

"Did he recognize you?"

"If he did, he didn't let on."

"Did you?" asked Radar.

"Let on? Lover, don't make me a mook."

Radar mused for a minute. "You say you thought he was a true believer. Why?"

"Resonant backstory. Conceived at a Dead show, born in a microbus, raised on a commune, home schooled."

"That didn't seem over the top to you?" asked Vic.

"Not at the time," said Allie. "I didn't have the eye I have now."

"Strange that he doesn't remember you," said Vic. "I'd

remember you. You're hard to forget."

"Thank you, sweetheart. Would you like to name my baby?"

"Oh, I already know the name," said Vic. "I've read ahead."

"You want to tell me?"

"And spoil the ending? I don't think so."

Radar thought, *Damn right Allie's hard to forget. And it ain't Adam's first chicken dance either. But if he recognized her he wouldn't say, because he wouldn't want to come off his true-believer docket. It's too valuable to give up.*

The true-believer cover is among the grift's most effective. It's durable and flexible. It stands up to scrutiny, and it withstands challenge. It's hard to attack anyone who wields a shield of belief; doubly hard to attack a hustler who hides behind that mask. Irrational acts, righteous indignation, intolerance: Any of these tools is available to a legitimate zealot—or to someone who looks like one. But the true-believer stance has a downside, in that you can never raise the stakes directly. You encounter someone else in the game, or someone overtly trying to block you, and you have no cards to play but your true-believer cards. *Outrage! Umbrage! Denial!* Good cards, thought Radar, but all from the same suit. Bottom line, if Ames made Allie, he'd try not to let on, and available evidence suggested that he could succeed.

Vic must've been thinking along similar lines, because he told Allie, "Maybe he made you. Maybe he just didn't say."

"No," said Allie. "I'm sure not."

"Why not?"

"I was lots different then."

"You couldn't have been that different."

"I was fat."

"You?" said Vic. "I can't see it."

"I could." Allie sighed at the memory. It put her someplace sad. "Guys were hitting on me all the time. I got so sick of it, I thought if I put on weight maybe they'd leave the fat chick alone."

"Poor you," said Radar. "Too hot for your own good. How much did you gain?"

"Seventy-five pounds."

"*Holy schneike!*"

"Radar, it wasn't just the weight. My hair, my clothes, my rap. My state of mind. I did everything in my power to desex myself. I hated men and I let 'em know it." Allie sighed again. "It was pretty messed up." She stared off into space for a moment. "It turns out men weren't the problem, *I* was the problem. My nature at the time. Low self-esteem, high self-loathing. A pretty toxic cocktail. In those days, I was trying to get as far away from me as possible, and doing a damn good job. Trust me, Radar, you wouldn't have recognized me, and you're a lot sharper than Ames."

"He's showing pretty sharp," said Vic.

"Not sharp. Just committed," said Radar. "He knows what we know: that true believers sell best." Radar thought for a moment, then added, "And whether he made Allie or not, he also knows we're in the game."

"How do you figure?"

"He can smell us, just like we can smell him."

"Well, alrighty then," said Vic. "I say we confront his worthless ass and send him packing."

"That won't work," said Radar. "He already has his hooks in." And that was the one thing he had told Sarah not to let happen. How could be people be so weak-willed? Or was it just weak will? He thought of young Allie, so angry and sad that she'd mutilated herself with food. He thought of himself at that age, always holding mooks in contempt for being such mooks, and then, after he'd ripped them off, holding himself in contempt for taking any pleasure in so hollow a win. A little approval from a trusted source would have gone a long, long way back then. So everyone has their blind spots, the seams in their personality where the hooks set best. Sarah needed a miracle cure for Jonah, but no less needed a validating ally, a lover perhaps, a fixture in her life. And why wouldn't Ames oblige? It's so much easier to pick the pocket when the pants are on the floor. "He's gonna pivot," said Radar with a sudden flash of insight. "Mark my words. He's going to say that the Institute's cure fell through."

"Why?" asked Allie.

"He doesn't need it anymore. Nor will he want to be pushed to put up or shut up. Not when he can be the boyfriend, and pluck Sarah a dozen other ways."

"But he's already got her tuned up for the snake-oil thing," said Mirplo.

"Uh-huh. And he knows we don't like it. So why not dump it? Then he'd be just her stalwart support in this time of crisis, and what could we possibly have against that?"

"You have to admire the move," said Vic. "It solves a lot of problems at once."

I don't want to admire this guy's moves, thought Radar. *I want to move him off.* Which, he realized, he'd already tried to do without much success.

And the chill he felt just then had nothing to do with the rain.

The next day, Sarah made a point of finding Radar and Allie at home. She wanted to apologize for kissing Radar, she told them. It was totally inappropriate, especially given Allie's condition.

Asked Allie, "What do you mean, my condition?"

"Well, it won't be long before, you know, you start to get blimpy." Allie reacted. "I don't mean that to sound mean," said Sarah. "It's just...that's when a man's eye starts to wander. It's when my ex-husband's did. I mean, he was a jerk to begin with, but when I stopped entertaining him...."

"Entertaining?" asked Radar.

"You know," said Sarah shyly. "In bed. Who wants to have all that sex when you're so achy and rashy?" She looked at Allie. "Oh, you may not see it like that now, but you wait, you will." She turned to Radar. "Anyway, that's beside the point. Radar, I want you to know that despite the kiss, I really don't have feelings for you. Our thing in the hall the other day? That was for Adam's benefit. Kind of a show."

"He wasn't watching."

"Oh, I'm sure he was listening. He's a listener, that one. But I have plans for him, and it would really help me if you acted like things between us were cool."

"Of course they're cool, Sarah. I can't tell you how to live your life."

She waggled her index finger at him. "I think you think you can, Mr. Morality. You think Adam is tricking me, and you don't like it. But what you don't know is, *I've* decided to trick *him*." Off their bewildered looks, she said, "I know he's a slime, you guys. You've convinced me of that. But you said I can't go to the police, so I'm taking matters into my own hands. I'm scamming the scammer! Isn't that great?" She fairly beamed. "I'm stringing him along, letting him think I buy his phony baloney act. Don't worry, he's not getting any dough from me. In fact if I play my cards right," she gave an amateur wink, "I'll get his."

Radar asked, "Sarah, why are you doing this?"

"Duh, revenge. Radar, I'm a single mother with a sick child. You don't mess with people like that. If you do, you deserve some payback." Radar and Allie both looked pained. "Oh, relax, you two. I'm not asking for help. I've got the whole thing planned out."

"You do?" asked Allie, flatly. She was a little beyond stunned.

"Uh-huh. Now, if what you told me is true, eventually he's going to ask me for money, right? And he thinks I can get it. That's why I brought him over to see you, Allie, just to make that point. But when the time comes, I'll say I can't!" She gave them a strange, manic grin. "Well, don't you see? Then I'll break down in tears and beg him to loan me it."

Radar couldn't imagine how Sarah missed the hole in her reasoning. "Sarah, what are you supposed to do with that money?"

"Well, send it to Switzerland for the serum." She self-processed for a moment, and a certain penny dropped. "Oh. Via Adam." Her face fell. "So even if I get his money, he gets it right back." She shook her head angrily. "Well, that won't work." She thought on, concentrating fiercely, and then said,

"Wait, what if I thought of something else? Maybe Jonah needs another medicine, something from somewhere else. Australia, say. And I'm supposed to pay, but I can't. Then he'd have to give me the cash."

"That's an incredibly dangerous game," said Radar. "Sarah, I told you, you just want this guy out of your life."

"But like Radar said," added Allie with sudden vehemence, "we can't tell you how to live it."

Sarah looked at Allie. "Do you think I'm being stupid?"

"I agree with Radar that there's a risk, but it's your risk, so...." She paused. "Thank you for telling the truth about your feelings for Radar. I wouldn't like to think another woman had her cap set for him." She added drily, "Especially when I'm about to get blimpy."

"Oh, I hurt you with that."

"Not at all. You've given me a good heads-up. I'll have to remember to keep my man entertained." She squeezed Radar's bicep. "In fact, I might get started on that right now."

Sarah looked at her blankly. "What? Oh. Oh! Okay, well...." Under the cover of fluster, Sarah withdrew

"So," said Radar when they were alone, "are we going to fool around, Blimpy?"

"Not if you call me that."

"I could call the kid—"

"Blimpy Hoverlander? You'd better not."

"Anyway, why'd you give Sarah the bum's rush?"

"Honestly? I was afraid you were going to overcommit again."

"No, I'm over that."

Allie wagged her finger at Radar in a conscious imitation

of Sarah. "I don't think so, Mr. Morality. I think you're more worried about her than ever."

"That's nonsense," said Radar. "Look, she's obviously self-destructive, so let her self-destroy."

But he was seriously starting to wonder if he could.

10

Sweetheart Scam

Vic Mirplo is giving a seminar.

"We now come to the sweetheart scam," he says. "This one's been around forever. All it takes is falling in love, and that's not hard. If you're older, you're particularly vulnerable. There can be a knock at your door and isn't it a winsome young thing looking for a certain address? You help her find it—apparently amiably so, because she delights in your company, and the next thing you know she's sharing hers in bulk. And when she tells you about her brother's can't-miss business venture, you're right there with a loan. Why not? It's what you saved for, right? To spend on what you want when you're old? And if she wants it, you want it, too. But she's got other relatives, and soon you've bankrolled them too, to the tune of your life savings, liquid assets, real property, and convertible goods. By then you're a coconut husk, and then she just throws you away.

"Ladies, don't think this can only happen to vain old

men. No one's immune. Everyone has holes in their guard,
and if yours are lightly defended, any snake of a charmer can
slither in. The male version comes equipped with proposals
of marriage, and trust me, these are well worn. He may have
wives all over; by now he probably does. Their stories will
all have the same sad refrain: 'He started out so loving, so
caring, so there for me when I needed him. And when he
needed me back, of course I was there, too. Why would he be
ashamed of borrowing money from me? That *is* why he left,
right? Guilt? Right? Gosh, I'd love to see him again.'

"I know what you're thinking. This could never happen
to you because you're way too smart for all that. Maybe.
Then again, maybe it already happened and you didn't
know. Are you saying you never fell for a line from a mooch?
Sometimes it's hard to tell where a real relationship ends and
a scam begins, especially if you're not motivated to look that
hard. Any time you're too polite or too scared or too conflict-
avoidy to tell someone to buzz off, you're being exploited,
which is to say conned. If it's your sister or your kids or your
mother-in-law, that just means they're keeping the business
close to home. Why not? They're in the market for a mark,
and if you're right there handy, why shop anywhere else?
Psychologists dress this transaction up in pretty clothes. They
call it codependency and enabling. Really it's just a scam.

"But make no mistake: Anyone who cold-calls your
phone or knocks on your door, ten times out of ten they're
on the make. They're doing construction work in your area?
And they have roofing materials left over? Isn't that swell?
Sure is—till the first time it rains. They're selling magazine
subscriptions to support the glee club? How come that lad

has a five-o'clock shadow? Shadow him for a while, you'll see: no magazines; no glee; no club; no compunctions whatsoever about plucking such cash as he can from the likes of you and your accommodating neighbors. Even the off-ramp panhandle bum dines out on your gullible kindness. That wheelchair? That wheelchair is a prop.

"You should be glad that they don't come at you with small arms or strong arms. Usually you can fend them off with a good, firm no. But get good at saying no. Otherwise get good at being broke."

Okay, it wasn't a seminar, per se. It was just a volunteer talk at a senior center, Mirplo the munificent giving back to the community, giving oldsters some weapons of self-defense. The seniors seemed to like it—so much so that they bought twenty advance copies of a book that didn't exist.

When Vic got home, the first thing he saw was the familiar sight of Allie crashed out on the couch. This had been her pose all week: facedown in a patch of her own drool. Apple cores and candy wrappers stood silent testimony to the awesome power of progesterone to make her eat, then sleep. Radar sat at the end of the couch, idly rubbing her feet. Upon seeing Mirplo, he rose silently and walked with Vic back to Vic's room. Once they were settled, Radar asked, "Why is Ames here?"

"For Sarah's money," said Vic. "So far as we know."

"So far as we know. I was just thinking, here we are, you, me, and Allie, playing citizen, acting all normal, and now there's another one of us parked just down the way? That seems like a coincidence."

"A coincidence and a half," agreed Vic solemnly. "Maybe

three quarters." Coincidences had crossed their paths before. More often than not they turned out to be not. "You think he's here for us?"

"The thought should cross our minds," said Radar. "He's being pretty sticky, and I don't think Sarah so much came around as got sent around to see us with her harebrained scheme. I see puppet strings. And the puppet show ain't over."

"That's pretty interesting, Radar, but can I just say it's one thing to know Adam's on the razzle and another to think he's coming after us. We have no evidence of that but coincidence. It's not…what's the word?…disposative."

"Dispositive," said Allie. She stood in the doorway, wiping sleep from her eyes. "Vic means he thinks you're looking obsessed."

"Tell me I'm wrong to be," said Radar.

Neither of them could.

The next day, Radar encountered Adam in the building lobby. Another coincidence? Radar had no reason to think otherwise, until Adam frankly admitted that he'd been trying to cross Radar's path. When Radar asked why, Ames said, "Sarah and I wanted to invite you to dinner. You and Allie, of course. And the other one? Vin?"

"Vic," said Radar. "Thanks. I'll take it up with the troops."

"No, look, seriously, Thursday. And let's consider it on. I still get the feeling you don't quite trust me. I'd like you to get to know me. You'll see that I help people. If you were in trouble, I'd help you."

For some reason it was a platitude too far, and Radar suddenly found himself blurting, "Cut the crap, man. I know who you help."

If Adam was affronted by this, he didn't let on. He merely said calmly, "If you mean I make money, okay I do. But the bottom line is, I define myself through service."

"I'll bet you do." Radar looked Ames in the eye. He saw no guile there, yet no honesty either. "You know what?" said Radar. "Thanks for the dinner invitation. I think I can speak for the others. We're gonna pass."

"I don't understand."

"Are you kidding me?"

"What did I do to earn your disapproval?"

Radar opened his mouth, closed it, turned, and walked away. He imagined if he glanced back, he'd see Adam looking outraged, or maybe perplexed, but he didn't look back. He knew that a good chunk of a con artist's power lay in the mark's unwillingness to say no. By playing the affronted innocent, you could often shame folks into giving you what you want, even get them to take actions against their own interests. Marks, as a rule, don't like to be rude. But Radar was no mark. He had no problem being rude. He just wished he hadn't lost his cool. Ames now knew that Radar had his true measure, and that was a card that Radar couldn't unplay.

He hoped it wouldn't come back to haunt.

Cortisol Surge

The weather stayed sour, with soaking, heavy mist and rain, low gray skies, and fog that froze into hoar overnight. Radar endured two grim days of it before donning his bright orange nylon waterproofs and driving over to Canyon View West to grind the hills. These hills were not at all challenging if he stuck to the contours of the roads and paths, so he chose guerrilla ascents instead, leaving the fastidiously blazed community trails and bounding up through the shrubs and sere grass. His feet pounded on the hard-packed sand, the suctioned rubber tips of his New Balance 940s gaining just enough traction to propel each next stride. Today the ground was wet and the surface sand had clumped into patches of slippery grit, but no matter. He attacked each hill hard, surrendering himself completely to the rhythm of the run, to the unity of lungs and limbs, and then to that sweet release at the top, where he would stop and subside and slide down into the full endorphin bath. Though this part of West Austin wasn't much to look at, and the crappy weather conditions hardly made for postcard panoramas, as Radar walked back and forth on a low summit, regaining his breath, he swallowed the available beauty whole. He felt alive and he felt blessed. He couldn't wait for the baby. *Milliner?* He thought. *Milliner Hoverlander?*

No. Too flowery.

Radar burned up the hilltop blacktops in a long loop back to Toro Canyon Road and the tiny trailhead parking lot where he'd left his car. When he got there he saw that it had been joined by a blue Score, the Song compact hybrid so popular with the reusable-grocery-bag crowd. Just as Radar realized that he recognized the car, the driver got out under an umbrella and ran at a crouch toward him.

"God, there you are. I've been waiting so long. How far do you *run?*"

"Sarah, what are you doing here?"

"I needed to talk to you, duh."

"So you followed me?"

"That's right." Her voice quivered. "Radar, I think I might've made a mistake."

"Great, now what?"

"Don't take that tone with me," said Sarah. "I feel bad enough as it is." She shuffled back and forth in the rain, hunched under her umbrella. "Can we get in your car, please? It's nasty out here." Radar made no move to open a door. "Fine," she pouted, "have it your way." Yet she moved in close, sliding the lip of her umbrella just above his sweat-steaming head. "So what I did, I kind of told Adam about you. How on the level you think he's not."

"That's no big deal. He knows it already."

"Really? Oh, Radar, I'm so relieved. I was afraid I spilled the beans."

"Then why did you do it?"

"I don't know. I thought it would help us outsmart him somehow."

"Us? We—" Radar thought of a dozen different things to say, but instead just walked around to the driver's side of the car and beeped open his door. "Goodbye, Sarah."

"What, you're just going to drive away? Is that even civilized?"

He looked at her over the top of the car. "Look, I can't, okay? You're making bad choices and I can't be a part of it. I'm sorry if you think I belong in your life, but I don't. I'm over here. You're over there. Okay? Goodbye."

She threw down her umbrella. It rolled and blew halfway across the road. She didn't move to retrieve it. Instead, she walked with purposeful strides to Radar, snaked her arms around his neck, and kissed him quite directly. He broke away at once. Almost at once. "This can't happen," he said.

"It already kind of is, don't you think?"

"No." He got in his car and drove off, watching in the rearview as she fetched her umbrella and stood under it, forlorn, in the rain. Damn, she was sticky. She and Adam both. What the hell was going on?

When he got home, he found Allie lying on their bed, her shirt pushed up under her breasts, contemplating her belly.

"How's that going?" he asked.

She ran her hand over the faintest of curves. "Well, it's not nothing."

"You know what? It's everything." He came over and kissed her. She drew him down on the bed beside her.

"How was your run?"

"Solid. The end not so good."

"How so?"

He told her about Sarah, sharing the details of their brief chat and, after a beat's hesitation, also its tawdry conclusion. "I kissed her," he said.

"I know."

"You do?"

"It shows all over your face. You were never a tough read to me, Radar. You still aren't."

"Why didn't you say something?"

"I know you: If you've got something to say, you'll say it."

"You'd just wait for me to fill you in?"

"As you're filling me in now, yes. And that's called being an adult. But if she kissed you, I know you couldn't help it. Radar, you have a weakness for strong women." She propped her head up on her elbow. "Hence, me."

"Sarah's not strong."

"She's strong enough. Needy and strong. That's her superpower, being naïve. But I don't think she's as naïve as she looks. She's into you, blatantly so, but she's also thinking things through. She's playing you kind of like...." Allie's voice trailed off.

"Like you did when we first met?" said Radar.

"Well, yeah. Like I said, you have a weakness for strong women. But hang on...."

"What?"

"Have you done the math, bub? If she's playing you like

I did, and I played you for a mark, then—"

"Holy smoke, I hadn't thought of that. Sarah's in the game?"

"Or maybe she just wants to bonk you." Allie moved in close. "I want to bonk you."

Radar said, "I don't get you. I just told you I kissed another girl."

"And I told you you couldn't help it. Now come on, you can't help it with me either."

They made love, and in the languid afterspace, Radar laid the length of his body against Allie's and drifted off to sleep. If the thought of Sarah's kiss entered his head, he kicked it right back out.

They napped until suppertime, then collected Vic and walked down to eat at Abel's on the Lake. The place was packed to the rafters with students from the nearby University of Texas, there to watch their beloved Longhorns play basketball on Abel's many projection TVs in its many dining rooms and bars. It took some aggressive scouting on Vic's part to find them a small, round pedestal table in a crowded corner of the main saloon.

Radar teased Allie with the menu. "Want some fried pickles, hon? Specialty of the house."

"Ugh," said Allie. "No, thank you. That phase is over." She scanned the menu, then stabbed at an item triumphantly. "I'm having *that*," she said. *That* was Abel's Famous Fumbler, and Allie read its description aloud with great gusto. "Chicken-fried steak topped with applewood smoked bacon, cheddar-jack cheese, and jalapeños, served on a sweet sourdough bun."

Phase not quite over, Radar thought.

While they ate, Radar asked Vic how the book was coming along.

"Not bad," said Vic. "I lined up a publisher." Radar and Allie exchanged looks. "What?" he said. "I sent out some emails. Some people said yes. Why not?"

"Why indeed, Vic," said Radar. Not for the first time, he admired his friend's ability to turn nothing into something. It was a talent he hoped his child would have. A child that he suddenly knew, or thought he knew, would be a girl.

When he voiced this thought, Allie laughed out loud. "How the hell do you know that?" she asked. "Psychic ultrasound?"

"I just know," said Radar. "I'm that tuned in. It's part of my pregnancy voyage."

Allie gawked at him. "Your pregnancy voyage?"

"Hey, I told you you weren't going through this alone."

"Oh, this is too easy," said Vic, prepared to take notes. "Please, Radar, do tell us all about your pregnancy voyage."

"Women think just because they carry the babies, it makes them theirs. And yes, on the level of hormones, weight gain, labor pain, I guess they're right. But men have hormones, too. Six weeks in, our fight-or-flight reflex peaks. It's called the cortisol surge. I'm on alert now, see? I'm sensing the baby coming." He waggled his fingers in a hocus-pocus gesture. "I'm seeing into the future." But then he took both of Allie's hands and said seriously, "Right now I feel a hundred percent sure we're having a girl. Maybe I'm wrong, but it's what I'm feeling now, and lover, if I'm feeling it, you're hearing about it. And if you're feeling something, I want to hear about it, too, and that's what I mean by sharing this thing."

Before Allie could respond with either *I love you* or *that's the dumbest thing I've ever heard,* Mirplo looked past her and said, "We've got company." The others looked and saw Adam and Sarah fighting their way through the crowd toward them.

"I just had a thought," said Radar.

"Another cortisol surge?" asked Allie lightly.

"Laugh if you want." He nodded toward Adam and Sarah. "I think they're about to jettison Jonah."

"What?" asked Allie. "Why?"

"They don't need him anymore. They'll make up some kind of excuse to send him away."

"Oh, now Jonah's in the game, too?" asked Vic.

"Why not? His whole disease could be a fake. Brain affliction? With symptoms that you manifest as you see fit? I could've pulled off that stunt at his age, no sweat."

Adam and Sarah reeled up, hand in hand, drinks in hand, sheets to the wind, two lives of the party. "Hey, you guys!" chirped Sarah. "What are you doing here?"

Allie looked down at her plate. "Eating ridiculous food."

"And yet you won't eat ours." She turned to Radar. "Adam told me you turned down his invitation. I'm here to say that won't do. I need us all to be friends, Radar." Her alcoholic haze seemed momentarily to lift as she braced him with her liquid blue eyes. "I need us all to know exactly how friendly we are." The implied threat—*don't make me tell Allie we kissed*—was not lost on Radar, nor of course Allie. She squeezed his hand to communicate that she'd back any play he made here, so he bowed gracefully to the pressure of her invitation.

"Then friends we shall be," said Radar. "Thursday. We'll bring wine."

"Great," said Sarah. "I knew—"

Whatever Sarah knew was lost just then in the roar of the crowd as the UT basketball team did something wonderful on every TV in the joint. "Yeah!" shouted Adam, as rabid as any alum, "Hook 'em, Horns!" He looked at Radar and the others and said with a shrug, "Just trying to fit in." He put his arm around Sarah's waist and gave her a pixilated kiss. "Got a feeling I'll be sticking around." Sarah murmured her approval and they smooched off into the crowd.

"They do put on a show," observed Allie drily.

"I'm writing them into my book," said Vic.

"And I'm taking a closer look at her," said Radar.

This he did the next day, starting with a search on social media, where he found her not. That was odd for this day and age, but he considered that she might have dropped off-line when she went con. Many do, for it's easier to maintain no internet presence than an elaborately fake one. Or maybe she just didn't go online. Some people were like that. Even in this day and age.

But Radar didn't give up. He pointed his Grape to an esoteric search engine and poked around among fake-patient scams, just on the off chance. He knew how these worked: You showed up in a small town with a supposedly sick kid and preyed on folks' generosity to generate a modest earn in cash and small checks. Sometimes your plight made news. Radar canvassed a country press archive for just such print-perpetuated tales of woe. He found a lovely one about a boy with brain cancer and his mother who'd been evicted, humiliated, denied health care, and run out of her own hometown. Now she and her suffering son were enjoying the largesse of the good people of Tyler, Texas. Though their names were pure bafflegab, their pictures were unmistakable.

Sarah and Jonah, oh-ho.

12

Backstory Wink

Bam! Bam! Bam!

Sarah hammered on the door in hysterics. "Radar! Radar!" she cried as she pounded. "Quick! Come here quick!" Radar and Allie rose and threw on clothes. Vic beat them to the door, pulling a T-shirt on over his gym shorts. He opened it and Sarah spilled in, her face blotched and wet with tears. "Jonah was having a seizure! Adam took him to the emergency room! Radar, can you drive me? Please, I need to see my son!"

Allie's eyebrows bounced. Vic pushed his tongue into his cheek. Radar's discovery of Sarah's shenanigans in Tyler had cast all of her actions in a new light, but even without that, the obvious question would have to be asked, and Radar asked it: "Sarah, why didn't you go with Adam?"

Sarah broke stride. "What?"

"Why did you not get in the car and go with Adam and Jonah?"

"I…" mumbled Sarah, "guess I should have." She threw herself down on the couch. "Oh, I didn't do that well at all."

"Do what well?" asked Vic.

"The dramatic flair thing. Like to get you all nervous and act rash, right? I believe con people call it rushing the mark." Off their reactions, she said, "What? I've been reading up."

"On cons? Why?"

"For my war with Adam." She looked at them, shifting her gaze from face to face. "Wait, you thought I was with him? I mean *with* him with him? Well, that's good, at least. At least I fooled you on that."

"So Jonah's okay?" asked Allie.

"Uh-huh."

"And this midnight hysteria is…."

Sarah shrugged. "Practice. But I think I need more." She frowned, then bounded back. "Oh, plus, tomorrow night I think Adam's going to make you an offer or proposition of some kind. I heard him talking about it on the phone. That smells fishy, right? Not that you'd be fooled. But play along, okay? I'm building a case against him, a legal case. I've talked to a lawyer and everything. I'm going to nail him for trying to rip you off."

"Sarah," said Radar, "A, that's entrapment, and two, it sounds like you're running another script here." Sarah cast down her eyes. "Sarah, look at me." She looked up. "Have you been to a lawyer?"

"No."

"Why are you lying?"

"I'm not. I'm being a con artist." Her shoulders sagged. "Just not a very good one. But I still want to hurt him, though," she said fiercely. "And I'm going to, whether you help me or not." She stood up and pivoted completely unself-consciously into hostess mode. "So, any special food requests? Vegan? Nothing with a face?" They shook their heads. "No? Okay, well, Adam won't know I was here. He sleeps like a log." She slipped out the door and closed it quietly behind her.

Said Vic, "That, to me, looked like batshit crazy."

"Was it intended to, I wonder?" mused Allie.

Before Radar could offer his observations, Sarah knocked on the door once more. This time she only stuck her head in and said softly, "I forgot to tell you: Actually I sent Jonah away. To his grandma's. She knows how to take care of him, and I need to focus all my energy on punishing Adam right now. Which is good for me, I think. You know? It takes my mind off things. Thanks for your support, by the way. You guys are good friends." She blew them a kiss and withdrew.

Vic said again, with exactly the same inflection, "That, to me, looked like batshit crazy."

"Yet Jonah is out of the picture," said Radar.

"As spake the cortisol forecast," noted Allie.

"I'm high on hormones," said Radar. "What can I say?"

They went back to bed, but Radar lay awake, reviewing Sarah's performance. It was contradictory, sloppy, emotionally promiscuous. It shifted shamelessly from mood to mood. It lied, got caught in a lie, and lied some more. What was the hidden logic of that? Maybe Vic's assessment of *batshit crazy* was correct. Maybe Sarah just lacked the remotest trace of self-awareness. Maybe she was on a script. Maybe even a script aimed at herself. People do that all the time, tell themselves a series of lies until it sounds like the truth.

In any event, her performance was consistently inconsistent, which meant that she no longer had to explain any irrational act, for irrationality was now firmly woven into the warp and weft of her docket. If docket it was. Radar still didn't know, and he realized that his best guess was just that—a guess. He was frustrated by this, but at the same time, he had to admit, intrigued. He felt himself embracing the situation in a new way. Leaning into it, almost. Whatever the true state of their union, Adam and Sarah now posed a pair of puzzles to be separately or severally solved. And when was that ever not fun?

Which may have explained his sunny mood the next night as he dressed for dinner, humming, for no particular reason, Matt Bunsen and the Burners' classic "Burnin' in a White Room" and pausing at intervals to play abortive games of fetch with Boy. Such games were always abortive because Boy always turned them into keep-away or tug-of-war, guarding his prize—in this case a bald tennis ball—with quick and jealous jaws.

Dog behavior, reflected Radar, *is an admirable quality if you are, in fact, a dog.*

Allie came out of the bathroom, naked and fresh from a shower—yet not quite as fresh as she'd like. "I wouldn't go in there if I were you," she said. "I'm beefing up a storm." Before Radar could speak, she added, "And no, I don't need you to make that part of your pregnancy voyage." She flowed to him and held herself against him, the buttons of his vintage Hawaiian shirt tickling her sternum. She inhaled the fragrance of him, tilted her head to kiss him....

And damn near burped in his mouth.

She stumbled away, laughing. "I'm so sorry, Radar." She tapped her chest with stiff fingers. "Internal combustion in here like you wouldn't believe. I feel like a frickin' fracking site." She returned to him and looped her arms around his waist. "Will you still want me when I'm blimpy?"

"You have to ask? Trust me, Allie, no woman attracts me like my frickin' frackin' baby mama, okay?"

"Okay," she said.

And they slipped in a quickie before dinner.

Mirplo was nowhere to be seen. They waited for him till half past polite, but when he still hadn't shown, they put on their party faces and trundled down the hall to Sarah's flat, holding hands. "Are we couple dating, Radar?" asked Allie. "This is weird for us."

He swung her arm lightly. "Honey," he said, "we're the crowned king and queen of bafflegab. If we can't make a night's worth of small talk, who can?"

The trick, of course, would be to ignore all available subjects in the subtext, and these were not few: Adam's snuke moves on Sarah; her potentially deranged ripostes; and whatever this impending pitch of his was. Nor did Sarah seem at all interested in dwelling on Jonah's suffering. Her perky party mood revealed itself the moment they knocked on the door and she responded with a lilting, "Be right there!" She threw the door open and squeaked happy greetings to them both, air-kissing Allie's cheeks and hugging Radar hard enough to telegraph the absence of a bra. She wore a linen blouse and flowing harem pants, and the glass of wine in her hand was evidently not her first. Ames strode up and gave them hearty handshakes. He had on charcoal khakis and a black polo shirt with a burnt orange Texas Longhorns logo. *Camouflage,* thought Radar. *Local coloration. The man is fitting right in.*

They were still settling in when Vic arrived, breathlessly monologuing. "Sorry I'm late," he said. "Got on a writing jag, lost track of time. You know how that goes. First you tell the story, then the story tells the story, then the story tells you. I haven't missed anything have I? Dinner? Yeah? No? Party games? Charades? Hors d'oeuvres? Hello, Sarah." He tossed her a wave, then turned to Ames. "I don't think we've really met." He stuck out his mitt like the last glad-hand standing. "Mirplo."

"Uh, mirplo to you, too?" said Ames uncertainly.

"No, that's his name, darling," said Sarah—and Radar noted the endearment she tucked in. How did that square with her attitude that Ames must pay? Well, it didn't. And that was the weird thing: He knew it didn't fit, he just didn't know how.

"Named after Saint Mirplo," prattled Vic, "patron saint of mixed drinks."

"Really?" asked Ames, blown back on his heels by the rushing wind of Mirplo's bafflegab.

"Not really," said Vic. "Help myself?" He made a beeline for the bar, for even this version of Mirplo, massively advanced over earlier builds, still felt the gravitational pull of free booze. Or did he? Radar recognized Vic's blast of white noise as a megaphone move, a standard grifter's grab for control of the room. But why had Vic chosen this script? To fight batshit crazy with batshit crazy? Or just to lay down a new docket? Sarah knew Vic only vaguely; Ames knew him not at all. Therefore, he could engage them now with any clean slate he pleased, and apparently he pleased to engage with the loud, non sequitur Mirplo, *all manic all the time.* "And by the way, it's Doctor," said Vic. "Dr. Mirplo."

Radar genuinely struggled not to snicker. Allie did, too, but, *why not a doctor?* she thought. *It's your docket. You can make it what you want.*

But please, God, good driving habits.

As Vic devoured a quick scotch and something, and started in on a second, Ames asked Allie where she was from. She gave him a backstory that Radar had never heard before, a myth of middle-class Midwest normality with a minister mother and a stay-at-home dad dwelling in, of all places, Ames, Iowa. Radar immediately recognized this as a backstory wink because…*Ames, Iowa?* It was so ridiculously on the nose, clearly intended to provoke a response. It either would or would not get one, but either way it would tell them something about Ames: how attentive he was; how good he was at hiding it. In the same vein you might use a name wink, like Olivier de Havilland, to rate your mark's cultural literacy. Sometimes it helps. People think grifters do these things for whimsy, but they don't. There's always a reason.

Ames left the remarkable coincidence unremarked as he forcefully percolated his own personality through detailed elaborations of his newfound love for Austin, Texas. To Radar, Adam's nonversation appeared almost formulaic. No, it *was* formulaic. 1) Name an Austin trait or landmark. 2) Express admiration for one of its qualities. 3) Make a self-deprecating joke. 4) Swear loyalty.

He did this four times.

"I mean, the *food* in this town? I had ribs at the Salt Lick. Seriously delicious. But I'd better be careful." He patted his stomach. "Flab city, right? Anyway, the locals tell me that Artz's is the real deal for barbecue. I can't wait to try them all.

"Hook 'em Horns, yeah? Big 12 champions, baby. If I had a spare arm and a leg, I'd get season tickets.

"South by Southwest, does anything rock harder? Not that me and my tin ear would know. Still, great for the city, huh?"

And so on.

Radar felt his mind starting to go numb. Was that Ames's intention? To make his own bafflegab so stultifying that Radar lost his edge? Feeling the need to clear his head, Radar retreated to the kitchen where Sarah was chopping salad. "Your guy's in love with Texas," he said.

"He hasn't been here in summer." She put down the knife and wiped her hands on a dish towel. "Radar, I'm sorry about barging in last night." She turned to face him, leaning against the kitchen counter in such a way as to pull her blouse tight across her breasts. Radar could see the high-relief outline of her nipples. "I know I've been acting weird," she continued. "I can't help it. You…you make me not help it." She took a step forward. Then, as if winning an internal struggle, she abruptly turned away. "Dinner will be ready soon," she said. "I'll let you know." He saw her rub her eye with the back of her hand.

He gave her the kitchen and went back into the living room, where Mirplo had captured the colloquy with his *true fact, bar fact* bit: how there's two classes of reality, things that are true and things that sound true in bars late at night, and you have to guess which. "For example," he said, "Napoleon invented Napoleon brandy. True fact or bar fact?"

Ames, forced into the role of indulgent host, pondered for a moment, then said, "True fact?"

"Honestly, I don't know. I think I just made it up, but I might have heard it somewhere. Reality is tricky that way." And while Ames contemplated the trickiness of reality, Radar found himself almost outside himself, lost in analysis. Adam hadn't risen at all to the "Ames, Iowa" bait. He seemed to be tolerating Mirplo's megaphone move with equal equanimity. In all, he gave not so much as a hint that anything here was anything other than what it was. Maybe they needed a stronger sort of probe.

Merging into the Mirplovian flow, Radar diverted the discussion back around to Adam's honeymoon with Texas. "It's not a honeymoon," said Ames. "It's true love. This state and I are going all the way. You don't know it, Radar, but I'm out there every day, meeting people, getting the lay of the land."

"Meeting folks," corrected Radar.

"Excuse me?"

"Around here you don't meet people, you meet folks."

"Okay, well, thanks for the tip."

"Will it be easy to pull up stakes?"

"What?"

"No ties that bind left behind?" This was a nod to Raluca. It said, *I know about the girlfriend, friend, and you don't know how much more I know.* Radar searched Adam's eyes for a flicker of acknowledgment—and got it! For a split-second, a different person was present there, a man of Adam's true past, not his ingenuine present.

But the flicker died and Ames said, "Nope. This ol' cowboy is footloose and fancy free."

"Then welcome to Texas, cowboy. Someone get the man a yellow rose."

A few minutes later Sarah served the meal, a spicy salchicha lasagna that she washed down with quantities of a quaffable Bulgarian red, which went straight to her head and made her the sing-songy life of the party. By the time she brought out her special dessert—homemade strawberry pie, thank you very much—she was calling the wine "Marilyn," as in Marilyn merlot, and regarding herself as the height of hilarity. As she doled out the pie, she yattered on, summing up the evening and how she thought it was going so far. "We're all having a good time, right?" she said. "A good time?" She handed Radar and Adam their plates. "Friends are friends, bygones have… bywent." She giggled tipsily, then continued, "So we're all good. We're all all good. And I think that's…" she cast about for the right word "…good." She cut Allie a robust slice of pie. "Okay, mommy, this is for you, blimp you up right and proper." She served Allie her plate—and flipped it into her lap. It sure looked like an accident, a triumph of alcohol over motor control, but Radar thought that situational faux clumsiness could not be ruled out. "God, Allie, I'm so sorry!" cried Sarah. "Such a clumsy clod!" She jumped up and immediately improved the situation worse by knocking her sticky pie knife off the table and onto the white condo carpet. At that she started laughing, a defense response to humiliation, and said, "Wow, I should definitely not drink."

She scooped up the pie knife and grabbed fistfuls of pie out of Allie's lap. "Come on, girl," she said, "let's get you cleaned up." She led Allie toward the kitchen and called back over her shoulder. "You boys go out on the balcony. I'll fix this all."

Ames took Radar and Vic out on the balcony. "In a sense," he said as he slid the glass door closed behind him, "that was a happy accident. I did want to talk to you men alone."

Here comes the pitch, thought Radar. He wondered what Adam would try to hit them up with. He anticipated maybe an insider trading gag or some other sort of can't-miss disinvestment.

He did not expect the Texas Twist.

13

The Texas Twist

I've been talking to a man from a university," said Ames.

"UT?" asked Radar.

"No, Saligny."

"Never heard of it," said Vic.

"It's small. But it's been around forever. Named after a French friend of the old Texas Republic. Its fans are rabid. And it has an interesting problem: money it can't spend."

"I love that sort of problem," said Vic.

"Apparently, there are these old endowments that have been on their books for years, money that was donated to the school, but with odd strings attached, terms that couldn't be fulfilled for one reason or another. So they've become orphans in a sense."

"Poor things," said Vic. He was rapt. Well, he had a rapt act.

"Some of the endowments are quite strange," said Ames. "Problematic, you might say. There's one from 1964, a bequest from an actual Ku Klux Klansman to set up a white-studies think tank on the Saligny campus. Can you believe that? Well, with Lyndon Johnson off in Washington getting the Civil Rights Act passed, no one had the stomach to fund a racist institute, so the money just sat. Technically, that grant is still open, if someone could find a way to meet its conditions. Not that anyone wants to promote racism. But there are medical grants as well, and one of particular interest."

"And that would be?" asked Radar, playing good cop, daft cop with Mirplo.

"The bequest of Eartha Wilson, widow of a rich alum named Scuggs."

"Scuggs Wilson," said Vic, "that's a colorful name. How about Scuggs, Radar? Scuggs Hoverlander?"

"Not now, Vic," said Radar. He turned to Ames. "Go on."

"Well, it turns out this woman had a deep and abiding faith in trephination."

"Trephination?" asked Vic.

"Trepanning," said Radar. "Drilling holes in the skull to relieve pressure or release bad humors."

"Yes, exactly," said Ames. "When she passed away in 1920, she left money to study the science—such as it is—and advance its practice."

"I doubt you'll be able to get a trepanning chair funded."

"Obviously no one has been able to. But it's a matter of interpretation. If the donor can be construed to have been interested in brain study in general, then that money can be put to work. You know, Radar, people laugh at me when I say I define myself through service. You yourself had an... adverse reaction, as I recall. But I see a resource like that going to waste, and I won't put up with it. Not when lives can be saved." Ames leaned against the balcony railing and stared out over the lake. "For almost a century, Widow Wilson's dream to advance understanding of the human mind has lain fallow. I'm going to make that dream come true. Not through caveman science, of course. Through cutting-edge investigation of the human mind. The Scuggs Wilson Center for Brain Studies. I can make it happen. And Radar, I want you to help."

"How so?"

"Join me. Be my director of fundraising." He looked at Vic. "You too, Mirplo."

"You don't need two directors of fundraising," said Vic.

"No, of course not. You'll be my head of special projects."

"I *am* a special projects kind of guy," Vic conceded.

"I know you are. That's why I want you with me."

"Why do you need fundraising?" asked Radar. "I thought there was an endowment for the spend."

"Well, yes, but it seems to require a matching grant."

"That's one of the conditions?"

"Mm-hmm."

Radar said nothing. He'd just been handed a Texas Twist, and though he had run the gag many times before, he'd never been on the receiving end of it. He found the sensation quite strange.

In the Texas Twist, a hapless do-gooder is roped into working for a worthy cause. There's never any problem finding such folk, for charity enthusiasts abound: people desperate to give their lives some sense of purpose. Those who take the bait are invited to take on roles of great responsibility within the worthy cause, but really they're just getting primed for the bleed: the key moment in the con when, for some bafflegab reason, the cause finds itself in sudden need of fast cash. Well, the mook is so passionate and dedicated and do-gooding and all, that he reaches for the first wallet he can find: his own. It's a trope of the Texas Twist that the charity's primary fundraiser is also its chief chump, and for Ames to imply that a grifter as savvy as Radar could be put in that position was really quite insulting. But Radar didn't know if Ames apprehended the gag on that level, so he kept his indignation to himself as he diverted the discourse to, "Special projects. What's that all about?"

"Whatever Mirplo wants," said Adam. "He's a charming character. *And* a character. Perhaps he'll be our spokesman." Ames waxed poetic for many long moments about the opportunities that awaited Vic as the public face of the Scuggs Wilson Center. Radar and Vic instantly understood that Vic was being magpied—distracted by something shiny. Radar decided to distract back. "You sure you don't want Dr. Mirplo on your medical staff?" he asked.

The question was so preposterous that it almost blew its own cover. But it also threw Ames. "He...he didn't name his specialty," stammered Adam. "It would be a huge coincidence if—"

"Neuroscience," said Vic. He allowed for just a beat of reaction, then said, "Nah, I'm just joshing. It's not neuroscience. Anyway, if Radar's in, I'm in. Whether he goeth, I goeth, too."

Ames looked greatly relieved. Apparently the prospect of Dr. Mirplo on staff was more than he had mapped. He drew a deep breath and said, "So, Radar, what do you think? Have I piqued your interest?"

"With all due respect, Adam, you can't know I'm right for this job."

"Because I barely have your measure, right?" said Ames.

"That's right."

"Radar, you're a close and guarded man. I get that, and I respect it. But your true nature shines through."

"Does it?"

"Definitely. The way you've protected Sarah, looked out for her interests, that shows me your integrity. I know I can count on you, and I know that the people you approach for contributions will see you in the same light."

"I appreciate your confidence," said Radar. "Have you run this by Sarah? I mean, what about Jonah and the Karn's?"

"On that front," said Ames, "I admit to a certain frustration. I had expected Dr. Gauch to be more forthcoming, but now he won't even release his serum."

Radar gave Ames some eyebrow. "No?"

"No. He says it's not ready. I accept that—you can't rush science right? But that's all the more reason to move on, find another approach."

"Substitute Karn's for trephination and research the hell out of it?"

"That's the idea. The intent of the original grant is honored and Karn's research gets a big leg up. And not just Karn's. My contact on the allocation board says my research will have a free hand."

"Allocation board?" asked Radar.

"The group at Saligny responsible for these orphan

endowments."

"I see. And you have a good ol' Texas hookup with them, do you?"

"With one of them, yes."

"Have you talked yapay?"

"Yapay?"

"Baksheesh. Lagniappe. This is Texas, buddy. Wheels don't turn without grease."

"Oh, I couldn't be a party to that," said Adam, upright. "And Radar, I'd appreciate it if you didn't mention it again. This will be a square deal, or no deal."

Of course it will, thought Radar. *Why wouldn't it be?* Through the glass door, he saw Allie and Sarah approaching. "Why are we talking alone?" he asked. "What's wrong with Allie knowing?"

"Oh, well, I don't have a job for her. I didn't want to hurt her feelings. Not that she'd want a job anyhow. I mean, she'll be occupied with the little one, right?"

"Oh yeah," said Radar, "she's got stay-at-home mom written all over her."

The girls came out on the balcony and the conversation turned elsewhere.

At a certain point later, Radar came out of the bathroom to find Ames waiting for him. "I wanted a moment alone," he said. "I want you to know how key you are to my plans." Radar said nothing. "You have a special quality, Radar. People gravitate to it. Sarah has, and she's not the fluffhead you think she is, not when it comes to judging character."

Then how'd she get mixed up with you, man?

"I want you involved," continued Ames. "I need you

involved. Of course you can say no, but think about it first. Really think; don't just pay lip service. Because I have qualities, too. And one of my qualities is commitment. I worked hard to find someone like Sarah, someone in need. When I set out to find people, I don't stop. I'm not boasting, that's just how I am. So you can turn me down now, go your separate way, that's okay. But next time, it could be you who's in need, you know? Or someone in your family."

"Viewed through a certain filter," said Radar slowly, "that could sound like a threat."

"Oh, no, no, no, you misunderstand me. Again." Ames looked exasperated. "Radar, I only mean that if you help me out here, I'll be in your debt, and that's a debt you can call in any time. That's all I'm saying. How could you think otherwise?"

"Must be the cortisol talking," said Radar. Ames wondered what he meant, but Radar didn't bother to explain. He just looked into Adam's eyes, and noticed for the first time how really dead they were.

The evening wound down. Radar, Vic, and Allie went home and sat up late deconstructing it. Allie wanted to know if Radar felt sure he'd been threatened.

"I'm sure," said Radar. "I saw Adam's hard side. He wanted me to."

"Meanwhile," said Allie, "Sarah says she's now disappointed that he doesn't seem to be a crook."

"Which she would," said Radar. "She's the queen of the clueless parade."

"Is she?" asked Allie. "I'm not convinced."

"I'm with Allie, Radar. She's bedlam-built for sure, but

she wears her stupid on her sleeve. It's there for show. I would know. I've worn that costume often enough."

"That you have, my dear Dr. Mirplo. So," he said "we have Ames in the game for sure. Everything from Athol confirms it." The others nodded. "And he knows we know it, but he won't come off his true-believer script, even though tonight would've been the perfect time to."

"Why should he?" asked Vic. "It's a great docket for dodging graft, or at least knocking down the price. And it plays well against us."

"And what about this allocation board? Is it anything but smoke?"

"He might've stumbled onto something," conceded Allie. "We know he prospects for leads pretty hard."

"Will his story track for them? Will it hold up to an undiscerning eye?"

"I would think," said Allie. "Precedent of concern for brain-sick kids. His own sad story, if you buy it. Finds true love in Texas and dedicates himself to a new dream. Who around here doesn't love to see 'love' and 'Texas' in the same sentence?"

"That's beside the point," said Vic. "He's running the Twist, right Radar?"

"What, past us?" said Allie. "He can't think that'll work."

"Maybe he underestimates us," said Radar. "He must be feeling pretty confident. After all, he does have us tar babied up pretty good."

"Agreed," said Vic.

"Which I'm sick of."

"Agreed," Vic repeated.

"As far as I'm concerned, he can stick his Texas Twist right up his—"

"Agreed," said Vic one more time.

"Vic, what are you doing?"

"Waiting for you to come around. It's obvious we're going to war with this guy. I wrote about it all day. This is the point in the story where you finally put it on the table that we teach the dude a lesson. But Allie and I are already onboard with that."

"You've talked about it?"

"We haven't had to," said Allie. "We're just at the same point of impatience. *Your* same point, Radar, otherwise why are we having this discussion?"

"No reason I can think of," said Radar. And with that, they went to bed.

The next morning, finding the apartment's feng shui antagonistic to his creative framework, Vic decamped to Java Man (the new one, slightly nearer than the old one) to write. Back at the flat, Radar was doing some dishes and thinking about stocking his bench. It might be useful to have a new player to throw at Ames, if and when the need arose. One came immediately to mind. Radar did a little mental math, contemplated a difference in time zones, and thought, *He's probably teeing off about now.*

The doorbell rang. Allie went to answer, and there was Sarah, breathless, bouncing back and forth from foot to foot, unrestrained elation on her face. "It's a miracle!" she shouted, throwing herself into Allie's arms. "Oh, Allie!"

"Sarah, what's going on?"

"It's Jonah!" crowed Sarah. "He's not sick after all!"

14

The Visine Gag

Two states away, a friendly dome of high pressure kept winter off Arizona's back, bringing buttery blue skies and scudding white clouds to Phoenix, Scottsdale, and the rest of the Valley of the Sun. The snowbirds were out in force at the Loco Creek Golf Resort, so much so that anyone wanting to play short of a foursome would likely have to pass the starter some serious change. The golfer known on these links as Chuck Woodrow had done just that, somewhat to the surprise of his guest, an average white dentist named Bleeth. Chuck was sixty-five but looked young for his age, unless he chose not to. Today he presented himself as a reasonable man of reasonable means who just happened to hate playing in crowds. Despite a considerable bribe, the best the starter would do was a threesome, and so they were joined on the first tee by a paunchy retired black auto worker from Detroit who called himself Honey. Honey was reluctant to gamble at first. He said the greens fees on these fancy Phoenix courses were killing enough as it was, but Chuck was persuasive, and Bleeth was just keen. By the end of the front nine, Honey was two grand to the good, having pounded them on stroke count, putts, first-on, first-in, closest-to-the-pin, bingle bangle bungle, and some just plain wacky proposition shots that the grizzled ebony veteran always seemed to make. With the contented sigh of a man on a roll, he dropped his golf bag at the tenth tee and headed for the snack bar to get something to eat.

"I know I damn shouldn't," he said, patting his girth. "But what the fuck. Beer, yo? My treat. Maybe a little buzz'll better y'all's games." Honey walked off chuckling and scratching his ass.

"That smug bastard," said Chuck. "I never should've brought him into our bets."

"I don't know how he does it," said Bleeth, whose successful chain of Bleeth's Teeths generated enough revenue to feed his considerable gambling jones. "He doesn't look that good. He's just damn lucky."

Honey placed his food order, then headed to the bathroom. He whistled to get their attention and shouted, "I'll be back. Gotta drop a deuce." He disappeared around the side of the snack bar.

"Know what I think?" said Chuck. "I think it's time we changed his luck."

"What do you mean?"

By way of answer, Chuck reached into a zippered side compartment of his golf bag and pulled out a small bottle bearing the label of a popular brand of eye drops. "Check it out," he said as he squeezed a drop onto Bleeth's fingertip.

Bleeth touched it to his thumb. "Tacky," he said.

"Uh-huh. They call this the Visine gag. See, that's a liquid resin. Pitchers use it to improve their grip on the ball." Chuck winked. "Till they get caught." With a furtive glance toward the bathroom, he crouched down and started squirting the stuff on the heads of Honey's clubs. "It dries clear," he said, "but wait'll you see what it does to his shots."

"You know, that's kind of cheating."

"What, you don't think he's been cheating all along? All those trick shots he's been making? He's a hustler, Bleeth. I figured it out on the first hole. Now he gets a taste of his own medicine. I'm going to get all my money back and then some. You want in?"

"I don't know...."

"Hey, if you don't want to get well, that's up to you." Chuck finished loading up Honey's clubs. "But make up your mind, 'cause here he comes." Chuck pocketed the bottle as Honey picked up his food and walked over.

"False alarm," said Honey with a self-satisfied grin. "Just a big, big ass flapper." He bit into a drippy taco—and explosively spat it out. Some shredded cheese and hot sauce landed on Bleeth's Footjoys. "Jesus Christ, that's disgusting." Honey yelled angrily at the Hispanic kid running the snack bar, "Hey, Pancho! What the hell do you put in these things, horse meat?" The kid flipped him the bird and cursed him elaborately in Spanish. (He'd been paid ten bucks to do so.) "Damn border bunnies," muttered Honey. "You'd think they'd know how to make Mexican food at least. I am throwing this shit away." He walked across the tenth tee to a trash can.

"What an asshole," whispered Chuck. "Come on, let's take him down."

Bleeth gave a terse nod. His liberal sensitivities had been inflamed by Honey's racial rhetoric, and he now felt like he and Chuck were secretly united against a common enemy.

Honey didn't need much urging to double the bets. More candy from babies, according to him. He did, of course, insist on knowing that the others could cover. Chuck obliged by showing a wad of bills bound up in an *I Love Boobies* wristband. Bleeth opened his wallet and fanned a thick sheaf of hundreds—possibly fifty or more—and Honey seemed satisfied. They set off down the back nine.

And sure enough, Honey suddenly couldn't hit clean. His drives savagely hooked or sliced. He topped his fairway shots and hacked his way through the rough. Nor could he chip or putt, for all of his lines knuckled off at odd angles. "What the fug is wrong with me?" he asked himself as the bogeys and double-bogeys piled up. A blowup in a sand trap left him cursing and sweating as he dragged himself to the fourteenth tee. His two thousand dollar winnings were smoke.

"This's bullshit," fumed Honey to himself. "Let these damn kabloonuks off the hook like 'at. A'ight, that shit stops now." He looked at Bleeth. "I know you got five grand." He shot a nod at Chuck, "How 'bout you?"

"About the same."

"Well, I got ten," said Honey, flashing his roll (a grifter's roll, as it happened, with big bills on the outside and smaller ones within). "I'll take on both of you peckerwoods. Five holes, best score, winner take all."

"No way," said Chuck. "That's too much."

"Come on, pussy. Man the fuck up."

Chuck looked at Bleeth and read his mind like reading a thought balloon over his head. Bleeth wanted to chase that buzz but he was scared, and in his indecision he had ceded control of the moment to Chuck. "We play partners," Chuck said at last. He wagged a thumb at Bleeth. "Him and me. Best ball."

"Nuh-uh," said Honey. "That gives away the store."

"Do I have to say man the fuck up? Or don't you want the action?"

Honey ground his teeth. Bleeth looked on, expectant. Best ball was a huge edge. Plus the shit on Honey's clubs… this was going to be sweet. But only if Honey said yes.

Which, at last, he did.

And proceeded to light up the final five holes.

His drives still took funky lines, but somehow they were the right lines. His approaches and chips were ugly but accurate; his putts wobbly but true. Of course with Chuck and Bleeth playing partners' best ball, the match was still competitive; the score was tied as they approached the eighteenth hole, a short par three over a duck pond onto a postage-stamp green.

"Okay, boys," said Honey, "let's see who likes pressure." He teed up his ball and addressed it with his seven iron. After taking a practice swing, he suddenly backed off. "Somethin' fucked up about this club," he said. "I don't trust it." He put it back in his bag and pulled out his nine iron instead.

Chuck laughed. "You'll never make the green with that," he said.

"Will if I hit it hard enough," said Honey. "Hard hit forgives a multitude of sins." With that he gripped it and ripped it, depositing his ball on the green about thirty feet from the pin. He grinned at the others, his yellow-white teeth shining between his sienna lips. He tipped them an imaginary cap and said, "Y'alls' turn, boys."

Bleeth went next. He teed up his ball, then backed off for a moment to consider his shot. With the back of his gloved hand, he wiped sweat off his upper lip. Honey's taunt— *Let's see who likes pressure*—rang in his ears. The truth was, he didn't like pressure. He didn't like that his whole bankroll was in play. *How did that even happen?* He addressed the ball, took a practice swing, set his stance, drew the club back slowly…and doinked his drive into the pond.

"Oh, ho ho," chuckled Honey. "Not your finest hour there, saltine. Better hope your partner comes through." He turned to Chuck. "Your turn, buddy."

"Not your buddy," muttered Chuck.

"Ooh," said Honey with exaggerated concern. "Someone's getting testy."

Chuck ignored him. He placed his ball on the tee, settled himself, took a smooth, measured swing, and dropped his drive on the green. It bit on the backspin and came to rest about eight feet from the pin.

"Not bad," whistled Honey. "Not bad at all."

As they walked to the green, Bleeth allowed himself a smile inside. All that had to happen was for Honey to miss a long putt and for them to make a short one. And they had two shots at it.

They got to the green. Honey sized up his putt. "This

baby's longer than I thought," he said, his brow creased with concern. He stood over the ball for an age. Chuck caught Bleeth's eye and mimed squeezing drops from a bottle. Bleeth just sighed. He felt a little sick inside. Honey, meanwhile, rested his mind, took a long, controlled breath, stroked on the exhale, and sent the ball straight and true to the cup. "Swish!" he shouted. "Yeah! Nothing but net!" He bowed extravagantly to the others. "Take it away, boys. One to tie, do or die."

Bleeth made a shambles of his attempt. With no faith in himself and desperate faith in his partner, he overstroked the putt and shot it clear off the green. Now it was up to Chuck to force a tie. He walked the line of his putt, inspecting it and flicking away the odd leaf or twig. In truth it was only an eight-footer, the kind of putt Chuck drained easily every day of his golfing life. But Bleeth could see the strain on his face as he grounded his club behind the ball, cocked it back… brought it forward…and stubbed the turf! He hit the ball on the short hop and knocked it somewhat less than halfway to the hole.

"He chumped the putt!" crowed Honey. "Mayonnaise motherfucker chumped the putt!" He held out his beefy black hand. "Let's have the luscious." Chuck pulled out his wad and slapped it angrily into Honey's hand. With a look of dull disbelief, Bleeth found himself opening his wallet and handed over his hundreds, which Honey snatched and pocketed with undisguised glee. "Pleasure doing business with you boys," he said. He hefted his clubs. "Oh, by the way." He licked the head of his putter. "Mmm," he said, "tasty," and strolled away laughing.

Back in the parking lot, Chuck couldn't look his partner in the eye. "I'm sorry I got you involved with that," he said, angrily hurling his clubs into the trunk of his car. "My wife always tells me not to play high, but I do it, and…fuck."

Bleeth could commiserate. He had a wife like that, too.

Chuck looked at his cell phone. "She left a message." He read the text aloud in a high, sarcastic voice. "'When are you coming home?' Oh, I am such toast." Chuck got in his car, shaking his head sadly. "Well, might as well go face the music," he said, and off he drove.

Five minute later—five minutes too late—Bleeth figured it out. Of course they were working together; how could they not be? But Chuck convincingly hated Honey. And had Bleeth hating Honey, too. That's where they got him—where ire shouted down logic. And then that bit about the wife.… Thought Bleeth, *I'll bet Chuck's not even married.*

He was right. Chuck wasn't married. Nor was Chuck even Chuck, per se. He was Charles Woodrow Hoverlander, known as Woody to those who knew him, including his old friend Honey Moon, no retired auto worker from Detroit but a circuit grifter like himself. They'd meet up later and split the get, twenty-five hundred each, less expenses. Not a bad way to spend a winter weekday.

Funny thing, though—there really had been a text message on his phone.

A message from Radar. Inviting his father out to play.

15

On Its Way to Pluto

ot sick?" asked Allie. "Cured?"

"Not cured!" said Sarah. "Not sick! Oh, Allie, can I come in?" She didn't wait for more than a nod, but skittered in and threw herself on the couch, then jumped right up again, too excited to sit. She wrung her hands as if to shake off static electricity. "Allie, they were wrong. The doctors were wrong all along. Jonah doesn't have Karn's! He has a virus, that's all, a virus they can cure with antibiotics. He'll ride out his treatment at my mom's and be home in ten days' time, good as new. Isn't that something?"

"That's quite a development. Sarah, I have to ask, is this more con practice?"

"What? No! God no! Do you think I'd lie about something like this? This is my boy's life. Allie, it's a miracle! And you know who's responsible?"

"Who?" She dreaded to hear Sarah say Radar.

"My Adam Ames," said Sarah proudly, holding her hand

to her breast. "He's the one who found us a second opinion. He *made* me send Jonah. I'm so glad I did. I can't believe my baby's going to be all right!" Now she collapsed on the couch, nervous energy wicking away as adrenaline shock ebbed. "God, I hope I never go through anything like that again. So worried. So many sleepless nights. You can't imagine the relief I'm feeling right now. I feel reborn."

"That's wonderful, Sarah," Allie said levelly. "I'm happy for you."

"I'm happy for me, too." Her eyes brightened. "Oh, and plus Adam told me the good news about the boys working for him. That is so great."

"That hasn't been decided, Sarah."

"Oh, hush, why wouldn't it be? It'll be so much fun, our men coming home from work together. We'll be all, 'How was your day, dear?' and they'll talk shop over drinks and the dinners we'll fix. And then later, when you need it, you'll have a built-in babysitter. You'll see. It's gonna be a full-time fiesta from here on out." Sarah's eyes gleamed. "Maybe I'll join you in, you know, blimpyhood."

"Sarah, don't you remember what Adam tried to do to you?"

"Oh, I don't think that was what you thought it was at all. Anyway, 'It's on its way to Pluto,' as my daddy used to say. The important thing now is that Jonah's getting fixed and we can focus all our energy on helping Adam. Do you know what, Allie? I just think he is a great man. It's funny…" She reached over and put a hand on Allie's knee, a gesture that Allie could only greet with widening eyes. "For awhile I thought your Radar was a catch. Not that he's not, but I mean a catch I missed out on. Now I see that Adam is the real catch. No offense to Radar."

"None taken," said Radar, coming in to join them. Boy sloped in with him, crunching noisily on an empty plastic water bottle.

"Oh, you sneak," scolded Sarah. "How long have you been listening?"

"Not that long." He came over to Sarah and put his hand on her shoulder. "That's great news about Jonah. As for Adam, please tell him that Vic and I have talked it over, and we'd be pleased to make any contribution we can to his cause."

That got Radar a hug whether he liked it or not, but he had decided that it would be useful to send his assent through Sarah, just to see how she muddied the message. She left a few minutes later, frothing with all her good news. Radar and Allie agreed that her performance was pretty low theater, but the only one who seemed not to notice that was Sarah.

When Vic came home, he announced, "I think Adam's going to try to write Jonah out of the script. Cure him or something."

Radar and Allie exchanged looks. "Cure him?" asked Radar, playfully. "Why not finish him off?"

"You mean let the fake disease take the fake sick kid down?" asked Vic. Radar nodded. Vic nodded back. "You could do that. It's a little downbeat, but hold the funeral out of town, come back in a big state of grief and then...." Vic paused. "No, that won't work. Mourning takes too long, and Ames is a man in a hurry. You'll see. He'll try to rush us. Rush us like rubes, I bet. Anyway, what's going on around here?"

That's when they told Vic Sarah's news, and all admired

the insight or foresight of the amazing Dr. Mirplo. But as the back-pattery faded, Radar said, "Guys, we have to ask again, Where is Sarah in this?" He made a grab for Boy's water bottle, but came up empty. "I mean, she's giving us a tight narrative, if you grant the glue of loopiness that holds her whole thing together, but we need to know: Is she that on script or just that florid in the tales she tells?"

"It occurs to me," said Allie, "that she's just that practiced."

"What do you mean?"

"We know she's run charity scams with Jonah at points in the past. Maybe this is always her exit strategy, the miracle cure from the unexpected source. She maybe even offers to return the donations, but by then she has so moved the townsfolk that they won't hear of it. Then it's out of sight, out of mind, and who bothers to follow up and see if little Jonah ever completed his recovery?"

Radar finally snatched the bottle away from Boy and flipped it across the room. Boy scampered after it and pounced on it with ungainly zeal. The crackle of flexing PET reverberated through the room.

"Hey Radar," said Vic, "I just had a funny idea. What if—?" He bit off the rest of the sentence.

"What if what?"

Radar could hear the stumble in Vic's voice. "What if Boy chews up that thing and swallows it whole?" But even as he said this, Vic sent Radar a text, *What if this place is bugged?*

Well, what if it is? Radar texted back. He knew it was possible. Sarah'd had plenty of access.

Do you think we ought to bug back?

"No chance," said Radar. "He's too smart for that."

While meanwhile texting back, *Why not?*

Upon later discussion, outside the apartment, Allie felt it was a bridge too far. After all, if they were smart enough to stay mum in their flat, then Ames and Sarah would likely be likewise. According to Vic, however, "When chasing wild geese, leave no stone unturned," so he headed up to the Spy Exchange on North Burnet to check out the latest advances in hooded surveillance.

The pretty little salesclerk (writes Vic) catches my eye like a touchdown pass. Hook 'em Horns. She presents as an erratic anarchist, serially pierced and tattooed, yes, wearing a *fuck authority* T-shirt, yes, but also sporting rhinestone cowboy boots, spray-on jeans, and a sassy Stetson. Spend any time at all in this town and you come to recognize the look: cowpunk chic, favorite of UT coeds and girl roadies. She greets my request for covert gear with amoral authority, and I can guess that here in the international house of spies she's sold enough lock picks, handcuffs, bogus badges, and blackjacks to become numb to their purpose or use. She directs me to the smallest mic in the house, no bigger than the watch battery that powers it, and covered in a mouse-brown powdercoat that'll blend it right in in a flower pot or china hutch. I also buy a snooper sweeper for counter surveillance. We transact. She throws in a link to a black-ops app store, where I can download YvesDropp, a highly programmable, highly illegal bug-management app. She tells me she's a whiz with these things if I need a consultant. Even as I tell her I can find my way around a tablet, I get a bright idea. I show her a digital picture of Adam Ames. It's a longshot but also a freeroll, because I'm really just sizing her up. I think I like the cut of her jib.

I find her jib shapely.

"So," I say, "you seen this mister?"

She gives me a sigh like the weight of the world and says in a syrupy Austin drawl, "Y'all know I can't tell you that."

"Could you tell me if I were a cop?"

"Nope."

"Why not?"

"'Cause I don't talk to cops."

"Good answer. What if I were a cop that controlled petty cash?"

"How petty?"

"At least a Big Ben."

"That's not much."

"Not bad for a first consulting gig."

She looks around furtively, as empty a gesture as any you could think of in a spy shop, and says, "If I had a name I could look it up. Customer database."

"Now we're talking," say I. "Now we are having a conversation."

I write the name on a piece of paper and slide it across the counter, along with a tightly folded C-note. She makes the cash vanish, then does a quick keyboard dance. In a minute, she's writing on the same piece of paper, which she slides back to me, which I pocket. She's fast, this one. In this game, fast is good. "The name's Mirplo," I say. "And you are…?"

She doesn't give me her name. Instead she just asks, "What's a Mirplo?"

"That question's too big to answer all at once," I say.

"Unknown stranger, is this your only job?"

"Well, yeah. I mean, it's only part-time. I'm in school at UT."

"Hook 'em Horns," I say. She does not say Hook 'em Horns back. Interesting. She's against everything she stands for, and that's just how I like 'em. "I might have something for you," I say. "Can you hang loose?"

"Like Mother Goose."

"Good," say I. "That's good...." I open another space where she might place her name.

This time she does. "Kadyn."

"Kaden with an e?"

"No."

"I?"

"Nope."

"Y?"

She gives me this devilish *you got it* smirk, and I decide I definitely like this pert little cowpunk.

I think I might write her right in.

16

Five Oh
Something Something

By Allie's reckoning, the first of March marked her eighth week. Dreams and food were bending her mind now, and they went hand in glove, like this one dream of waffles that got her up before dawn because, *waffles, what a good idea!* And then when she was done making them, she threw them away. She couldn't stomach eating them.

She still had no bulge to speak of, but a snug waistband here and a taut bra there told her that the change train was coming to town. This put her in a giddy mood, even though she knew that her moods were not her own. She pictured the peanut down in her womb throwing open her hormone valves, releasin' the relaxin. She had trouble visualizing a girl fetus making such mischief, no matter what Radar said. *A boy,* she vibed. *Definitely having a boy.*

In the end it was Allie who planted the bug in Sarah's apartment. They had become coffee-break buddies, as per

Radar's plan to have Allie normalize relations with Sarah and try to discover where the truth of her lay. In this she had been largely thwarted, for it seemed like when she scratched the surface of Sarah all she got was…more surface. But was it surface or artifice? Allie couldn't tell, and when the needle of doubt wouldn't budge either way, she decided to go along with the listening in. *Make the latest possible decision based on the best available information,* right? So one morning at Sarah's, while she was off in the kitchen on her phone, Allie upended an ottoman, used a ballpoint pen to punch a tiny hole in its underlining, and popped the bug inside. By the time Sarah returned to the room, Allie was reading a magazine with her feet up.

"That was Adam," bubbled Sarah. "He's decided he needs a foundation."

"A foundation?"

"To start the brain center. An organization that can cut through red tape and write grants and stuff. He called it a… five oh something something?"

"A 501(c)?"

"That's it. Adam says with a foundation he can fund feasibility studies, see what research has promise. Oh, I hope he finds something. You know, I hadn't realized what a pity party I was on. When Jonah was sick? I saw prions eating away at his brain and all I could think was, oh poor me, you know? I forgot that life is a gift, and you have to make the most of it, especially my boy, with his time so short. Now that it's not short, well, now I know how big a gift I got. And then Adam comes along and he gives and gives and gives and now that Jason's okay, I feel like I want to do that too, you know? Don't you? Feel like you want to give back?"

"Now that Jason's okay?"

"Huh?"

"Your son. You called him Jason."

"No I didn't."

"Yeah, you kind of did."

"Really?" Sarah rolled her eyes comically. "Woo-hoo, guess who else better get her prions checked, huh?" A cloud passed over Sarah's eyes, and to Allie it registered as a glimpse of some other level of her. Sarah must have noticed it, too, for she said, "To tell you the truth, I'm actually feeling a little lightheaded. Would you mind going now? I think I'd like to lie down."

"Of course not. Feel better."

Later that day, Allie and the boys bundled Boy into the back of the Staccato and headed out to a local dog park, privately sponsored by Paws That Refreshes brand dog water. The trip may have been unnecessary in terms of grift hygiene, since a sweep of their flat had turned up no hidden ears, but the day was warm and it felt good to be outside, especially for Allie, who lifted her shirt to expose her belly to the sun. Radar, still spouting the derived wisdom of his baby books, had predicted that at this point in her pregnancy she would start to become flighty and distracted. She supposed that thinking of her belly as a solar panel might qualify as that. Boy didn't care. He had butts to sniff and exotic balls to chomp. Humans never quite recognize it, but dog parks are an orgy of almost unbearable sensation to most dogs.

The three of them sat on a concrete bench, dissecting Sarah's gaffe. Allie thought that since Sarah changed her son's name from time to time and scam to scam, on this occasion she might have conflated her Jason and Jonah. Vic took it as a sign that Sarah was losing what limited cheese she had. Radar was more interested in Adam's new foundation. "He must know," said Radar, "that a 501(c) will be of interest to people like us."

"'People like us,'" agreed Vic, "would see it as a license to print money."

"Is it bait?" asked Allie. "Or are we just intended to see it as such?"

Before Radar could speculate, Mirplo's Rabota made a sound like a Chinese gong. "This might shed a light," said Vic. I programmed the YvesDropp app to voice activate."

"You can do that?" asked Allie.

"Dr. Mirplo can do anything," said Radar.

"And don't you forget it." Vic touched the tablet screen twice and put it on speaker, though what they heard from the apartment was primarily TV, some reality show, probably that new one, *Nudity Island,* that's getting all the talk. Adam and Sarah had mild words about it, but this was just couple stuff; if you were listening in on anyone else, you'd think it was cute.

Eventually, Radar said, "This is starting to creep me out. Can you refine the voice activation on that thing?"

"What, like, train it with keywords?"

"Exactly. So we don't have to be bored and…creepy."

"I wouldn't have expected this reaction from you, Radar."

"I wouldn't have expected it from me, either. But, God, they sound so normal."

"So boring," said Vic.

"So maybe they're wary like we're wary," said Radar, "and they only speak freely outside the home."

"Or he's still gaming her."

"Or she's gaming him."

"Gosh," said Allie drily, "who'd have ever thought that a bug would clarify things *so* much?" Radar gave her the benefit of a grin, but they all knew that in any case Vic's trip to the surveillance supermarket had not been in vain, for his hundo had bought the information that Ames now owned a blank-firing Walther P22. Radar cast a glance at Allie sunning her belly and loved his unborn child with all his goofy heart. The thought of a gun in the picture, even a blank gun, made his cortisol jump. Meanwhile, infuriatingly, Radar still felt the need to keep letting Ames call the shots. This was Adam's script, his scam, and Radar wouldn't know how to break it until further pieces of the puzzle were revealed. But it galled him just the same. No grifter likes to ride another man's script, especially when he doesn't know where it's headed.

Not that he wasn't devising scripts of his own.

The next day Ames texted Radar and Vic and asked them to meet him at the Yoghurt Yurt on Guadalupe Street across from the UT campus. Yogurt and niceties later, he led them down Guadalupe to a door between two stores, where a flight of stairs rose to a small second-floor business suite overlooking the street and the UT campus beyond. The suite had a tiny reception area, an open administrative/work space, and one private office. Exposed brick walls and weary secondhand furniture gave the place an austere feel.

"Well?" asked Ames after they'd looked around. "What do you think? Not too lavish, right?"

"No," said Radar, "I wouldn't call it lavish."

"Because this is one foundation that's going to be run lean and mean, and Radar, that means I'm counting on you for your…what shall I call it?…gift of gab. I don't want you going out and all wining and dining potential donors. If you can't sell the Wilson Center on its merits, then I don't want you selling it at all."

There was nothing, absolutely nothing, in Adam's words that put him anywhere but on the level; yet, at the same time, not a single word rang true. Radar sorted through appropriate replies and settled on, "Well, I'm your man, man."

"Good. Excellent." Ames turned to Vic. "Now, Dr. Mirplo—"

"Oh, I'm not really a doctor," said Vic.

"What?"

"I was just jerking your chin the other night."

"Jerking my…?"

"Chin. You know, pulling your log."

Ames stared at him blankly for a moment, then laughed in a broad, theatrical way. "Of course," he said. "I knew that. I knew that." His tone perfectly conveyed the inner tension of a man caught on the wrong side of a joke trying desperately to demonstrate otherwise. "So you're not a doctor?"

"No, yeah, I am," said Vic.

"What?"

"A doctor. See, and now I'm pulling it back."

This elicited damn near a sneer from Adam, who realized that Vic was now simply dissing him—and may have been doing so just to see how he would react. Ames quickly bottled his reaction and played what his script demanded that he play: the good sport. He threw a convivial arm around Vic. "And that's just the kind of whimsy I'm looking for. So, Doctor or Mister or Doctor Mirplo, how are we coming with special projects?"

"We have something in mind," said Vic. "A party."

"Party?"

"A launch event for the foundation. A fundraiser. Can't ever raise too many funds."

Radar held his breath. Looking down the length of the snuke toward what he imagined would be its endgame, it seemed necessary for Vic to lay this particular section of pipe. But would Ames go for it?

Ames templed his fingers and nodded, "Sounds good. Sounds real good. But nothing too pricey, okay? Please. I hate those charities where most of the money just goes to attract more money."

"Me too," said Vic. He paused, then said, "I can book Willie Nelson for free."

"Can you really?" For just a moment, Adam was keen as a kid in a candy shop, but then he read Vic's face. He wagged his finger in admonishment. "This is more whimsy, isn't it?"

"Whimsy it is," said Vic. "Don't worry, I'll whomp up something."

"There you go," said Ames. "The chief cook in charge of whomping things up." He turned away from Vic, and seemed greatly relieved to do so. "Now Radar," he said, "as you know, I've made friends with some influential people...."

"On the allocation board."

"Yes, exactly. And they're very enthusiastic about my

plan. But as I explained, they don't feel that they can take on the whole risk of the project by themselves."

"Hence," said Radar, "the need for matching funds."

"Yes, that's right. Now Radar, my question to you is, do you think you can attract the kind of investments we need?"

Radar swallowed the urge to play this moment for the farce it was, a farce based on the fiction that Ames was interested in any money other than Radar's. He said, "I could make some calls. To philanthropists, like."

"No, no, no, I don't want that," said Ames with a vehemence that took Radar and Vic by surprise. "That's that same old money. Guys, I don't know if you know it, but there are people in this world whom you might think of as professional givers." Radar and Vic played sufficiently dumb to create space for Ames to continue. "Yes, they get involved with all sorts of organizations, organizations like ours. But they want things. Authority. Privilege. Next thing you know, your good work has been completely diluted, and the only people getting any benefit at all are the professional givers, through the projects and the budgets they control."

"You sound like you know a lot about this," said Mirplo.

"I know a bit," dissimulated Ames. Then he shook his head and said, "No, that's not true. I know a fair deal. Radar, Mirplo, I want to be entirely honest with you."

Oh, please do, thought Radar.

"The truth is, this isn't my first charitable foundation. Well, attempt. The last one didn't go so well. But I learned a lot from my mistakes, and the main thing I learned was to keep those professional givers at bay. You have to find folks who are genuinely committed to the same goals as you are.

Radar, that's the kind of person I want you to find."

"A true believer?" asked Radar.

"Exactly," said Ames. A knowing light flared and died in his eyes, and Radar mentally kicked himself for waving such an obvious semaphore.

"Well," said Radar, "I'll throw it out the window and see if it lands."

He knew the words rang lame, but Vic helped him out with a quick misdirectomy; he looked around the empty office and said, "It's a little lonely in here, dude. When are you going to start staffing up?"

Ames smiled like a seigneur. "Oh, no, no, I'm not going to start handing out salaries until the need is really there," he said. "For now, we'll manage well enough on our own. Like I said, 'lean and mean.' Shoestring budgets all the way around."

"Are you serious?" asked Vic, seemingly massively affronted.

"What do you mean?" asked Ames.

Mirplo said, "Look out your window, man. What do you see?"

Ames glanced down at the throng of college kids on Guadalupe.

"Students," said Ames, uncertain. "So what?"

"Mr. Ames," said Vic, "I'm sure no one would call you stupid to your face, but why did you rent space across the street from a college campus if you weren't thinking about interns?"

"Interns?"

"Interns," repeated Vic, his eyes aglow. "Of the hard-working, *unpaid* type."

Ames smiled. "You see?" he said to no one in particular. "That's why we put up with the whimsy."

Sure it is, thought Vic. But in his head he was already running his bogus recruitment campaign.

Bogus because he already knew who the intern would be.

And so it was that when Radar returned the following week, the sparky young cowpunk at the reception desk quite professionally identified herself as Kadyn, welcomed him to the offices of the Scuggs Wilson Foundation, and informed Mr. Ames that Mr. Hoverlander was here to see him. In his office, out of her earshot, Ames proclaimed himself well pleased with the girl who'd answered the ad Vic never placed, and who had so far proven so eager and capable in her work. Thus did Vic put eyes and ears inside Ames's operation, and no additional bugs need apply.

That they started keeping company after-hours was a happy accident.

Meanwhile, in certain oncology intake clinics around town, a quirky hypochondriac was making his presence known to a series of receptionists, insisting in resolute and unreasonable terms that tumors in his brain were blowing up like balloons and deranging him by the day. Had these receptionists compared notes, they would have agreed that he certainly appeared deranged, but their credit checks on him passed rigorous muster, so they passed him along to doctors who could schedule the extensive, expensive tests that his condition seemed to demand.

One obliging soul passed word of him to Adam Ames.

17

Leave Wellinov Alone

T hanks for coming in, Radar," said Ames. "I know it's a nicer day to stay home."

Radar looked out the window of Adam's office into the heart of a cold March rain and found that, for once, he agreed with Adam Ames. After a run of balmy days, winter had closed in again, like an aging diva taking extended bows, unwilling to surrender the stage. First came the icy blast of an arctic front, then a ground fog that ate hills whole, then measurable snow, rare for around here and cataclysmic to traffic. He wondered what the weather would be like when the baby was born. Autumnal. She would be born in autumn.

Autumn? Autumn Hoverlander?

Allie had started to show. Not a bulge, exactly, but measurably a mound. Just getting started. But Radar already could hardly remember a time when she hadn't been knocked up.

Nor, frankly, could he remember a time when she'd been

more randy. She jumped him at bedtime, commandeered his morning wood, and grabbed any afternoon delight that offered itself when Vic was off working with Kadyn, which these days was almost all the time. Vic had decided that the specific whimsy called for was an April Fool's spectacular. At first Adam had been skeptical; just a month to get the word out, it didn't seem like enough time. But Vic had reassured him, saying, "These things land hardest when they come out of nowhere." Actually, the telescoped time frame suited Radar's evolving script; he wanted Adam focused on an event in the future, though not too distant.

In the meantime, he had a baby mama to serve.

Just now, back home, he had found her at the bedroom mirror, naked to the waist, gawking at her own breasts.

"Look at these monsters," she said. "I've never seen them so big. You should take pictures."

"Okay."

"Later," she said as she backed him up against a wall. "I want you now." Though it was of course the hormones talking, he knew better than to talk back. Nor did it take much time, for these days Allie put the "quick" in "quickie." Radar easily got to his meeting with Ames on time. Though his mind was still very much not in the room.

"Radar? Hello? Anybody home?"

Radar turned away from the window. He flopped into one of the cheap-chic folding chairs that Ames had procured from some down-market source of prefab furniture. Ames sat behind a similarly flimsy desk, one that looked like it had been quickly thrown together for the express purpose of slowly falling apart. Surely anyone visiting the office would see the pains taken to maintain austerity, and surely that was the idea.

"I'm here," said Radar. "What's up?"

"How's it going? With the investors and such?"

"Not so good," Radar confessed. "Since I can't reach out to my usual guys, I've had to develop leads from scratch."

"I see. Well, not to say I'm doing your job for you, but I've heard about a lead you might develop."

"Really?"

"Yes, through a friend. He could be just the sort of benefactor we're looking for." Ames gave Radar a smarmy smile. "Buddy, I think it's time you put that ol' Hoverlander charm to work." It took pretty much all of that ol' Hoverlander charm to keep Radar's bile down, for the more time they spent together, the more Adam's smug self-assurance and loudly proclaimed do-gooder's zeal scraped across him like fingernails on a blackboard. Just the same, Radar couldn't help admiring how Ames had repackaged himself as as good a good ol' boy as ever graced the Lone Star State. He oozed *Don't mess with Texas* and no doubt remembered the Alamo. Though Radar was a gifted chameleon who could dissimulate across a stunningly wide range of identities, he knew he'd never master Texan. He just couldn't channel his inner blowhard, not like Ames, whose dress had drifted westward to boots and big-buckle belts. But that was just protective coloration; what Ames really had going for him, Radar realized, was fabricat bonhomie, a talent for counterfeit charm that rivaled Radar's own.

Ames now had ample time to devote to that task for, as surprised exactly no one, it had been arranged for Jonah to stay on indefinitely at Grandma's, where he had cousins to play with, kids his own age, a salutary school district, and many other most likely imaginary advantages. Radar wondered if Jonah wasn't already back out on the razzle, playing brain-broken kid for another allegedly desperate mom on the medical-scam circuit. The idea may have seemed outlandish to a normal person—who farms out their own son to road hustlers?—but was not foreign to Radar's own experience. He'd spent his ninth summer as the waiflike "adoptee" of a man selling fictive cemetery plots to the religiously devout, for everyone knows how a kid dolls up that act.

Ames handed Radar a business card, raised black ink on weathered white stock. "Here's the man I want you to meet. These are his details." Radar fingered the frayed card. That it looked like it had been sitting in someone's wallet for years was a tribute to the skills of a certain printer who specialized in making new things seem old.

When he read the name printed on the card, he snorted an explosive laugh.

"What?" asked Ames, taken aback.

"This is a great one," said Radar, continuing to chuckle. "I haven't seen this one before."

"What do you mean?"

"Didn't you read the name?"

Ames took the card back and looked at it. "Henry Wellinov. So?"

"Well, it's a fake name," said Radar. "A goof."

"Okay, now you've really lost me."

Radar said, "Let's say for the sake of argument that I'm at least a bit of what you think I am."

"Comfortable among those who play fast and loose with the rules?"

"As you put it. Then wouldn't you think I know something about that world? Its language? Its codes?" He retrieved the card and tapped it with his fingertip. "This name here, 'Wellinov'? Don't you get it? 'Leave Wellinov alone'?"

"That's a weak jest."

"It's not a jest. It stakes a claim. It tells the competition to back off."

"Competition?"

"Other scalawags. People like me, according to you. I'm not saying I'm people like me, but if I am, then this Wellinov is, too."

"And you get all that on the strength of a name. Amazing. But I don't think you're right, Radar. He's been vetted."

"By whom?"

"People."

"Oh, well, people do a good job at vetting. Vetting is what people do best." As was common in conversation with Ames, Radar felt himself split between the need to stay on his own script and the burning desire to laugh at the moment's absurdity.

"They—"

"Your people?"

"Yes, *my people*. They think he's a lonely older guy who nurtures nonexistent health problems for, as much as anything else, the pleasure of simple human contact. I've met many such lonely sufferers in my time. When they find that they can channel their loneliness into something productive, well, they're grateful."

"Ah, they get a VPM."

"VPM?"

"Verbal prostate massage."

Adam shook his head. "Radar, the things you say." He pointed at the card. "Speak to this man. Get him to think less about his own problems and more about the greater good. Maybe he's what you think he is. Maybe he's something else. Either way, his money could make the difference, and we don't have much time."

"Is that right?" said Radar.

"Yes. It's already March. The academic year ends in May. That's when my friend at Saligny leaves his position. He's termed out, Radar."

"Termed out of an allocation board?"

Ames raised his hands in overstated despair. "I don't make the rules in Texas. I just know that this fellow Wellinov is the first legitimate prospective donor we've seen. I'm not saying you've been slack, but I do notice that I'm bringing him to you when it should be the other way around." Ames waged a visible war with impatience and allowed himself to win. "In any case, Mirplo's party is timely. I'm hoping to announce full matching grants that night. I have to, or else I lose my window of opportunity and the Wilson endowment goes begging.

"Meet the man, Radar. Give him the benefit of the doubt."

"Funny," said Radar, "that's what Sarah asked me to do with you."

"And see how well that's worked out?" Adam amped up his enthusiasm to the highest wattage, and this was when

Radar loathed him most. "We're a good team, brother. We've both been working hard. And when the funds are in place.... Look, Radar, I know I come from an altruistic space that you don't share, but don't worry: You'll be rewarded for your efforts. Even for your overactive imagination." Ames shook his head again. "I honestly don't know what to make of that. I suppose it's the downside of your gift. You see things so keenly that you sometimes see things that aren't there."

"Well, you know what they say," said Radar, "the invisible and the nonexistent look very much alike."

"That's clever," said Ames. "Did you make that up?" He keyed the office intercom. "Kadyn, can you come here for a second, please?"

Her disembodied voice responded promptly, "Be right there, boss."

"Bright girl," said Ames. "Turns out she has a real knack for research. Watch this." Kadyn stepped in and Ames asked, "The name Wellinov, how common is it?"

Kadyn dropped her head over her Serengeti Smartphone, a mini-tablet that packed the punch of devices ten times its size. In seconds she had the answer. "Plenty common," she said, "in Belarus."

"There you go," Ames told Radar. "He's an immigrant. An immigrant with money. He could be our guardian angel, the matching grant that opens the university's trove. So see what you can rustle up, pard."

"Pard," said Radar, "I'll do my best."

In truth, he knew that his best would not be necessary.

After all, how hard can it be to schmooze your own old man?

That Saturday, Radar and Allie drove down to visit the Cathedral of Junk, a stunning three-story tower of welded jetsam rising from the backyard of an otherwise unassuming house in suburban South Austin. Through years of obsessive diligence, its owner had created a honeycomb of rooms, chambers, grottos, stairwells, catwalks, and dens, all assembled from accretions of abandoned shopping carts and scaffolds, rusty lawn mowers and bed frames, rebar, teakettles, empty propane tanks, anything you can think of. The Cathedral of Junk was rather a touristy trip to take, but the couple was in a touristy mood, for they'd spent the morning buying baby items, and now a little recreational eccentricity was just the thing to put thoughts of impending parenthood at bay for the day. And the Cathedral of Junk certainly qualified as recreational eccentricity or, if you cared to glorify it thus, art. Behind high sturdy walls, it was its own little world of enshrined ephemera: hanging dangles of CDs and DVDs; pillars of paperback books; playpens filled with old Smurf dolls and skateboard decks; landline telephones; CRT TVs; calendars from 1996. In all, it was a reliquary, a walk-through reminder that everything's junk at the end of its day. But if you wanted a place away from prying eyes—apart from the goggle eyes of photo-snapping Japanese sightseers—you could do worse than this shrine to the notion that all things must pass.

Radar and Allie found Woody bent over a large flowerpot filled with upended food blenders. He had gained a little weight since Radar saw him last, and the fullness of his face gave him an elfin quality. He tentatively flicked the chopper blades that rose like the propellers of tiny *Titanics* and smiled with satisfaction as they whirled.

"Mr. Wellinov, I presume?"

Woody lifted his head and broke into a broad grin. He gave them both big hugs and topped Allie's with an avuncular kiss. Though he hadn't seen his son in six months, it had been his pleasure to drop everything at Radar's request, invent Henry Wellinov, and bring the circus of him to town. Woody liked acting rashly like this. It kept him light on his feet—deft, even into the depths of late middle age. And he loved Radar's play here, first allaying Adam's suspicions by introducing Wellinov through Ames's own channels, and then raising them again with the red-flag ridiculousness of Wellinov's name. That could get a man leaning two ways at once. A good thing, if you wanted him on the wobble.

After Woody released Allie, he stepped back and pointed at her belly. "Start with that," he said. "Don't start with anything else."

"You could tell I was…?" asked Allie.

"In the family way? From a mile away."

"That seems like a safe distance," said Allie. "Soon I'll be so big you won't even recognize me."

"Trust me, my dear," said Woody, "I would recognize you if you gained a hundred pounds."

Whatever reaction Woody thought his comment would elicit, he didn't get it, for Allie suddenly stared at him, eyes wide. "Would you really?" she asked.

"Of course. Allie, you're distinctive. And beautiful. You could be the size of a shipping container and you would still be beautiful. And distinctive." Allie looked thoughtful and, it seemed to Woody, distressed. "That was supposed to be a compliment," he said.

"Oh, I know," said Allie. "It's just...."

"Just what?"

"Just," said Radar, "if you're right that she's that recognizable, even in a changed state, then we have to rethink some things."

"No we don't, Radar," said Allie with unexpected fervor. "I stand by my stand. Ames doesn't know me. We worked the same turf, that's all. Besides, like I told you, I wasn't me back then. I certainly didn't glow." She turned to Woody. "Do I really?"

"Like a radon refrigerator, hon." He turned to Radar. "So, when do I meet Ames? I don't suppose I should look too eager."

"No, actually, in this case that would be okay."

"Won't it seem like rushing the mark?"

"It will. But according to his script, I'm a clever scumbag and rushing the mark is what clever scumbags are expected to do."

"Then let's do it Monday."

"I'll set it up." Radar pulled out his device and fired off a quick text to the effect that his meeting with Mr. Wellinov had gone swimmingly, and the quirky gentleman was now ready to get with Ames to discuss the particulars.

Vic arrived just then, barking his head on a low-hanging bower of laundry baskets filled with ancient encyclopedias. "Woody, hey!" he said brightly. "Great to see you, man!" He gave the old man a hug and an enthusiastic smooch on the cheek, then turned to Radar and said, "Hey, are we sure Ames doesn't know Allie from before?"

"Man, Vic, stop doing that," said Radar, stunned again, yet not surprised, by Mirplo's uncanny jumps to relevant conclusions. "What makes you ask?"

"Actually it's something I found," said Kadyn, who did a better job than Mirplo of navigating the laundry baskets. She went to Vic's side and laced a fingerless-gloved hand in his.

"Tell me about that in a minute," said Radar. "First, Vic, are we comfortable with her here? Wouldn't we have been more comfortable discussing it first?"

"We might have," Vic agreed somberly. He put his arm around her. "But I'm comfortable now. Plus…" he tapped her noggin with his fingertip, "she smart like whip. Kadyn, tell 'em what you did."

Kadyn said with dark defensiveness, "Ames left his tablet unattended. It's not my fault."

"Fault? What fault? Who fault?" said Vic. "It was great." He turned to the others. "Guys, this gal's a natural."

"I just did a search."

"Which is what a natural does. Tell 'em the rest."

"I searched for images of you three in all of Adam's apps and files."

"Face-recognition hacks," said Vic. "TSA shit. She won't even tell me where she gets it."

Kadyn asked Radar, "Were you Olivier de Havilland, some kind of scientist?" Radar nodded. "He has pictures of that." She turned to Allie, "And did you wine and dine some guy at a steak joint in Tulsa?"

"As Fabrice Traynor, yeah."

"He has pictures of that, too."

Said Radar, "I can't believe he'd leave pictures like that

just lying around on his device."

"They weren't just lying around," said Kadyn. "They were password protected." She gave a schoolgirl smile. "But passwords are easy to guess."

"Told you," said Vic. "A natural." She pinched him in protest and Vic jumped, but not too high.

"Anything else?" asked Allie.

Kadyn replied with a question. "What's Green Girl Solutions?"

"Nothing now. It's defunct. It used to be a multilevel marketing scam. Around 2003 or so."

"Were you in it?"

"I had a cup of coffee with them."

"They have a uniform?"

"Oh, God, I forgot about the uniform."

"Ames didn't. He has pictures of you in it. At some kind of trade show in some kind of booth."

"A franchise expo, yeah, that could easily be."

Asked Radar, "Any pictures of Vic?"

"Not just pictures," Kadyn laughed. "Video."

"Karaoke," explained Vic.

She teased him in the manner of the newly encrushed, "Apparently he wants to fly like an eagle to the sea."

He nuzzled her nose. "Well, that's only because time keeps on slipping, slipping, slipping into the future." He turned to the others. "So what do you think? Can she play for our team?"

"I really want to," said Kadyn. "Ames is a dick. He's gropey."

"Really?" asked Radar. "I wouldn't have thought that."

"No, you wouldn't, would you. He's one of these guys who make it look like they don't know what they're doing. But he knows."

Radar gave Kadyn a long, searching look. To the unschooled eye, she looked exactly as she represented herself to be: a young girl pushing through post-adolescence with insolent insecurity, heavy mascara, and perhaps a fantasy con scenario nurtured by too many viewings of *The Sting* and *Ocean's Eleven*. Could she know what the con life really entailed? Could anyone at that age? But she met his gaze frankly and openly, communicating this much: that she knew enough about herself and enough about them to make an informed choice. "We'll let you know, Kadyn. In the meantime, stay under Vic's wing. He seems to have room for you there."

"Indeed I do," said Vic.

"Okay, then," Allie suddenly said with a sigh. She patted her belly. "Baby tired, we go now."

They drifted to their various parts of Austin: Allie and Radar back to the Doke, Vic and Kadyn to her place in SoCo, and Woody to a Home Sweet Suites near the airport. Radar felt a pang as he parted company from his dad. On the one hand, Woody was back in his life, so yay. On the other hand, the old jackalope was in deep mufti as usual. And wasn't that their coconspiracy? To stay within roles with each other? Wasn't time inside these roles a lost opportunity to be with each other for real? And what about little Fundament? Didn't she deserve a genuine grandpa, not someone so permanently on script? Masks were no good for the sort of daughter Radar wanted to raise. He wanted her loved ones to be real. Real with her, real with each other. Real, like he was real with Allie.

Real enough for him to say to her as they drove home, "I have to take a shot at Sarah."

"What do you mean?"

"Engage her. See if I can flip her. I haven't tried it yet. I think it needs to be tried."

"I don't disagree," said Allie, "but how far are you willing to go?" She turned to face him. "I really don't want you sleeping with her."

"I don't want me sleeping with her, either. I want me hearing how Ames plans to play us."

"It could backfire."

"Put him on a jealousy tip?"

"Or a turf one. That's you horning in. On his gal or his business, either way it's still horning in. It might piss him off."

"Well, good. He could use some pissing off. The time to pussyfoot has passed."

" 'The time to pussyfoot?' " She mocked a swoon, "Oh, Mr. Hoverlander, you do turn a phrase. Maybe you should write a book, too."

"Uh-uh," said Radar. "Only kids' stories for me." He playfully patted her belly, but as he did so he thought about Ames and those pictures, and a shiver ran through him. That was some kind of stalker shit at minimum. Up till now, Radar had thought this was a straight money touch. But if so, what was with the pictures? How long had Ames been on their trail? *No wait, wait, Radar, don't assume. Just because he has pictures doesn't mean he took pictures. Maybe he's collected them since we all crossed paths.* That sounded plausible to Radar—but he couldn't make himself believe it. It seemed clear to him that Ames had intended all along for their paths to cross.

They rolled through the back of the Doke and approached their building from behind. *I thought this was a redoubt,* thought Radar. *Now it seems like a trap. What kind of mess have I made?*

"Radar, where are you?"

"Blaming myself for the world."

"Really? Me too."

"You? Why?"

"Over Ames. Over what I just remembered or just let myself remember." Radar didn't say anything. He waited for her to continue. "We fought for a seat on a bus once. I belittled him pretty good. It was just one of those moments where you're a harasshole because you can be. Because even though I was a swollen, sullen, man-hating self-loather, I knew I was still hotter than anything a smelly hippie could hope to have. So I put him down. Maybe I pissed him off, I don't know. I wasn't even sure it was him until Kadyn mentioned Green Girl, because—" Allie stopped short. "Radar! I met him again. At that expo. He wanted to buy me a drink."

"You shot him down?"

"No doubt in flames. Back then I chased everyone away."

"I'm glad you got over that." He patted her belly again, and this time through his unborn child he felt his own strength. At the same time, this new information caused him to recalibrate his take on Ames. He now saw Adam's true-believer gloss not as a temporary veneer applied for this snuke or any snuke, but rather a permanent condition, and one that precisely defined the distance Ames kept from himself. Kadyn's comment about his wandering hands certified him as the kind of creep who doesn't know he's being one. The pictures, though, the pictures changed everything. They made the situation more dangerous. But how dangerous? *Run away* dangerous—the ol' shade 'n' fade if it's not too late? No. Ames found them once, he could find them again. So what about the opposite tack? Just confront him, lay out everything they know with a great, thumping, "See, dude? We're onto you."

And then what? Call the cops? Swing a baseball bat? How do any of those moves do anything but bounce off Adam's bland do-gooder docket? And with that, Radar realized that the pictures didn't really change anything after all. *I still have to get to the bottom of him. I still have to make him show his hand. Until I hear who Ames thinks Ames is, I'm nowhere.*

And nowhere is no place for a father-to-be to be.

18

A Captain Kirk Kiss

On Monday morning, Radar and Allie had a fight about, of all things, baby names.

From out of nowhere (from a particularly irrational place, thought Radar) Allie had thrown a moratorium on the game that he, and he thought she, had been enjoying so much. She had decided that it was bad luck to inflict names, even highly speculative or colorful or imaginative or ridiculous ones, especially ridiculous ones, on the unborn. "I don't want to jinx him," she'd said, and Radar had joked, "How about Jinx, Jinx Hoverlander?" Well, the trouble with too far is you never know you're going till you've gone, and Allie's stormy cold shoulder informed him that he had. Considering what was coming up with Sarah, he wondered if she had picked the fight just to put herself in a verisimilitude mood. He hoped so. Otherwise it was just her being mad at him and that was never big fun.

Radar arrived at the office to find Vic proofing posters,

wall cards, handbills, web pages, and evites for the foundation's fete, the magniloquently named *Inaugural First Annual April Fool's Fundraising Celebratiathon and Auction: A Fool and His Money Are Soon Partying.* "That's a mouthful," said Radar. "You sure folks won't write it off as a joke?"

"Nope. They'll be charmed 'n' disarmed."

"And how are we going to pay for it?"

"What, this part? This is legitimate enterprise. It pays for itself."

"I don't know," said Radar, still dubious. "It seems a bit much."

"Anything that's worth doing is worth overdoing, my friend. You'll see."

Radar noticed the call for costumes—*Come As Your Favorite Fool*—along with attendant examples: Dan Quayle, the Three Stooges, and, with smug self-reference, Mirplo himself. "Costumes, too, I see," said Radar.

"Oh, yeah. You'll want to look your best, man. You'd better put your thinking cap on." Vic considered his own statement, then said, "Of course, you could just wear a thinking cap."

Radar studied Vic's promotional mélange. In true Mirplovian fashion, it was six ways over the top, but he had to cede to Vic the savantry of knowing what would draw a crowd. The amazing Mirplo had long since ceased to amaze. Now he just got things done.

At that moment the office door opened and Kadyn stepped in, followed in stride by Adam Ames and a rugged, leathery, ten-gallon Texan that Radar and Vic didn't know. He was a large, stocky man wearing Austin-standard boots and jeans, a snap-button shirt strained by his gut, and a bolo tie adorned with a chunk of turquoise that could choke a tortoise. Radar and Vic didn't need to be told that this was Adam's inside man. He had allocation board written all over him.

And he had his eye on Kadyn. "Are you in school, little cowgirl?" he asked from the condescending depths of a drawl.

"Part-time."

"Mmm, you got a little ol' part-time for me?"

Kadyn's look may have been intended to wither him, but it seemed just to bounce off the man as he moved in and more or less occupied the room.

"Everybody," said Ames, "this is Cal Jessup."

"How's university life, Mr. Jessup?" asked Radar, immediately regretting it, for that sort of demonstrative self-indulgence had no place in an orderly snuke.

But Ames just nudged Jessup and said, "Told you. Misses nothing. Radar, will you join us?" Ames led Radar and Jessup into his office and closed the door. At the reception desk, Kadyn opened her Serengeti and activated YvesDropp, and with wireless earbuds she and Mirplo went about their work, listening in on the conversation like catching the local news.

Inside the office, Ames offered his guests Dollar Tree bottled water and made a self-consciously self-deprecating (and therefore largely unsuccessful) joke about how frugal he was. Once they were settled, he said, "So, Radar, as usual, you seem to be further ahead in the textbook than anyone, you with that crafty mind of yours. What do you think is Mr. Jessup's business here today?"

Radar figured that Jessup was here to detail conditions of

the grease, but having oversold his cleverness once, he wasn't about to do it again, so he said, "Adam, I have no idea."

"Shame," said Ames. "I was hoping we'd get another wild theory about scoundrel code or whatnot." To Jessup he said, "Radar has some jaundiced views. I think his brain must be a difficult place to live." He turned back to Radar. "Well, as it turns out, he's here to talk to you. There are some particulars concerning the matching funds that he needs to discuss." *Yep, detail the grease.* "And, well, you understand numbers better than I do, I think."

The intercom crackled to life. "Mr. Ames," said Kadyn, "Mr. Wellinov is here."

"Be right out." Ames stood up. "Well, Radar, this is your meeting. Mine's out there." He smiled. "I'm taking our new best friend to lunch." He started to leave, then suddenly, theatrically, chuckled. "Wellinov," he said. "You know, I didn't get that at first."

Ames departed. Jessup pulled out a pack of cigarettes. "Y'all don't mind if I smoke?" He went to the window and opened it. "Oh, out the window, of course. And don't tell me it's illegal, I already know. I fought that ordinance tooth and tongs, I can tell you." He lit up. "I love Austin, but it's gone and got infested. Too many damn lib'rals with too damn many rules."

"Liberals with rules?"

"What, you don't think? No smoking. No chaw. No plastic bags. No whale hunting inside city limits."

Radar chuckled, as much at Jessup's effort as at the joke.

"Know which one's the funniest? Nuclear-free zone." He pronounced it "nucular," George Bush style, and Radar wondered if that wasn't a bit of misdirectomy on Cal's part, designed to make him look less swift than he was. "There's a sign, you know. I seen it. Right outside of town. 'Austin is a nuclear-free city.' Like some Jihad Johnny with a dirty bomb gonna pay any attention to that." He shook his head. "Funny ol' world."

"So, Mr. Jessup...." said Radar.

"Mr. Jessup's my daddy. Call me Cal."

And with that, Call Me Cal laid out the, as it were, proposed fiduciary relationship between Adam's foundation and Saligny University. He started by showing Radar a plastic-protected copy of the original Wilson Trust deed, the one that detailed Widow Wilson's terms and conditions. It was, thought Radar, a very authentic-looking document. Which meant next to nothing; it's not like period paper and inks were hard to come by. Nevertheless, he gave the supposedly ancient conveyance the attention that Jessup intended it to deserve. After he'd read it, they discussed its stipulations. The allocation board, Jessup said, was satisfied that Adam's proposal honored the intent of the trust. "That is," said Jessup, "they might could be satisfied. But that'll depend on the matching funds. Ain't no way I can release the full endowment 'less I can show the board a partner in earnest."

"How earnest?"

"Something in six figures."

"And when we say earnest, are we to gather that we mean cash?"

Jessup took a drag and blew a smoke ring out the window. "We are, sir. And may I say I'm right pleased that you can say so so frankly." He cocked his thick chin toward the door, which Radar took to infer Ames. "I know that one understands, but he plays so high and mighty. Can't talk straight with the man. I like a man I can talk straight to. Round here, bein' that kind of man really pays off." Again he looked toward—through—the closed door. "His kind, they don't last."

"Then why are you backing him?"

"Oh, business is business, son. That million bucks has been on the books too long."

"Million?" Radar almost blurted *Is that all?* And even though he didn't, his dismay was easy for Jessup to read: A million dollars was too small a sum to warrant a six-figure kickback.

"It was a million at the start," drawled Jessup. "Back in 1920. It's been managed well since. It's worth nigh half a billion now." Radar gave the sum a respectful whistle, but he knew then that he'd been played, set up to reveal just what he'd revealed: knowledge of how to price a bribe. Score one for Cal. Radar didn't like anyone scoring one.

Jessup went on talking and puffing, puffing and talking, lighting one cigarette after another off the dying stub of the last and lining up the butts like toy soldiers on the window sill. "So, understandably, we ain't lettin' the trust go for cheap. Now your ol' boy out there, he stumbled onto a play he could make. He found hisself a pot of legal, free money that'll set him up for life, or for however long he wants to pretend he's doing a damn thing with it."

"Won't there be some oversight? To make sure the center's properly run?"

"Aw, hell, the board don't care about that. It ain't their money. But they damn sure gonna get their taste, and that's a point seems lost on your boy. Now I'm counting on you to get it found."

"In cash."

"Yep. To show the board y'all are serious about bringing a world-class brain operation to little ol' Austin."

"And you speak for the entire board?"

"Them as matters. We all on the same page on this. Sauce is sauce." Jessup stubbed out his last cigarette on window glass. "But sauce there will be." With a sweep of his hand he knocked the entire line of butts down onto the street below. "Littering," he said, shaking his head. "Look at me, ain't I a felon?"

Jessup strode to the door and threw it open. Vic and Kadyn had hastily removed their earbuds and Kadyn was back at her desk. The big man tipped his hat to her on the way out. "Little lady," he said. "You sure I can't take you out someplace nice? Paris? My place?"

"That's a sweet offer," she said. She reached across the desk and adjusted Jessup's bolo tie, playfully sliding it up his neck so far so fast that he had to pull her hands away to keep from being playfully choked. "But I think I'm gonna pass."

Jessup glared at her as he loosened his tie and walked out.

"That wasn't exactly nice," said Vic.

"You kidding?" said Kadyn. "Guys like him, that just keeps 'em coming back for more."

"Where's Ames?" asked Radar.

"Out with his pal Henry Wellinov," said Vic. He tapped his skull. "Ames could tell right away that the old guy's not all there. But Henry told Ames that he sees you as a—how did he put it?—man of destination. And damned if he doesn't want to get down a bet on brain science."

"His answering machine's set on *announce only*," said Kadyn with a mischievous grin. "It's gonna be a tough lunch."

Indeed it was. Down the street at a Chinese deli, Adam Ames listened with growing impatience as the lavishly unraveled Henry Wellinov ootled randomly from thought to disconnected thought, with no nod to causal connection or the niceties of polite conversation. Just now, and for no discernible reason, he was talking at length about his grandson's bar mitzvah. "Of course I gave the little pudwhacker cash, and that's lots, sir, lots and lots. A wad this thick." Henry aggressively poised his thumb and forefinger two inches apart, and two inches from Adam's nose.

"Cash says you care," offered Ames.

"Damn right it does." This sent Wellinov off on a rant about, as near as Ames could tell, overdue library books, how people's failure to return them showed the depth of the country's moral decay. Then came something about his ex-wife, how she wouldn't go down on him with a gun to her head. Then his spin class. Some guy he knew in high school. How his kids never call. The lameness of professional wrestling. Comparative creation myths around the world. And on and on and on. At last Ames could stand it no more and cut Henry off in the midst of his discursive assertion that genetically modified crops were a national menace on the order of fluoridated water.

"Mr. Wellinov," said Ames, "Henry. I need you to focus on me."

Henry ground to a halt. "You don't care about corn?"

"I care about corn. I'm not going to die from it."

"You could be disfigured."

"Mr. Wellinov, please."

Wellinov blinked. "Go on."

"Now I gather that Radar told you about our work."

"Yes. Impressive young man. Impressive. He says you'll be building buildings. I suppose if I donate you'll name a wing after me."

"That's something we'd consider."

"I'll settle for a breast!" Henry guffawed, spewing a bit of spittle on Adam's shirt. "I'm sorry, I'm sorry," said Henry, still chuckling. "I'm funny. Go on."

Ames went on, all the way down to how he'd prefer to take Wellinov's contribution in cash.

Henry said, "You'll give me a receipt for that, right? For the donation?"

"Of course."

"Then what do I care how you take the dough? Hell, I'll put 'er in a bushel basket if you like. Just like baby Moses." And with that, he was off again, explaining at length how the real Bible, the original Bible, had been replaced by early Rosicrucians, and that's when all the trouble between religions really began. Personally he thought that the almighty God should be a goddess with almighty boobs. Certainly that's who he worshiped when he was alone.

The conversation never drifted back to the money. Ames couldn't drag it there, and he honestly wasn't sure whether they had concluded their encounter at all on the same page. Then, out on the street, after thanking Adam for lunch,

Wellinov suddenly said, "You'll match my donation, of course."

"What?"

"With cash of your own. For the foundation. As a show of good faith."

"I thought a receipt was a sign of good faith."

"This is another." Wellinov spread his hands. "Well?"

"I…I guess it could be arranged."

"Then mine can, too."

Ames smiled sourly and watched Wellinov depart, not at all happy with this last-minute pivot to cash of his own.

In reviewing his performance later, Woody was satisfied with how he had dizzied Ames and then forced a mistake on him. *Now he's agreed to a matching fund to the matching fund,* thought Woody merrily. *This is starting to get fun.* At the same time, he realized that his leverage had come much from the element of surprise and from his decades of practice at this sort of art. You could say that Ames had simply been outplayed by a strong player. But this was just a moment in time. Who knew what Ames would think, or how he'd counter, once he reflected on the meeting and had a heart-to-heart chat with himself?

Woody related this concern to Radar and Vic later when they convened a discreet meeting at a Farmer Boy restaurant well outside of town.

"What, you didn't have him fully wool-pulled?" asked Mirplo.

"No, just cornered. For the role he's playing, he couldn't blow my cover without blowing his own."

"Either way," said Radar, "that's his money in play at a

time and a place of our choosing, and to that I say nicely
worked, old man."

"I bask in the glow of your approval."

On the drive back home, Radar texted Allie and asked if
she'd teed up Sarah for him.

I had us both in tears, she texted back. *You can be a real
bastard sometimes.*

It grieved Radar to think of Allie bad-mouthing him,
even for the sake of the snuke. But in order to flip Sarah, he
had to give her hope: the sort of hope that might come to
her if she thought he and Allie had had a big falling-out. Yet
here they were, once again creating fabricat conflict for the
sake of setting a hook. *That's got to stop,* thought Radar. *Sets a
bad example for the kid.*

That evening, Sarah stepped out on her balcony and
noticed Radar leaning against his railing a few balconies over,
staring out at the lake in a manifestly melancholy mood.
They nice-nighted each other with nods. Sarah could tell
by the set of his shoulders that he was a man still smarting
from a spat, and she mouthed the words, "Are you okay?"
He answered by waggling his hand to indicate *comme ci,
comme ça.* Then, boldly, he pointed down to the lakeshore
and conveyed the idea that they should meet. She countered
with a questioning look, but he just essayed a sad shrug: *Why
not?* She smiled and went back inside.

Five minutes later, Sarah found Radar waiting for her
outside the building. He led her north a few hundred yards
along a lakeside path until they came to a boat landing, a calm,
still place illuminated by a single sodium-vapor streetlamp,
where tiny wavelets rippled up twin slabs of slanted concrete

and floating Styrofoam bumpers made hollow knocking sounds against a dock. Though it had been warm earlier, it was chilly now. Radar wore a substantial wool greatcoat, but Sarah had on only a short jacket, which she pulled close around her. "This is naughty," she said through chattering teeth. "Does Allie know you've slipped out?"

"I suppose," said Radar, downbeat. "At this point I don't think she much cares. What about Adam?"

"He's not home from work yet. He's working so hard."

"Well, that's what you want, isn't it? A hard worker? He'll make a good husband."

"Oh, husband. No one's thinking about that."

"No? Sarah, you know I'm pretty good at reading people. It wouldn't be the first time I guessed what's going on in that pretty little head of yours."

"Maybe not. But it would be the first time it didn't feel like an attack." She turned to face him. "Why is that, Radar?"

"I've been rethinking some things," he said.

"Such as?"

"Such as giving you such a hard time. I've done that too much. I want to say I'm sorry."

"Well, thank you, Radar. You have been a little mean."

"Are you cold?" he asked. She nodded. "Come here." Radar opened his coat. She eagerly accepted the invitation, wrapping her arms around him under the coat and resting her head against his chest.

"Mmm," she said, "that's more like it." They stood like this for a moment, then Sarah said, "Adam thinks you hate him."

"I suppose I do."

"But see, I don't get that, Radar. If you're right about who he is, then you're just like him, aren't you? A cowboy? You boys, you all want to be cowboys."

"Cowboys with different agendas. He tried to hurt you. I suddenly find I don't like that."

"Why?"

Here we go, thought Radar. He cupped her chin in his hand and tilted it upward. Then he kissed her as he imagined she imagined he'd kiss her if this moment ever arrived. He kissed her with conviction, vehemence; passion. He kissed to communicate commitment. To inspire loyalty. He kissed to bond. He kissed from his soul, from that place where a man tells a woman he's hers forever. It was a Captain Kirk kiss, hard enough to flip an alien.

It flipped Sarah.

She opened like a can of beans.

19

The Leveling Game

There comes a time in every snuke when the mark needs to be ignited, whipped into whatever flavor of frenzy the scam demands. When Radar kissed Sarah, he applied accelerant to available fuel and she just combusted. Was she that ready to flip or was it that great a kiss? Hard to say; professional kissers abound, that's not the point. The heat needed turning up. It takes a lot of heat to make a frenzy.

Sarah took a breath and looked up from the kiss. "What will Allie say?"

"That's a conversation for another time," said Radar.

He kissed her again, and now she was all over him, hands everywhere, as she urgently whispered, "Oh, Radar, I want to wear you like a coat. Can we do that? When can we do that?"

"Soon, Sarah, but first: How did you really meet Adam Ames?"

Sarah stiffened. "Is that what this is about? You giving

me the third degree? I thought you wanted me."

"My kiss told you what I want. But the you I want is the real you. So tell me: Where did you meet Ames?"

"I was bringing Jonah to see doctors."

"You knew he wasn't sick?"

She nodded. "But the doctors still wanted to do tests, so we played along. Kind of they paid us to."

"Kind of?"

"No, they did. They paid us. They passed us around. Everyone had a fake look at Jonah and then overbilled someone. Radar, I didn't like doing it. I felt dirty. I'd never done anything like that before."

"Sarah, I know that's not true. You knew what you were doing, working the system." He placed his hands between their chests, letting his palms rest on her breasts. "If we're going to have a future, you and I, you're going to have to come completely clean about your past."

Her eyes widened. "We have a future?"

"We might. It depends on you." He leaned in and whispered, "Tyler, Texas." He saw her face go white.

"You know about that?"

"I found out."

She buried her face in his neck. "God, you must hate me."

He wrapped his arms around her. "Babe, you've got it all wrong." He kissed her again. "I told you I want the real you. That means the con you. You're a cowboy, too, you know."

Sarah blinked. "You think I'm a cowboy?"

"Oh, yeah. I mean, you're pretty raw right now. You don't think your moves through. But you could be trained. I can see us being a team."

"A real grifter road gang?"

"Mm-hmm. But that's a conversation for another time, too. Right now I need to know where you are with Ames and how you got there. Now you know what I need, Sarah. The rest is up to you."

She looked at him with doe eyes, measuring the moment. At last she said, "It's like you say, we were working the system. Jonah and me. But I never meant any harm, and Jonah adored the attention." She searched Radar's face for approval, but he just waited for her to continue. "Adam found us somehow. I suppose through one of those girls that keep a lookout for him, we were in and out of those offices often enough. When we first spoke, it seemed he still took Jonah for sick, but then later I understood otherwise. It was as though he knew the truth about us but wouldn't say it out loud and, if you really thought about it, didn't much mind.

"Anyway, he told me about a condo he rented, this place, here in the Doke, how he wanted to hold onto it but couldn't live in it right now, and if I would move in and sort of house-sit, he'd be grateful for that. That was a good deal for Jonah and me. But then Adam started having me do things."

"Like what kind of things?"

"Like get a dog. Have it befriend Boy. And me befriend you. Let on about Jonah."

"And the story you told us? About meeting outside the medical center?"

"Oh, he made that up. He coached me on how to tell it." She thought for a moment, then said, "He's coached me on pretty much everything I've said to you all along. Radar,

I've been with men. I'm no stranger to men. I don't usually let them boss me, and I didn't even think that was what was happening, but now I see that it was." A flash of something... jealousy?...crossed her face. "And all of it about you," she said. "He's way more interested in you than he is in me."

"Why do you think that is?"

"I don't know. He never talks about you, but he thinks hard about you, I can tell. Radar, can I tell you something?"

"Anything."

"He doesn't like you."

"I know that."

"He wants to hurt you. I don't know why." She hugged him hard. "Oh, Radar, I want our future, too. But Adam, he *could* hurt you. I mean he's capable."

"Capable?"

"Down deep he's dark. I fear he contemplates evil."

"Don't worry about it."

"Why? What are you going to do?"

"Don't worry about it."

She pulled back from her hug and looked up into his eyes. "Radar, am I just a pawn to you?"

"No."

"I don't know if I believe you."

He kissed her one last time. "Then you'll just have to wait for proof."

She moaned against his mouth. But he broke off the kiss abruptly and said, "When's Adam getting home?"

"Soon, I suppose," she said, disappointed.

"Then we'd better go. Not a word of this to him, okay?"

"Of course not."

"Good. I'll walk you back. I have an errand to run."

Radar drove into Austin and met up with Vic and Allie at a new Tex-Mex-fusion restaurant, Paco Houston's. When he recounted his encounter with Sarah, Allie said, "Wow, she cracked like an egg."

"Overwhelmed no doubt," intoned Vic, "by the power of the Hoverlander lips."

"Does anyone think it happened too easily?" asked Radar.

"You doubt the power of the Hoverlander lips?"

"We weren't there, hon," said Allie. "We can't take her measure. Only you can. At least now we know they have history."

"We just don't know if she's his partner or his patsy," said Radar. "And the power of the Hoverlander lips notwithstanding, we still don't know where her loyalty will land in the end."

"In other words," said Vic, "will she stay flipped?"

"In other words, is she flipped at all?"

By the second week of March, the buzz around Vic's costume ball was impressively deafening. Everyone who was anyone in Austin, from Kadyn's college gal pals all the way up to the heavy cream of Texas aristocracy, had the date circled in red on their calendars (well, entered in red on their digital devices). Vic's talent for making something out of nothing had proven nothing less than epic. Vic Mirplo: the undisputed king of the self-fulfilling prophecy.

"There's no trick to it," said Vic as he and Radar walked to the office one sunny morning. "You just talk about things you imagine as if they're things that are."

"That's the trick right there."

"If you say so. All I know is, this little ol' foundation is going to put on a party the likes of which the Austin Convention Center has never seen."

"You booked the *convention center*?"

"I had to. At first I thought the Marriott, but demand… sheesh. For a while there I was eyeing Darrell Royal."

"Darrell Royal?"

Vic hooked a thumb in the direction of campus. "The stadium over there. Hook 'em Horns."

"Hook 'em Horns."

"Yeah, so, stadium. But then I thought, you know, what if it rains?"

"What, Vic Mirplo can't control the weather?"

"Come on, Radar, I'm not God." He paused, then added utterly without affectation. "Though admittedly a bit godlike."

Not for the first time, Radar reflected on how far he and Vic had traveled together down their common, crooked road. There was a time when he'd thought of himself as Vic's mentor, but that time had long since passed. Radar now understood that Mirplo was the singular sum of his gifts: unquenchable enthusiasm; bent perspective; and the superpower of someone who knows no no. In that moment, Radar's heart actually overflowed with love for his friend—love and regret, for he knew that one consequence of Allie's pregnancy would be an irreversible change to the dynamic of their friendship. When Mommy and Daddy started focusing on the needs of little Lavender Rho Hoverlander, a Mirplo must necessarily find himself the odd man out.

Nor did it surprise Radar—he was well past being

surprised by Vic's sick synchronicity—when from out of nowhere Vic voiced a similar thought. "You're gonna have a tough time getting along without me. You and Allie and the baby."

"What, no Uncle Mirplo?"

"Maybe for visits but…no, largely it's time we each chart our own course. After we button up Ames, of course."

"Of course. But Vic, why?"

Vic looked off to the south, where the dome of the Texas state capitol dominated the view. "This is a small place," said Vic. "It's just not enough."

"Austin? Texas?"

"The whole country. There's too many Perus and Katmandus out there waiting for me to see. Besides," Vic spread his hands expressively, "no little girl wants to see her father consistently outshined by his best friend."

"So you think it's going to be a girl, too."

"Not think: know. I already told you I read ahead."

"You are aware, Vic, that there's at least a barely discernible difference between the real world and the world of your imagining."

"Barely," conceded Vic.

"So then with one foot in the future, do you know how this all plays out with Ames?"

"Well, now, that's a little trickier. I know where and when, and that's the convention center, April first, cocked and locked. As to how, well, I've mapped some scenarios. I'm sure you have, too. But they all come back to the leveling problem."

"Tell me about it."

"What, I have to explain the leveling game to you?"

"No, Vic, I was speaking rhetorically."

But Vic was already off and running down another Mirplovian byway. "I explained it to Kadyn. I told her how there's truth, then lies, then truth disguised as lies, then lies disguised as truth disguised as lies, and so on unto the umpteenth level. I said that's the leveling game: figuring out what level of deception your enemy is on. Know what she said? She thinks there's only two levels."

This took Radar aback. Like every dedicated grifter, he had spent much time in contemplation of the leveling game, trying to get to the bottom of the bottomless *I know that he knows that I know that he knows that I know that he knows* conundrum. "Only two levels?"

"That's what she said. A person is either A or not-A. If he starts out as A, he can flip and become not-A. But if he flips again, then he's not B or C or sassafras tea, he's just A again, a different version of A, but one that plays the same. He might have a thousand reasons for choosing either truth or lies, but none of them matter, since what he gives you in the end can be only that: either truth or lies. Once you've figured out broadly whether he's not-A or A, you've got him. Anything beyond that is oversolving the problem."

"Interesting," said Radar. He was genuinely impressed, for original thought on the leveling game didn't come along every day. "Vic, I gotta say, she sounds like a good match for you."

"I know, huh? I believe I might have to fall in love with her."

"What, you don't know? Haven't you read ahead?"

"No, that would be cheating," said Vic solemnly. "One never cheats in affairs of the heart."

"Well, she's put some good thought into it," said Radar, "but I'm afraid it's not that simple."

"Why not? There's only two parties: the collective us and the collective them."

"Except we don't know if half of them—Sarah—has genuinely flipped, so that doubles the number of levels we have to think about."

"Ooh, you're right," said Vic.

"Plus, what's Jessup? A confederate or a free agent? Did Ames approach him on this deal, or was it the other way around?"

"And the levels double again."

"And then heads start to explode." They had reached the street entrance to the office and loitered there for a moment before buzzing themselves in.

"Well, how are we going to run this, Radar? On the night, I mean?"

"Money-go-round," said Radar.

A money-go-round is a particular kind of scam, one in which competing con artists bring cash to a certain place at a certain time, and the object of the exercise—played for bragging rights and bankrolls—is to romance or trick your enemy's money away. Money-go-rounds are usually one-on-one, but in this extraordinary case there were eight players that Radar could name: himself, Ames, Allie, Vic, Sarah, Woody, Jessup, and Kadyn.

"Money-go-round," nodded Vic. "That sounds good. So long as we get the money."

"I wish I could persuade you, Vic: Money is just how we keep score."

"I wish I could persuade you, Radar: Money is just how we buy cars."

"I wish I could persuade you both," said a low voice behind them. "Money is just how we have fun." Radar and Vic turned to see Woody's familiar features peering out from, of all things, a dented and extravagantly cracked football helmet emblazoned with the head and horns of an orange steer in silhouette. Along with matching padded pants and jersey, it looked like the real UT McCoy, which wouldn't surprise Radar at all, for Woody was handy at putting his hands on stuff, and Radar imagined that he'd made this skill part of the Wellinov docket as well.

"Mr. Wellinov," said Radar, "so good to see you again."

"You as well, Mr. Hoverlander…Mr. Mirple."

"It's Mirplo," corrected Vic.

"Is it? I'm terrible with names."

"And apparently with dressing yourself."

"What, this?" Woody rapped the side of the helmet. "It might be my costume. I'm trying it out."

"So your favorite fool is a concussed quarterback?"

"Exactly."

Radar opened the door and together they ascended the steps. "I like it," he said.

By the time they reached the office door, Woody was deep in character. "Frankly, sir, while it pleases me to hear you say so, it isn't your opinion I seek."

"No? Then whose?"

"Why, the young firecracker who works in your office,

of course."

"Her opinion matters, does it?"

"To me, yes."

Radar opened the door and immediately thought, *In that you're not alone,* for there stood Cal Jessup looming over Kadyn at her desk, attempting to flirt. Her prior put-down had, as predicted, indeed brought him back for more. With no more success than before, apparently; Radar read the glower on Kadyn's face and heard Jessup comment to no one in particular, "Well, it's the wildest fillies that's most worth breakin'." He tipped his hat to Kadyn and turned to go.

As Jessup passed Wellinov, Radar caught the two exchanging looks. On Jessup's part, it may have been the incongruity of seeing an AARP candidate in a football helmet. To Wellinov, Jessup might have looked like competition for a lady's affection. They cycled through a number of expressions before settling on mutual wariness. After Jessup left, Henry struck a caricature of a Heisman pose and asked Kadyn, "Well, my dear, what do you think? Am I appropriately foolish?"

All she said was, "Hook 'em Horns."

"Hook them indeed," he said. When they shared a smile it looked like he'd scored a point. "Would Mr. Ames be in by any chance? I have a matter of some weight to discuss."

Kadyn buzzed Ames, who strode out of his office and greeted Wellinov effusively. "Henry! So great to see you. What brings you in? Nice look. Is that what you're wearing to the bash?" Radar watched as Ames overtly surrendered status to Wellinov and tried to level the move. An Ames on the straight, he knew, would act exactly this way: showing deference to a donor. However, so would an Ames on the snuke. So, for that matter, would an Ames who didn't buy Wellinov's docket but didn't want to let on. So there were three different motivations for the same action. *But if they all lead to the same action, does it really matter what the motivation is?* In other words, if he could predict Ames's behavior, he could ignore the question of which level informed it. *Huh. Beat the leveling game by just not playing it.* That was a new thought for Radar. He knew it was inspired by Kadyn's notions, and she correspondingly rose in his estimation. *Girl's got game,* he thought. *Now what to make of that?*

Ames led Wellinov into his office. As soon as the door shut behind them, Mirplo activated his listening software and tossed wireless earbuds to the others.

"When I bring you my cash," they heard Wellinov say, "I don't want to just hand it over. I want to make a splash."

Radar turned to Vic and mouthed the words *money-go-round.* Vic nodded. Off Kadyn's questioning look, he mouthed, *I'll explain later.*

"A splash?" asked Ames guardedly. After his last vexing conversation with Wellinov, he may have been wondering—and worrying—where this one was headed. "What kind of splash?"

"A damn big one!" said Henry. "Show that money off! Make it do some work. Inspire others to give." Wellinov now laid out his (cockamamie to Adam's ear) theory that big displays of money, if done with the proper panache, could create an atmosphere of, as he put it, "sympathetic donation," especially among partygoers drunk enough to let down their guard. Ames claimed not to understand what Henry was driving at. "Don't you? But it's simple. Giving inspires giving. If we flash enough cash at the bash, we'll open every wallet in the house."

Adam tried to dampen Henry's enthusiasm. "It seems risky," he said. "I can't let you expose your money—"

"Oh, your money, too, don't forget," said Henry with some glee.

In the silence that followed, Radar could imagine Ames coming to terms with Wellinov's genteel extortion. He may have been planning to meet Henry's contribution in name only. Now, however, he'd be pressed to produce—to show green, in grifter cant. He grasped at a last straw. "I don't know," he said. "Won't it turn the party into a circus?"

"It already is a circus, son. Haven't you heard? This town has fool fever. Now you made me an offer to be your—how shall I put it?—foremost fool, and I was happy to accept. But you accepted too, yes? So, do we have an understanding or not? Because if you don't want my money, I'm sure some home for stray dogs will."

"No, no," said Ames with quick reassurance, "you stick with me."

"That I will, sir. We'll be two admirable fools standing up in front of everyone saying, 'Be fools like us and give from your heart.' Oh, it'll be epic."

"Epic," muttered Adam, with all the false sincerity he could mount.

Henry, apparently satisfied with this, got up to go. At the sound of scuffling chairs, Radar and the others pocketed their earbuds. Wellinov passed through the outer office, Heisman-posed once more for Kadyn, and departed down the stairs.

Adam's forced smile vanished as soon as the outer door

closed. "Radar," he said, snapping his fingers, "my office." When Radar joined him there, Ames outlined Henry's plan, and now his disdain fully flowed. "First, it's gauche," he said. "Just bad taste. Second, I don't think it'll have the intended effect."

"It might," said Radar. "People get funky around cash. I've seen it happen before. Do it right, you can get a real feeding frenzy going. I think the old man has a good idea."

"Do you? I wonder." He paused, then continued. "I don't know if you know it, Radar, but I've learned a lot from you. I'm starting to think your way of looking at things isn't all wrong."

"So now you're suspicious?"

"I see where it might be useful to be." Ames sank back in his chair and sighed. "He wants the matching funds to be truly matching, Radar. His cash and my cash, right out there in front of God and everyone. The problem is, I don't think I can pull it off."

"No?"

"Not until the endowment is in hand. My personal resources are not what you seem to think they are. Things are leveraged, you know?"

"Things usually are," said Radar.

Ames pursed his lips. "Radar, I hate to ask, but…" he puffed out his cheeks. "How about you?"

"How about me what?"

"Could you get that liquid? Am I using the word right? Could you lend me the money? I'd just be holding it, of course. Literally just for the evening. To show Wellinov that I honored my word."

"Wellinov who may or may not be remotely what he seems?"

"Ah, yes, we're back to the joke name and what it represents. Well, I haven't gone completely over to your way of thinking, Radar. I've looked in the man's eyes and I judge him to be sincere. But even if he were a scoundrel, wouldn't it be that much more meaningful to turn his bad money good?"

"I suppose," said Radar.

"I'll put up a bond, of course."

"A bond?"

"Security for your cash. Right now I'm thinking about something from my great-great-grandmother. She…well, Radar, she was royalty."

"Was she now?"

"Yes, a duchess of Schleswig-Holstein. Certain heirlooms have been handed down to me, including one in particular. A ring, quite valuable. Of course I'd never want to sell it, but I'd let you hold it as my promise that your money will be safe."

Radar couldn't look at Ames just then.

He was afraid he would laugh out loud.

20

Collateral Glass

Later, Allie did. "Collateral glass," she said, shaking with amusement. "I can't believe the dude offered you collateral glass."

"I know, huh?" said Radar. "That's more than a little insulting."

They lay together on a big bed at the Four Seasons Hotel downtown, in a spacious suite on a high floor with a broad view of Lady Bird Lake, for one of Radar's baby books had sung the praises of giving the mom-to-be a romantic-retreat treat. As dusk fell they watched millions of Mexican Freetail bats stream forth from the crannies of Congress Bridge and ribbon away east across the sky on their collective mission to hasten reincarnation for ten tons of insects a night. The last red rays of the sun spilled across the suite and found Allie's belly, now convex as a soup spoon. She laced her fingers behind her head, which pulled her breasts upward and flattened them against her rib cage. To Radar she never looked more lovely, nor more matter-of-fact.

"But you have to admit," said Allie, "it plays both ways. It's something a doofus would do, but also a trick what hustlahs try."

"Which clarifies exactly nothing," said Radar. "Which is exactly what I want to think about now." He ran his hand up the length of her thigh and was a bit surprised when she stopped it.

"Whoa there, hot stuff. You're awful keen these days."

"I'm keen? You should see you."

"That was last week. Anyway, what are you afraid of? That you'll run out of turns? Trust me, lover, you'll never run out of turns."

"Well, that's romantic as hell. I think."

She sat up and straddled him. "You want romance? I might have some here somewhere." She scooted up his chest. "I think I can show you just where." He felt her inner thighs on his neck, then his chin. As he was intimate with her, with the taste and smell of her, he felt, and not for the first time, just in awe of her: her beauty, her heat, her frank sexuality. If he were completely honest with himself, he'd have to say he felt privileged to have access to her. *Access,* he thought, *that's a funny word. But pleasing, though. Pleasing.* He hoped she found access to him as pleasing. From her throaty moan just then it seemed that she did. She let him be for a bit, then dove on him and occupied him like territory. Somewhere subtropical in them a storm started to form. It grew, then raged, and then actually shook them loose from each other. Allie spilled away and rolled into a lotus seat. He could see her glistening nexus. "You are so much the man I love," she said. Then she climbed back upon him and rocked him like the hurricane they became.

Later, Radar and Allie lay together in the gathering gloom. Radar could feel sleep creeping up on him—until a lucid dream suddenly snapped him awake. "Allie," he said, "I just thought of our costumes."

"Which are what?" murmured Allie, herself more than half asleep.

"Bride and groom."

She raised her head and looked at him through half-open eyes. "Fools in love?"

He nodded enthusiastically. "Fools in love."

"I love it."

"You haven't heard the best part," he said. "We could actually do it for real."

"What, get married?"

"Uh-huh."

"Of course we could," she said with the same mock seriousness she assumed he was using. "I mean, what else do we have to do that night?"

Okay, rock of my life, let's go. Let's be the life together we already know we're going to be.

"Okay, let's," said Radar, and his tone conveyed something so different that Allie came fully awake.

She propped herself up on her elbow and read his eyes. What she saw there—the earnestness and honesty that she knew was such a reach for him—made her leak tears. She threw herself over him and held him close. "Okay, let's," she said breathlessly. "Let's really let's."

It was full dark now. The bats had returned to the bridge

and tucked themselves in for the night, sated and content. If the collective happiness of several million bats could be measured in insect-pounds, all of it taken together wouldn't tip the scale of happiness by which the newly betrothed couple now measured themselves.

The next day, over pints and burgers at Al's House of Pints and Burgers, they shared the news with Vic. As an ordained minister (as were they all), he immediately offered to preside, and they happily accepted, not pausing to wonder how a Mirplo might preside. "Of course," he said, "I might have to rethink my costume, for no end of fools put themselves up as the definitive link between man and God." He mentioned Jimmy Swaggart, Ted Haggard, and some others. "Funny how the most rabidly anti-gay crusader is somehow always the one found in bed with the boy-toy." Then, striking a serious tone, Vic said, "You realize that this wedding is a stunning offensive weapon. Ames won't know what to make of it."

"That's not why we're doing it," said Radar. He grinned goofily as he and Allie twined their fingers together, going-steady style.

"Still, it puts him in a bind. He's going to want you focused on the money at a time when you're focused on love. To the extent that he loses control of the moment it might make him careless."

Asked Allie, "Do you think he thinks we buy his collateral glass?"

"He can't possibly," said Vic. "It's so bogus on its face. But maybe it's like your wedding: another level; another layer of smoke."

"Except our wedding is real," Radar and Allie said as one, which made them giggle as one.

"That's too cute," Vic said dryly. "I should of videoed that."

A few days later, high pressure rolled into West Texas, served up warm with a side of puffy blanched clouds and cerulean sky. Stripped to their shirtsleeves, Mirplo and Kadyn crossed the UT campus to the south mall, just below that clock tower with those historic lines of sight. They spread out a blanket and lay in the sun, watching Frisbee players throwcialize nearby. Vic chose that moment to invite Kadyn to the fete as his date. To his surprise, she said no. "I can't go with you, Vic. It's not my best play."

"You…wait…what?"

She sat up and patted his knee. "Honey, you're great, but frankly either Jessup or Wellinov would be more my type."

"I don't believe you."

"I don't know what to tell you. I only get to show up on one arm that night, and who I choose matters."

"Well, but we can date later?"

Kadyn leaned back on locked elbows. "Let's get to later later," she said.

Vic felt rocked, soul shaken. This was not the outcome he'd expected.

Riding on a puff of cliché, a cloud passed before the sun and the day turned suddenly cold.

It didn't get much warmer, on either the literal or metaphorical level, when Mirplo met Radar later at the Vegan Holiday Restaurant ("an Austin tradition since late last year!") and, over yummy bowls of yeast flake soup, brought him up to date.

"Crap," said Radar, "now we have to worry about her levels, too."

"What? No."

"Yes, Vic. She just about told you she's jumping ship."

"No way she's jumping," said Vic. "She got glued good."

"I thought she did," said Radar. "Now I'm not sure." Getting glued, as they both understood it, was a tyro's tendency to imprint on the person who first taught her to grift. The phenomenon could usually be counted on to lock a player's loyalty to her team for at least the first few snukes. But never forever; that's not how grifters roll. With Kadyn, smart and confident and naturally gifted as she was, it was reasonable to think that she'd go indy sooner than most.

Now, thought Radar, *how can we use that best?*

21

Savransky Cut

When Radar got home, Sarah pounced on him the minute he parked his car. He had no idea how long she'd been waiting, but as waiting for him had become something of her leitmotif, he took it in stride.

"Radar," she said, "we have a big problem." Telegraphing an urgency that may have been real or maybe just telegraphed, she grabbed his hand and dragged him to a secluded spot behind the building.

"What is it, Sarah?"

He anticipated—and got—another vivid piece of her active imagination, for she drew him close and whispered, "I think Adam's going to bunny."

"Bunny?"

"Isn't that what you call it when someone runs away?"

"Rabbit," said Radar.

"Well, rabbit, bunny, whatever. As soon as he gets your money he's out of here."

"Uh-huh. How do you know?"

"I did that history thing on his computer. History browser?"

"Browser history."

"That's it. I saw all the websites he's been to. Airlines, hotels. I think he's going to Brazil."

"Brazil? Really?"

"Rio de Janeiro." She demonstrated great, brow-furrowing thoughtfulness. "Isn't that what you do when you're on the lam? Fly down to Rio? I've heard of it before."

"I imagine you have," said Radar. "Which is why I imagine you've made it up now."

"Wait, you don't believe me?"

"As it happens, no. But it doesn't matter either way. Your actions, your interpretation—or your invention—of Adam's actions, none of that can affect my thinking."

"But…" sputtered Sarah, "I'm trying to help you!"

"Sarah, I'm sorry. I judge you're talking nonsense."

Sarah put her hands on her hips. "Oh, you judge I'm talking nonsense?" He tried to step around her but she moved to block his path. "You're mean, Radar Hoverlander," she said with rising ire. "You think you're nice but you're not. You kiss me and cuddle me and promise me tomorrow, but I know you're never going to pay off. 'Cause now I hear you're getting married." She gave him a saucy look. "Yes, bride and groom costumes, I know all about it. It's cute. Very original. But what does it say about us? Huh? That there never *was* any us, right?" Now she looked genuinely sad, little-girl sad. "You tricked me. You used me for information. And now you just dismiss me." She quoted him in a mocking voice. "'I judge you're talking nonsense.' That's just great. That's just fricking wonderful." She crossed her arms and said, "So what's the deal, Radar? Am I in your heart at all? Or did you just play me like you warned me Adam would play me? Tell me the truth if you can."

Radar thought for a moment before he spoke. He now understood that it had been a mistake to try to flip Sarah in the first place. Her docket was too chaotic to yield any sort of reliable line. Here, at least, was the chance to clean up a level or two. "I used you for information," he said at last. "I'm sorry."

"Oh, you're sorry." She spat on the ground next to his foot. "Well, we're done then, Mr. Radar Fucking Hoverlander. I hope Adam does get your money." Radar watched her stomp off and wondered if he had really cleaned up her levels or just created more noise. He was reminded of a piece of grifter wisdom from way back: *You can't figure out their strategy if they don't have one.*

When Radar got inside, Allie was waiting for him with a jotted note. "Ames called," she said. "He wants to meet you at a place."

Radar looked at the note. "Well, that's the middle of nowhere," he said. "Want to roll with?"

"He kind of said come alone."

"So it'll wobble him if I don't. Maybe shift him off his script."

"Okay, I'll come." Allie suddenly grinned. "This is fun," she said, "moving people off their script. This is how we used to have fun." Radar started to respond, but Allie cut him off. "I know, I know," she said, "no life for our daughter. I'll tell you one thing, mister, our *son* is going to be great, no matter what he ends up doing."

"You're so sure it's a him?"

"As sure as you're sure it's a her."

"Sure enough to bet?"

"What stakes?"

Radar answered without hesitation, "Naming rights."

"Oh, no. No, no. Nice try, bub. What is she today? Oleander?"

"No. But Oleander's nice."

"Oleander Hoverlander? I seriously don't think so."

"Okay, so not naming rights. Well, we'll think of something."

"You know what, Radar? Let's not. I don't want to have to tell our son that his birth was a coin flip for us."

"Agreed, then: no bet."

"No bet." They shook on it.

Shook on it and then some.

The car Radar and Allie had leased was a Song Subdominant, and the fuel-cell-powered, active-navigation smart car practically drove itself out east on US Highway 290 to County Line Road, then south to the intersection of County Line and Monkey Road. Why there should be a Monkey Road in the middle of Texas Radar couldn't guess, but just down it a bit was a neglected pocket park with a sandbox and rusting jungle gym, a battered ball field, and a couple of netless soccer nets. They pulled into a parking lot composed of dirt and coarse gravel. "There he is," said Allie.

"I'm thinking..." said Radar slowly, "that it might be time to unbag the cat."

"Huh?"

"Ping him about your and his past. See how he reacts."

"What do you want me to do?"

"No, nothing. I'll take care of it," said Radar. "You just stay mum. Give him the stink-eye."

"One stink-eye, coming up."

Radar parked the Subdominant, and they walked to a nearby band of struggling dogwoods, where Adam sat at a splintered picnic table, wearing a bulky daypack over one shoulder. He stood as the pair approached and blinked at the sight of Allie. "I don't understand."

"Don't understand what?" said Radar.

"I asked you to come alone."

"I forgot she was in the car. It happens. Don't worry, she's quite quiet." Allie said nothing, just focused her gaze on Adam, trying with no success to make eye contact. "Or do you want us to go home?"

"No, it's…I would think the fewer people involved the better."

"We're few enough," said Radar. "What's up?"

"That's it? No preamble?"

"Preamble? What, chitchat? This isn't a date. What. Is. Up?"

Ames removed the daypack and unzipped it. Inside lay a poorly organized olio of money: stray twenties and fifties; attempted bundles of hundreds; and then just random wads of cash.

"That looks like a lot of money," said Radar.

"It's a hundred grand."

Radar and Allie studied the money for a moment. They

made no move to touch it or inspect it more closely. They exchanged looks. Then, seemingly in unison (though the trained ear would hear Allie a beat behind), they burst out laughing.

"What?" asked Ames in near panic. "What? Do you want to count it?"

"What are you doing, Ames?"

"Showing you I'm serious. I scraped together such cash as I could, but it's still not enough. Look, Wellinov's money doesn't work without mine, and mine doesn't work without yours. I need you to know I'm committed. Plus, there's this." He reached into his pocket and pulled out a small square velvet box. Allie turned away and bit down hard on her laugh. Ames handed Radar the box. Inside gleamed an antique ring, whole-karat diamonds squared around a spectacular center stone. The setting looked to be platinum or white gold, handwrought and classic.

Radar squinted at the artifact and muttered, "Wish I had a loupe."

"I'm sorry," said Ames, "I didn't think to bring one."

"Understandable." Radar examined the ring at length, then said, "Well, that's a Savransky cut. Beautiful stone." He looked up. "What's it, from the 1880s?" Ames just shrugged. Radar returned his attention to the ring. "Russian design," he said, "but executed in Britain." He held it up to the sun, intently studying the refraction pattern. "Yep. South African stones, original De Beers Pipe."

Ames allowed himself a smile. "Somehow," he said, "I knew you'd know about diamonds."

"Yeah," said Radar noncommittally. "This the duchess

heirloom?"

Ames nodded. "What do you think it's worth?"

"Shit, who can say? Half a million?" Adam's eyes gleamed until Radar added, "If it's real."

"You don't think it's real?"

"Can't tell from here."

"Then keep it," said Ames.

"What?"

"Take it home. Give it a closer look. Test it. Do whatever you like. Radar, I trust you." He added emphatically, "and I need you to trust me. Bring your money to the ball. I promise it will be safe, and that ring is my guarantee."

"I'll check it out," said Radar, pocketing the ring. "I'm surprised you never gave it to some girl." The word *girl* drew Adam's eye to Allie. Radar watched her stare him down for a moment and then, abruptly, turn and march away to the car. Radar followed her with his eyes. "I know that look," he said.

"What look?" asked Adam.

"She knows you from somewhere." He turned to Adam. "She know you from somewhere?"

"No, not that I...no."

Radar absorbed his reaction. "Weird. I thought I knew her looks."

A few minutes later, the silent Subdominant was cruising up County Line Road, back to the highway. "Well, that was a joke," said Radar. "Pure amateur hour. He handed over the ring like he knew it was fake. Gave himself completely away."

"Yet here we are," said Allie, "holding collateral glass. What did he do when you pinged him about me?"

"I would say he went opaque. There's something there,

but he's not letting it out." They drove on in silence. "Well, it solves one problem at least," said Radar at last.

"What's that?" asked Allie.

He patted her knee. "Where to get your wedding ring."

22

The Big Misinformation

Allie went shopping for a gown, which was tricky because was it a costume doubling as a wedding dress or the other way around? Radar had a tux, and it worked but it wasn't special. Allie wanted something special. So she borrowed Vic's truck, took Boy for a romp along the river, then trekked down South Lamar to the ghetto of funky consignment shops and secondhand stores clustered around the Alamo Drafthouse Cinema. But the trip was a bust; among the cast-off cotillion gear and self-conscious country-club chiffons she found nothing she could stand to wear.

She was coming out of Gertie's Goodies when, for the first time, she felt her cargo shift. It wasn't movement exactly, more like something tickling her innards. Still, it caused her to think *Whoa, girl, this is really happening,* and the thought made her feel quite good.

Then the scent of char-grilled hamburger drifting down from the Drafthouse made her feel quite sick.

She had noted with some irony that her stubbornly lingering morning sickness seemed not at all constrained to constrain itself to morning. She got that this was her body's way of standing sentry against toxins that might hurt the baby, and she admired the strategy's endocrine elegance. Still, not a party with candles and cake for mom. She vectored upwind of the Drafthouse and made her way to the truck. She had some soda crackers in there. She'd feel better soon.

As she approached the black behemoth, she got the sense that there was someone behind it, which was odd because she'd left Boy in the truck bed, and he'd be raising a ruckus against some kind of stranger. Peeking around the cab she saw Adam Ames stroking Boy's head. He gave her a smile: his bright, guileless one. "Allie? Hi!" He nodded toward the cinema. "I'm just going to a show. I was passing by the truck and I saw Boy. I couldn't believe it. What a coincidence, huh?"

"A coincidence and a half," said Allie. "Some would say three quarters."

"We can't think of costumes," said Adam at his sheepish best. "Sarah and me." He nodded toward the cinema and Allie read the marquee.

"Monty Python marathon?"

"We hope to be inspired."

"Where's Sarah?"

"Oh, she's already inside."

"Getting popcorn?"

"I suppose."

"That's good," said Allie. "You kids have fun." Allie opened her door and said to Boy, "Saddle up." Boy bounded down from the cargo bed and jumped into the cab.

"That's a smart dog," said Adam.

His voice couldn't have been more temperate, yet it triggered something in Allie, perhaps something from her homeless teenage time when she defended herself with nothing but bravado against the pimps, thugs, junkies, muggers, and maulers who would otherwise see her as bait fish. Which may be why she said, "He's no Adam Ames," as she climbed up into the driver's seat.

"That sounds like it means something," said Ames. "If I didn't know better, I'd say it's meant as an insult."

"You don't know better. It's not."

"Allie, do you not like me? Did I wrong you somehow? Radar thinks I know you, but if I do I don't know it."

"Is that right?"

Ames let his frustration show. "You're just like him, you know? You never give anything away."

"Is that right?"

"Look, I know: Why don't we sit down together, you and I, see if we can figure it all out?"

"Tell each other our stories? Find our connection?"

"If there is one."

"That sounds good," said Allie, thinking it sounded exceedingly not. "We'll set that up." She went to close the door. "I have to go."

He slid his knee between the door and the frame and leaned in close. "Your boyfriend is a very strange character," he said. "So mistrustful. But it's rubbed off on me and now I'm mistrustful, too. Well, why wouldn't I be? I've fallen in with con people, you clan of liars." Adam's tone became flinty. He said, "You think I'm a pushover but I'm not. I will defend my interest." It was an odd turn of phrase, and odder still for the way the tone carried past the words to a deeper meaning that unmistakably resonated of threat. And when she raised her eyes, she saw anger in his: anger and history; a clear, unspoken declaration that whatever Adam claimed to have forgotten, he certainly had not.

In the next moment he papered the whole thing over with a forced and frozen smile. "I'd better go," he said. "I don't want to keep Sarah waiting." He closed Allie's door and walked off.

Allie sat alone in the truck for a few minutes, eating crackers and then getting the shakes. Ames had rattled her, not just by the threat but by the whole encounter, and by the fact that he'd obviously followed her and lain in wait. Despite her display of brittle attitude, he had owned the moment—and momentarily owned her. At last she took some deep breaths and headed up north on South Lamar to meet Vic and Radar downtown.

Though they'd deemed their apartment to be bug free, snuke hygiene still required that they not talk shop at home, so they'd established the habit of a happy-hour confab in a back booth at a 6th Street watering hole, Santa Margarita. There Allie found Mirplo plugged into his Rabota, listening with half an ear. Radar sat across from him, lost in thought. Allie slid into the booth beside Radar and quickly unbundled her tale. She took a sip of Radar's beer to calm her nerves and hoped it wouldn't make the baby a monster. Radar and Vic agreed with Allie's assessment, that Ames had confronted her for the purpose of running a certain script. When Radar asked her to level Adam's performance, she described it as genuine yet tactical, authentic but deliberate.

"That's a lot of strands," said Radar. "What does your gut say he was up to?"

"Showing me a card," said Allie, "and saying, 'Don't make me play this.'"

"Do we play back?" asked Vic.

"Not quite yet," said Radar. "It sounds like Adam kept a lid on. Didn't say anything he couldn't walk back, right?"

"Right," said Allie.

"So he wants it to be a card he can still unplay. We'll leave him that option for now." But even as he spoke, Radar was aware of a seismic shift, for when the threat of violence, even its veiled version, entered the game, the game changed. The snuke world was unique in how it conducted—and how well it concluded—its business without resorting to force. To some grifters it was an absolute point of pride: If you couldn't give the mark a satisfying reacharound, you didn't deserve the get. So no, it wasn't a strong-arm community. But that didn't say strong arms never entered in.

However, his confidence buoyed Allie, who sipped a soda and began to relax. "Monty Python," she said, chuckling. "I can't believe he tried to sell that past me."

"Sarah for sure wasn't there," said Vic. He tapped the Rabota. "She's been home all afternoon, loudly mangling the lyrics of pop songs. Did you know there's fifty ways to leap your lover?"

Radar, as was his habit, had been scanning the crowded bar. This was, again, simple grift hygiene. You kept your eyes peeled, always. Now, abruptly, he leaned across the table, drawing Mirplo close. "Hey, Vic," he whispered, "does your girlfriend know that we meet here?"

"My whatever," corrected Vic. "But whatever. No, I don't think so. Why?"

"She just showed up with Jessup is all."

"What?" Vic started to turn and look, but Radar held his shoulder. "Be cool," he said. "They haven't seen us. You sure she doesn't know?"

Radar looked down at his Rabota. "Maybe she gaffed my tablet," he said. "I wouldn't put it past her." By now Vic had resigned himself to having Kadyn play her own role in the endgame, and intellectually he understood its purpose. Nevertheless, she had maintained a strict radio silence between them—apart from what their coetaneous party prep required—which never sits well with the seriously love struck. Now, seeing her actually out and about with Jessup, well, it made Vic's heart break a little. And this was news to a Mirplo. He didn't know his heart could do that.

Allie asked, "What do you suppose she's trying to tell us by showing up here?"

"That I can go screw," said Vic, ruefully.

"Vic," said Radar, "you know it's more textured than that." He turned to Allie. "And I wouldn't be surprised if you, doll, had to go to the bathroom."

"You know," she said, "I do believe I do." Allie got up and headed down the back hall to the door marked *Señoritas*. Shortly thereafter, Kadyn passed by, pointedly not looking at them. Radar kept an eye on Jessup, who seemed satisfied to focus his attention on the basketball game on the bar TV. Hook 'em Horns.

Mirplo moped. Radar tried to jolly him out of his funk. "Come on, man," he said with a grin, "appreciate the moment. This is fun. We're watching a rookie phenom."

"*My* rookie phenom, don't forget."

Now Radar's grin became sly. "Not yet she's not. But she can be. You've got to win her." His eyebrows bounced. "That's fun, too."

"Radar, I don't know what you're impuning...."

Radar laughed. "I'm not impuning, friend. I'm just saying you're in love and it tickles me. Seriously, have fun. Love is fun. It's worth the ride." He saw Allie returning and whispered jovially, "But don't say I said so. Women have too much power as it is."

"Including super hearing," said Allie as she sat down. She patted Radar's hand. "You boys. Where did you ever get the idea that you call the shots?"

A moment later, Kadyn emerged from the bathroom, passed silently by, and returned to Jessup's side. She occupied him for the space of one drink, then escorted him onward, down 6th Street toward one or another of the boîtes and blues joints that lined it. Vic hoped they weren't heading farther, back to someone's somewhere, but at that moment the matter passed out of his hands. He supposed that if Kadyn was a woman worth winning, part of the prize of her was her strength of will. She'd steer her own ship, by God, and Vic knew that's what he wanted: a woman who'd steer her own ship.

Radar asked Allie, "Well, what did she say?"

"Nothing. Just chitchat. She told Jessup and Ames that she'd feed us some misinformation."

"So they knew we were here?"

"Sure. She told 'em. She wants them to know she has a channel to us. So they'll trust her more."

"And what's on the channel?" asked Radar. "What's the big misinformation?"

"That Ames is shopping for sidewheels."

"Muscle? Why?"

"Notionally for party security, but really to bully you if necessary."

"It's not misinformation," said Vic suddenly. "It's true." He tapped his earbud. "Ames *is* hiring thugs. He's meeting with them at his place right now."

"No he's not," said Allie. "That's ridiculous."

"I agree," said Vic. "But Thing One and Thing Two are running it down for him: what they charge, how they work, what they're willing to do." Vic listened for a moment, then added, "He's impressed. Apparently they come highly recommended by friend Jessup."

"Oh, this is all for our benefit," said Radar. "He must know his flat is gaffed."

"And still trying to put the fear on us," said Mirplo. "Well, Radar, I would say he is now officially going to extremes. What are we going to do about that?"

"Just what we planned," said Radar. "Go to extremes back. And break him like a thing that breaks."

23

Kxx

Radar lay awake that night, listening to Allie's breezy breath as she slumbered beside him. Instead of sheep, he counted the ways Ames had tried to put the fear on them. Three just today, if you count Jessup's misinformation as a double-misdirectomy, which it might be. What, he wondered, was the real intent of all this manifest bluster? *To panic me and rush me through the endgame? Or to create enough expectation of violence that I'll want to preemptively buy my guys' safety with cash—give up our dough and go?* Radar supposed you could call that a reacharound of a sort, extortion in congruence to con artistry: Just play along and be grateful to leave in one piece. He could see Ames trying to promote that outcome, but he couldn't see the logic of the relentless hard sell. *Does he think I'm that dense, that I somehow might not get the message?* Once again Radar felt a certain wounded pride at being treated like a cheap trick. For someone whose own moves had ranged from bald-faced to comical, Ames sure displayed some arrogance. But maybe that, too, was just for show. Maybe all of it—the ignorance, the arrogance, and the threat of violence—was just to preoccupy Radar with Adam's script instead of his own. *Stay on your script, Radar. You have a good one.* With that, Radar declared his inner skull session over and set out to find sleep.

But sleep eluded him, and after an hour of tossing and turning he decided that maybe a breath of lake air was what he needed, so he threw on a ratty tracksuit and went outside.

He walked down to the shore below the condo complex and sat on a bench there, thinking his thoughts. After a few minutes he heard footsteps behind him and turned to see Sarah hustling down toward him, hastily dressed in a long vinyl raincoat.

"I saw you from the window," she said. "You won't believe what Adam's up to now."

"You're right, I won't."

She pouted but let it pass. "He's in cahoots with the coot."

"The coot?"

"The money one. Wellington?"

"Wellinov."

"Yeah. They're teaming up to screw you."

"Hmm," said Radar blandly, "that is bad news."

"You're still not taking me seriously, are you?"

Radar didn't answer. After so many iterations of the same conversation, there seemed to be nothing new to say. But, as usual, Sarah's stunning revelation was just a pretense to another agenda. An agenda she revealed quite unequivocally with the unzipping of her raincoat. "How about this? Can you take this seriously? Huh?" She was naked underneath, her breasts high and hard, and her nipples crinkling in the cold. She moved quickly to Radar and held herself against him. He tried to back away, but she clasped her hands behind his back and whispered hotly, "Shh, let's be quiet. We don't want to wake the neighbors."

Radar wore nothing beneath his track pants, and to the sight and feel of her his reaction was evident. It pleased her. "See?" she said, looking down. "You want me, too."

"I'm sorry, Sarah, but really I don't."

"Ooh, Radar, so icy, so in control. Let's see what we can do to melt you a little."

She groped for his goods, but he pushed her hand away. "That's not going to happen," he said.

"Well, that's what *you* say, but your tented trousers say otherwise."

"My body has a mind of its own, Sarah. That means nothing."

"Nothing, huh? Really? She backed away a step and faced him, frankly daring him not to stare. But he just kept looking at her face, and after a lengthy stalemate she harrumphed and closed her coat. Then she reached into her pocket and withdrew a pack of cigarettes. "Guess since I'm not going to kiss you or blow you I might as well smoke." She lit up. "You missed a good time, you know. I'm a damn good time."

"I'm sure you are."

"Oh you're sure, are you? You're sure I'd be worth the time and effort it took the great Radar Hoverlander to mount me?"

"Sarah, I didn't mean—"

"Oh, shut up," she said. "You know what? Why don't you get over yourself?"

Radar's heart went out to her then, her pain and her need, her confusion, her broken past and future. "Sarah," he said gently, "where do you see yourself after all this?"

"Not around you, that's for sure. You're just a jerk."

"Yet a jerk you keep coming back to. That's not because of me. That's because of you, something inside you that's drawn to wrong men. Can I make a suggestion? Find something real to do. Something for yourself. Then you won't need guys like Adam and me."

"Oh, that's very pastorly. What do we call you now? Reverend Radar?"

When she blew smoke in his face, Radar finally gave up. "Forget it, Sarah. Forget I brought it up. Whatever you want from me, I can't give it. But I can give you this advice: Come Saturday night, just steer clear. Let others sort this one out."

"Yeah, right. Then I'll end up broke and with nothing. No, I'll be there to defend my interest. Maybe you won't recognize me. There's a lot of fools in sheep's clothes, you know." She flicked her cigarette into the lake and flounced off upstairs. Radar looked up to his bedroom widow. Allie was a light sleeper these days. He thought she'd be watching, and she was.

He wondered if Ames was, too.

Later, back in bed, Radar noted that Sarah and Adam had used the same phrase, *defend my interest*. To Radar it put Sarah firmly on Adam's script, breathless revelations and naked propositions notwithstanding. But talk of naked propositions turned them on and they made love then with

THE TEXAS TWIST

a fierce urgency that had nothing to do with hormones, parenthood, last turns, anything like that. This was pregame sex, leavened with anticipation and spiked with fear, for even the tightest snuke could come unraveled in the end. And this one was more ragged than most. It made them feel more fraught. So they climbed all over each other and had hard at it. As the color ran up in her face, Allie gloried in their two bodies, in the relentless chemistry and elegant physics that made sex work so well. *Whoever thought this up,* she thought, *definitely earned their pay for the week.* Radar's mind lighted momentarily on Sarah's naked body and her hand on his pants. Some other time, he suspected, he might be replaying that tape; tonight, however, he needed no fantasy. The woman who moved and moaned beneath his touch more than took his mind where his body wanted to go. The sound or perhaps scent of them caused Boy to snuffle in his sleep. He didn't bother waking up. He'd seen this show before. It held no interest for him.

On March 29th, the Baby Bluebonnet beauty pageant that had been occupying the convention center's grand ballroom finished its run, and Vic and Kadyn finally got access to the cavernous space, which they proceeded to transform into a fool's paradise. Under their effortless joint direction (it drove Vic crazy how well they worked together), capable minions hung tufted clouds of cotton batting above the entrance and installed floating plump cherubs and cupids. Greek columns rose up to the clouds, and then more clouds crowded the floor. On the night there would be dry ice, creating the impression of strolling through heaven. But this was just the first of dozens of dizzy motifs. Some were large, like the *Is It Art?* department, filled with common objects in uncommon contexts. Others were merely moments in passing: your map of a flat earth; your Lucille Ball–bearing TV. A massive labyrinth of their construction offered new foolishness around every bend. Have you painted your face yet? Played the shell game? How about a hit of this helium balloon? Or that funny balloon over there? Then out you pour into the display of auction items, there to drool like a fool over sparkly baubles and spa getaways. Hired hosts and hostesses will be on hand to take your bids via wireless register. Very engaging young people. Very persuasive. You might bid more than you like.

You'll easily drink more than you like if you like. Tequila runners on roller skates will see to that, as will the champagne waterfall and the beer-pong contests. Smoking is not permitted in the ballroom of course, but there's that terrace over there that you can step out on. It's very discreet. If you want to pot up, pot up, but then *bid* up, for while your organizers don't condone illegal activity, they do enable it, all for the good cause. When you get hungry, visit the junk food bar, but don't be surprised if those Cheetos are actually risotto; our chefs can do some pretty clever trompe l'oiel. Oh, speaking of fooling the eye, be on the lookout for counterfeit guests. Don't think of them as prostitute partygoers, paid to entertain. Like the hosts and hostesses, they're just here for your good time.

We're here for your good time. Don't forget to give.

Pay no attention to the music. Let it sneak up on you. It will start off playful, a dumbass jukebox of forgotten one-hit wonders and candy-floss melodies that get stuck in your head. Then will come ballads of teen tragedy, of Dead Man's Curve and other fatal mistakes. Finally we'll quit fooling around and give you words you can dance to till dawn, till you're exhausted and sated, and you spill yourself out into the world. Did you have a good time? Did you see it all? The Civil War reenactment with troll dolls? The funhouse mirrors? The couple getting married? You didn't drive, did you? Good. Find a cab and go home. We'll see y'all again next year.

And that's called party planning. Credit Vic with the vision and Kadyn with the execution, and damned if that didn't just make him want her more. They were such a good team, a genius team. And yet when first Jessup and then Wellinov came by to woo her that week, she fawned shamelessly over them both. With Jessup she was a julep, grown flowery on his flattery. It was a little disgusting to watch. But with Wellinov, she tracked more like a classic gold digger sizing up her sugar daddy. Watching Wellinov feast on Kadyn's attention like any lonely solo gentleman would, Vic almost forgot that Woody was in there. This sensation doubled whenever Wellinov and Jessup crossed paths (as they did frequently in their respective efforts to canoodle Kadyn), for the two men circled each other like bull elks, and since when did Woody Hoverlander ever play the alpha-male card? Yet in this case he played it well—you could almost see him snorting smoke. This gave Mirplo pause. Woody had betrayed Radar before. Could he be counted on to stay true glued? Pretty young girls make excellent solvents.

Kadyn gave Henry a present: a sleek and supple black money vest, ballistic nylon, with clean lines and myriad pockets and concealed compartments. He happily accepted the gift and enthusiastically agreed with her thesis that he would find it more comfortable to wear his money than carry it.

She had a vest for Mirplo as well, and one for Radar, specialty items from her store, as Vic explained to Radar when they next met at Santa Margarita. "Please tell me this was your idea," he said. "All these vests."

"Of course it was," said Radar. "But it goes back weeks, to before she went rogue."

"Or whatever," insisted Vic.

"Or whatever." Radar started exploring his vest's many pockets. He didn't know exactly what he was looking for. Eyes and ears, maybe? Silent alarms? But the vest was clean, so far as he could tell. However, in one tiny zippered compartment he found something that brought a smile to his lips. It was a small slip of paper assuring the buyer that the garment had been "inspected by #6." But what really delighted Radar was the handwritten message on the back side: *Kxx*. He showed it to Vic.

"Kadyn with kisses?" asked Vic.

"That's how I read it."

"How do I know she means it?"

"I gotta tell you, Vic, this is not the Mirplo I know and love."

"I know, I know. I'm that sad a sack. But she's that young, Radar, and we've put a lot of power in her hands. If she gets a choice between a good man and big money, how can we be sure she'll see the value of choosing the good man?"

"Now you're a good man?"

"I could be for her."

"Well, let it play out," counseled Radar. "And keep the faith."

"I'll be fine," said Vic without much conviction. "I just have to find my inner fool."

Radar actually found that quite reassuring, for if a Mirplo couldn't find his inner fool, who among them could?

24

We Play with Pain

On Saturday morning, Radar went for a short run to balance his energy and review his script one final time. Upon his return, he found Adam loading several large suitcases into Sarah's blue Song Score. "We have a room at the Driskill Hotel," Ames offered by way of unsolicited explanation. "For tonight."

"That's a lot of gear for just overnight," Radar observed.

"Elaborate costumes," said Ames.

"Uh-huh," said Radar. As he walked away he thought, *Well, it certainly looks like a shade 'n' fade. Is Sarah right? Is he going to bunny? Or does he just want me to think he is?* With this, Radar knew, he was right back in the leveling game, trying to unsnarl the knot of Adam's actions and the engine that drove them. Now, suddenly, he saw the levels in a different light. Part of Radar's strategy for simplifying the game was to make Adam play that true-believer card over and over again. But suppose Ames was working the same trick on him? What card was Adam making Radar play with predictable consistency?

This one right here, thought Radar. *The suspicion card. At all times, in all situations, he wants me to think the worst.* In which case, the packed blue car was just a stuffed red herring. Interesting.

Of course, booking a room at the Driskill was such a good idea that Radar had thought of it and seen to it long ago, and Saturday afternoon found Allie alone in that room, standing near the window in new white satin briefs and matching bra. She gazed down on the street below, lost in thought. Downtown Austin was quiet for a change, with no bustle, no big music festival or film festival or food festival going on. In the few months she'd been there, Austin had struck Allie as self-consciously busy, and its relentless effort to keep itself weird seemed to take more energy than it was worth. No matter how tonight played out, she thought, soon they would be moving on. This wasn't home. It couldn't be home.

She crossed to the bed and looked at the dress she'd laid out, a flowing white Chantilly silk whose art deco stylings betrayed its Jazz Age provenance. She had found it in the umpteenth resale store she tried, and paid just a resale price for it, but she knew it had been a classic once, and with restoration could be made so again. So, costume? Gown? In the end, the dress she bought was both, and what did that say about her? That she gave everything to Radar, yet held a little bit back? Well, maybe that's what marriage was: giving your all, almost. In any case, she liked the gown. It made a complex and contradictory statement, and that seemed a bit like marriage, too.

She took off the dress and hung it up in the closet as she thought about the evening ahead. There were, she knew, two parts to the snuke. The first part was the money-go-round. The second part, the crucial part, was getting to the bottom of Adam Ames. Allie understood that everything about the first part was really just there to serve the second. She hoped to hell it worked. She wanted Ames out of her life. She still couldn't figure out why he was in it.

Allie cast her mind back to her time with Green Girl Solutions. Green Girl had been a tricky sell for her. All MLMs are culty, and this one was heavily draped in sexual mystique. She made good money with it, but never felt comfortable with the sensuality it peddled at a time when she was trying so hard to desex herself. Put plainly, the docket didn't fit, and her whole time with Green Girl she felt edgy, tense, and inadequate, her self-loathing projected back to her with every sale she made or deal she closed. That night in the bar when she shot Adam down…had she been very drunk? She may have been; it was a trade show and she always played those loose, for you wrote as much paper at the bar as you did in the exhibit hall. So then: drunk and sullen. Not a good combination. Still, if all she did was blow off a guy who tried to buy her a drink.…

Then, suddenly, she remembered.

She had been walking back from the bathroom, feeling claustrophobic in the noisy and sweaty (and sexy and self-confident) crowd. A man had surreptitiously assaulted her there, shoving her into a small space between a pay phone and a cigarette machine and jamming his hand right up her skirt to her crotch. In other circumstances, she would have

just pushed him off and walked away because...*pawed by
some asshole, who cares?* But that night, drunk and sullen, she
had fought back: kneed him in the groin and then kicked
him when he fell. And now, like turning on a light, she
remembered the guy's face, his look of pain—and shame. It
was Ames.

Allie went to the window and stared out at nothing,
mentally kicking herself for letting something so key get
so forgotten. No, not forgotten: buried; blocked from her
present as a black part of her past. Sometimes it seemed to
her that the whole of her pre-Radar history was myth, the
story of somebody else.

Often she wished that it was.

You were who you were, doll, she told herself. *Deal with it.
Just get on top of your energy and let the game come to you. You
know how to do this.*

Allie sat on the edge of the bed and waited for time to
pass.

Longtime residents of Austin will tell you to enjoy spring
while it lasts—all ten temperate minutes of it—because
summer will be on you before you know it, and summer
arrived that day with a vengeance, riding a hot Mexican
wind to thermometer readings in the low 90s. As Vic drove
into the service yard of the Austin Convention Center, the
Staccato's air conditioner going full blast, he guessed that a
lot of tonight's partygoers would find themselves ruing the
panty, sleevy costume choices they'd made a month ago. *Not
my problem,* he thought as he parked his truck and unloaded
a small wheeled cargo bag. He rolled it up a ramp to the
delivery entrance where a guard recognized him—he'd been

in and out often enough that week—and waved him through to the service elevator, which he took to the fourth floor. He exited the elevator and walked down a long hall lined with meeting rooms until he came to room 23. He unlocked the door with one of several key cards he held and went inside. Placing his bag on the polished-granite conference table, he unzipped it and inspected its contents. Yep, everything was there, neat and orderly, just like he'd packed it. Getting into costume wouldn't be a problem—but getting into character might.

Vic mentally braced himself. "Get your head in the game," he said aloud to the empty room. "This is not how a Mirplo rolls."

Leaving his gear in the conference room, he went back down the hall to the main ballroom and slipped in through a rear entrance. This brought him directly into the Woodstock installation, *Fools in Mud,* with its rock and soul dance track and authentic Family Dog light show. From there he made his way to the Midway, a broad double row of classic carnival games: ring toss, dip bowl, tic-tac-toe. Every booth wore a garland of trinkety prizes, worth no more than Mardi Gras beads—until a certain gluttonous *gotta have it* consensus reality kicked in, at which point no price would be too high, and patrons would find themselves draining their wallets to win a stuffed dog or a kewpie doll they could buy down the block for a buck. The Midway was the party's main thoroughfare, just slightly too narrow for the traffic it would carry, and that was by design, for tight spaces create energy, and Vic was looking for a very energetic response to the Midway's games, all heavily gaffed and so favorable to the house.

He found Kadyn standing near the dime toss, talking on a wireless device slaved to her Serengeti mini-tablet. When she saw Vic, she switched off the phone. "Well, it's official," she said. "We're a sellout."

"That's good."

"Yep. Uh-huh."

"Good gate, good get. Good. Everything else dilated in?"

If she caught his playful play on words, she chose to ignore it. "Uh-huh," she said. "I was just about to go home and change."

"I'll hold the fort," he said. "My costumes are here."

"Costumes?" she asked, then quickly amended, "Oh, yeah. I forgot about the second one."

"The second one's the important one. You won't forget your part?"

She closed her eyes and then opened them. "Don't micromanage," she said. "I know what to do. I just hope I don't hurt you."

"I'm a Mirplo," he said. "We play with pain."

"Okay, then."

"Okay."

She walked away. He almost called after her, but she was already tapping her Bluetooth, making another call.

I like her too much to hate her, thought Vic. *I hope that won't hurt the script.*

25

Fools in Motley

The first group of fools to arrive was a troupe of talking mimes. They loitered just inside the ballroom entrance amid the cotton clouds and the dry ice, leaning on imaginary walls of their own construction and discussing the news of the day. Next came a glittery pop foursome, self-identified as Drabba, flaunting chartreuse jumpsuits and bad Swedish accents. Behind them came Casey Jones, forever doomed to die on his runaway train. A convincingly clumsy Kramer stumbled in, as did another; and it was momentarily Kramer versus Kramer till they decided to be friends and go find a drink. A trio of cigarette girls arrived, wearing hot pants and pillbox hats and giving away free Old Golds. Then came some fairly run-of-the-mill fools, your Mad Hatter, your Don Knotts. Then there was a lull, and the first guests milling self-consciously exposed in the vast open space wondered if they were the fools who had chosen the wrong party. But this was by Mirplovian design, for the rainbow of feelings associated with foolishness certainly includes self-consciousness, and on this night guests would experience every stripe of foolery they cared to try—as well as some they hadn't bargained for. Soon the admission logjam was relieved and the ballroom quickly filled. A handsome bride and gorgeous groom swept in, the first of a dozen such couples that night, including many bride and brides and groom and grooms and the occasional bride and groom and bride, all of which made Radar's brainstorm seem, say, fifty percent less brainy than he'd first thought. With the contemporaneous arrival of some Hairy Krishnas, a Jehovah's Witless, and the Moron Tabernacle Choir, the rush was on. Unicyclists. Balloon-animal twisters. Rodeo clowns. Seal hunters. Peace activists. Evolutionists *and* intelligent designers. Luddites. Hussites. Scientologists. Naked San Franciscans. Ghost hunters. Jar Jar Binks. Sun Myung Moon. Richard Simmons. Richard Dawson. Charles Darwin.

Charles Darwin? Well, when you think about it, everyone is someone's idea of a fool.

At the entrance to the Midway stood a money wheel, blatantly offering even-money payouts on ten-to-one longshots. Only a fool would take that action, so of course it was already thronged, especially because, as the sign above it announced, *All Proceeds Go to the Benefit!* Radar loitered near the money wheel, watching the passing parade. Uncle Fester. Bertie Wooster. The Doctors Doolittle, Who, and Daneeka. And then, oh lovely, a whole ship of fools, each with an albatross (well, rubber chicken) around his neck. Radar saw enough fools in motley to field a football team, especially if you counted those who decided that a jester stick and two dabs of makeup were all the costume they could muster. A full Spike Jones band marched up the Midway playing the crap out of "You're a Sap Mister Jap." There were Beetle Bailey with his Sarge and Gomer Pyle with *his* Sarge. Was that Colonel Kilgore loving the smell of napalm in the morning? And who would be foolish enough to wrap himself in a Nazi flag, saying over and over again, "First, we kill ze Jews"? Radar pitied the fool who had realized too late that he'd sentenced himself to playing Hitler all night—worst costume ever. But when a singing quartet of Don Quixote, Sancho Panza, Dulcinea, and a windmill tilted past, he set his mind at ease for the state of humanity's creativity, or at least its party cleverness.

"See, Radar?" an arch voice beside him said. "Other people are as half-witty as you." Radar turned to see Sarah standing there, dressed in something of a cleavage-spilling toga. She wore flowers in her hair and a golden torque around her neck, and she carried a small cedar chest with a brass clasp and a baby doll padlock.

"Pandora?" he guessed.

"Oh, very good," she said. "Go to the head of the class. Wanna peek in my box?"

"Thanks, I'll pass."

"Of course you will," she said smugly. "You're Radar Fucking Hoverlander, too good for everything and everyone. Hell, you can't even play along at a party. You know, Radar, I don't think you realize it, but you have a really big stick up your ass."

"Is that right?"

"Uh-huh. It took me a while to figure it out, but I did. So I'm just here to tell you: Have fun, fool, you're not going to spoil my night." She kissed his cheek, then lasciviously licked it, and sauntered off exactly like a lady who'd gotten over a man. A little too exactly, thought Radar. That didn't feel like Sarah at all. It felt like a pulled string. He looked around to see if Ames was watching, but couldn't spot him. This proved nothing; many guests wore masks.

Radar drifted up the Midway. It wasn't too crowded yet, but you could see that it would be later, with long, snaking lines for fried Twinkies and funnel cakes further serving to impede pedestrian flow. Just beyond the Midway he found an Adam Sandler retrospective and paused to watch loops from *Happy Gilmore* and *The Waterboy.* That's where Allie caught up to him, and the sight of her took his breath away. She simply dazzled, from her elaborate coif to the diamonds on the soles of her shoes, and all he could think to say was, "I thought it was bad luck to see the bride."

"Screw that," said Allie. "Have you heard the klezmer band? They're hot like sun. Let's go dance."

"Allie, we're not here to—"

She leaned in and whispered, "I know what we're here for, Radar, but the night is young, and this is called letting the game come to you, yeah?"

"Yeah."

"So let's go dance."

She led him to the end of the Midway, where a yellow brick road led past a kaleidoscope of installations, one of which was a shtetl courtyard, very Old World, very *Fiddler on the Roof.* Later tonight there would be a pogrom, but for now the *klezmerim* made merry on a low stage of hay bales, ensnaring costumed madcaps in their driving 2/2 beat. Odd

pairings hoofed around the dance floor: Ratso Rizzo and
Joe Buck with Papa Smurf and Smurfette; a massively fat
Falstaff and a bevy of blonde cheerleaders, all wearing short
skirts and none wearing undies. The Emperor's New Clothes
romanced Lady Godiva, and both costumes were completely
authentic. It was that kind of party already.

The music slowed. Allie pulled Radar in close—as close
as her nascent baby bump allowed—and started whispering
in his ear. Not sweet nothings; the dredged memory of her
ancient encounter with Ames. He took in the news and
danced with her in silence for a moment, processing. At last
he said softly, "Didn't we suspect this was a revenge tip?"
She nodded. "Okay, then nothing has changed. The truth is
revealed under pressure, and everything we're up to tonight is
about using pressure to get truth." He touched his forehead
to hers. "We trust our script," he said. "We end this tonight."

Radar essayed a confidence he didn't entirely feel. After
all, he'd mapped out his moves to the best of his ability and
hoped they would have the intended destabilizing effect. But
there's a difference between putting the mark *on* the wobble
and just *near* the wobble. If Ames bent but didn't break....

He put the thought out of his mind. *Trust your script,* he
told himself, and he danced with his bride-to-be.

The music heated back up, and the couple heated with
it, so that they both wore a sheen of sweat by the time the
set ended and the band took a break. As they walked off the
dance floor, a flash of clashing colors caught Radar's eye: the
purple trench coat, blue swallowtail jacket, green hair, and
deviled eyes of the Joker—and damned if it wasn't Adam
Ames, standing there rigid, glaring at them. Sarah stood by

his side, her cedar chest tucked under her arm. The sight of
Ames chilled Radar, for looking at Adam's chosen role, that
of a cartoon psychopath, you'd have to conclude that Mr.
Nice Guy had been given the night off. Then Radar chided
himself, for all Ames's costume choice really revealed was a
lack of imagination on his part. The Joker was practically
the first fool that came to anyone's mind. As if to prove the
point to himself, Radar scanned the dance floor and spotted
three other Jokers, including one in the klezmer band. It was
a common costume.

*Stay on your script, Radar. Trust your script. You have this
under control.*

Adam and Sarah vectored over to meet them. Radar
expected Ames to make at least a vague attempt to inhabit
his character, but he seemed to know nothing about the
Joker, his mannerisms, motivations, backstory, or riffs. He
just asked in a low, dark voice, "Do you have the money?"

"Wow," said Radar, "so much for foreplay."

"You're the one who doesn't believe in preambles."

"True," said Radar, "but we're not all here yet."

"Here come more of us," said Sarah brightly. She
pointed to an archway that separated the shtetl courtyard
from the splashy chromatic landscape of the next installation
over, *Pepperland,* where Jeremy Hilary Boob, the original
Nowhere Man, battled an array of Blue Meanies. Framed
against that display's resplendent spray of jelly-bean colors
stood Vic Mirplo, looking like something straight off a tarot
deck. He wore leather ankle boots, yellow tights, and *calzon
flojos:* loose shorts that billowed out around his waist like
a poltroon's pantaloons. Having accessorized the look with

a feathered cap, a bindle, and a beaming smile of radiant stupefaction, he struck a momentary pose, then walked up to join them.

"Well, Mirplo," said Radar. "I should have known."

"But what else?" asked Vic. "The Fool. Forever seeking enlightenment. Forever walking off his cliff." He pointed across the ballroom to another installation, *Dave's Drink 'n' Drive Dive*, where the house specialty was always one too many. "It's not too crowded over there yet," he said. "We can talk." As they walked over, Radar surreptitiously eyed the custom job Vic had done on his vest, first inverting it, then dolling up the lining into kind of a harlequin camouflage. It fit perfectly with the rest of his look and seemed to serve no other purpose than that.

Mirplo led them into the Dive—and pulled up short, for there was Kadyn, sitting at a table, her legs primly crossed at the ankle, looking like the librarian of his most moist adolescent fantasy. She sported horn-rim glasses, a starched white blouse, blue wool skirt, and sensible shoes. With her hair pulled back in the severest of buns, you could almost feel her rapping your knuckles with a ruler. To Vic it was the most deeply erotic thing he'd ever seen in his life. If he wasn't a goner before, he was sure a goner now.

She held a prop paperback—a case for her Serengeti—and closed it as she rose and moved to join them. Vic's heart melted at the sight of her naked knees. Ames, however, once again cut brusquely to the chase. "You," he barked. "Where's Jessup?" Kadyn darkened at his tone of harsh unceremony, but Radar took heart, for Adam's no-nonsense stance actually betrayed the nervousness of a man who wasn't sure where he stood in the snuke. And that was good. It raised the possibility that Ames was putting the wobble on himself.

"Cool your jets," said Radar, matching Adam harsh for harsh. "He'll be along. We don't need him yet."

"Well, we need Wellinov," said Ames. "And where the hell is he?"

"Hanging out," said Vic, waggling a key card. "Someplace quiet. He thinks it's too noisy in here."

"Ha," said Sarah. "Wait till later." She looked around, admiring, at the swelling crowd of revelers. "I think the roof's gonna come off." This comment earned her a glower from Ames. "What?" she said. "It's a party, isn't it? Can't I have fun?" She gestured with her little cedar chest. "Careful, I'll open my box."

Ames looked like he wanted to say something, but then apparently decided that the best thing to do with Sarah was ignore her.

Meanwhile, Mirplo was staring balefully at Kadyn. "So," he said in a flat monotone, "Jessup's your date? Well, good times there, huh?"

She gave him a cold look and said, "What's your problem, Fool?"

"No problem," he said in a voice betraying not the slightest hint of conviction. "I'm happy as a cow in Calcutta."

"Oh, please." She kissed him hard, then pulled off his cap and tousled his hair. "My sweet dummy," she said. "He's a *date,* nothing more. Now, no more jealousy, okay?"

Mirplo said nothing. The shape of his mouth said he wanted to buy it but wasn't sure he could.

"What's that all about?" Ames asked Radar.

"The vicissitudes of true love," Radar replied in a whisper. He glanced at Sarah, then gave Ames an elbow nudge. "I don't have to tell you what a rocky road that is."

Ames seemed not at all happy to be tarred with the brush of true love. "Whatever," he said. "Let's get this damn show on the road."

More self-inflicted pressure, thought Radar. And in a voice tinged with pugnacity, he demanded, "What's your hurry, man? All you've got to do tonight is collect the green and get it where it's going. That won't take too long, will it?" Adam said nothing. "So let's slow down, let the moment breathe." He looked around. The pulse of the party was definitely starting to quicken. "Apart from everything else, this little bash is shaping up to be a major earn. Doesn't that excite you?"

"All that excites me is getting Jessup paid."

"Okay, Joker," said Radar with a sigh. "Have it your way." He turned to Mirplo. "Vic?" At a nod from Radar, Vic turned over the card key.

"Room 23," said Vic. "We'll be along shortly."

Ames grunted and led Sarah away. She wanted to stop and ogle a deliciously muscular Rocky Horror, but Ames grabbed her elbow and steered her swiftly past. *Yep,* thought Radar, *close to the edge.*

Getting closer all the time.

In meeting room 23, the redoubtable Henry Wellinov inspected his wizardy garb. It presented somewhat less well here than it would have in the forgiving light of the darkened ballroom—but then again, it was never intended to present as anything other than the slapdash haberdashery of the borderline daft. Here, under stark fluorescents, the verdict was especially grim, highlighting every strained seam of his black velvet robe and the crude haste of the runes and pentagrams he'd chalked on it. In places the velvet was worn shiny and smooth, evidence of repeated Halloween rentals or hard low-budget movie use. His shoes were brown brogans dusted liberally with glitter and tricked out—who knew why?—with cardboard wings. The conical stiff satin hat decorated with moon and stars was pure cliché, and the wand, well, the wand was a chopstick.

At the sound of a card key slotting in, Wellinov turned toward the door and struck a frankly ridiculous pose. As Adam and Sarah entered, he raised the chopstick high above his head and demanded, "Frog or newt!"

"What?" asked Ames, taken aback by Wellinov's nonsensical mien.

"Frog or newt!" Henry repeated. "Which would ye be turned into?"

"Oh, it's a game," said Sarah. She smiled indulgently at the old man. Though she barely knew him, she found him charming—just as marks had been finding Woody Hoverlander charming for a half century or more. "Well, newt," she said.

Woody tapped her on her head and of course nothing happened. He rapped the chopstick against the flat of his hand. "Dead batteries?" he asked. Then he just kind of stared at the stick and said, "I don't even know why I'm holding this." With that he opened his hand and let it drop onto the conference table, where it clattered and bounced and rolled to a stop. He sagged into a seat beside it, visibly distressed. "I wanted to be Neville Chamberlain, you know. One of the genuine great fools of history. But try finding a Neville Chamberlain costume these days. No, I had to be Bumblebore or whatever he's called."

"You're fine," said Sarah, moved by this naked show of shame. "You'll be fine. Would you like something to drink?"

Wellinov scooped up his non-magic wand and touched Sarah again. "Ye will bring me a sparkling water," he intoned. Sarah giggled and went to fetch a bottle from the conference room's mini-fridge. While she was doing this, Radar and Vic came in. Kadyn slipped in behind them and quietly occupied a place beside the door, which she kept open a crack.

Sarah looked up from the fridge. "Where's Allie?" she asked.

Radar shrugged. "Bride stuff," he said.

This seemed to vaguely trouble Ames. He grumbled but pushed past it. "Let's get started," he said. "Who goes first?"

"Oh, I will," said Radar. "That's no problem at all." He took off his tuxedo jacket, revealing one of Kadyn's money vests underneath.

"Ooh," said Sarah, "striptease." She clapped her hands like a little girl. "I like this show already."

Radar removed the vest and tossed it on the table. It landed with a considerable thump. Another thump followed, equally considerable, and that was Vic's vest, its harlequin colors a stark contrast to Radar's solemn black affair.

"What's that?" asked Ames.

"The rest of my money," said Radar. "We split the load. It was too heavy for one."

"Oh, not for me," said Wellinov brightly.

"Well, we're wimps," Mirplo assured him.

Ames waved away the nonsense. "Come on," he said, "let's see the green." He nodded to Sarah, who picked up Radar's vest and opened the first pocket she came to.

She turned to Adam, her eyes shining bright, and she whispered quite reverently, "Jackpot."

26

Grifter Fill

Sarah checked out the rest of the vest, opening each pocket with the avidity of a child opening windows in an Advent calendar. Just the same, though, she examined all the contents with a critical eye, and Radar knew that she was hunting for grifter fill, the renegade fives or tens that pad a grifter's roll to make not much money look like lots. He also knew she wouldn't find any—the count was kosher. Finally Sarah handed the vest back to Radar and told Adam, "Fifty grand, I think."

"Well, do you think or are you sure?"

Sarah reacted petulantly to his tone of voice. "I'm sure," she said, and stuck out her tongue for good measure.

"Good." Ames turned to Vic. "Shall we have a look at yours now, *Doctor* Mirplo?" Radar and Vic both heard it. With a word, Ames acknowledged the mockery they had occasioned to make at his expense; acknowledged it and telegraphed his festering resentment on that score. To Radar it was an unforced error. A great grifter would never have let such animosity show, no matter how deeply felt.

Vic picked up his vest, flashing its impressive hand-painted harlequin lining. He held it out to Sarah, but before she could take it, Kadyn, who'd been keeping lookout by the door, suddenly hissed, "Someone's coming."

She opened the door wider and peeked out. "It's okay," she said. "It's only Allie."

Said Sarah, "I thought she was doing bride stuff."

"So did I," said Radar. There was an edge of displeasure in his voice—not much, but enough to draw Adam's and Sarah's eyes to the door in anticipation of conflict to come. Into that modest moment of distraction, Radar and Vic inserted several actions. Radar flipped his vest inside out and deftly stripped off a tear-away sheath of black fabric, revealing a harlequin lining that was a twin to Vic's in every respect. Mirplo took the black fabric and Velcroed it into place over his harlequin handiwork. They exchanged vests and then Radar pushed between Ames and Sarah, striding to the door to confront his bride-to-be as she walked in.

"What are you doing here?" Radar demanded.

"Nothing," she said lightly. "Just joining the fun."

"There's no fun here," he said. "This is business." Everyone could hear the steely tone in his voice. "Business we agreed would happen without you."

"You agreed," she said. "I never did." She patted his cheek. "Happy wife, happy life, darling. Get used to it." Then, unexpectedly, she went to Ames and took both his hands in hers. "Adam," she said, "Radar thinks we should keep this affair strictly on the money tip. He thinks that if you're not going to address your—" she made a mockery of the next two words "—dark subtext, then neither should we."

Radar growled a warning, "Allie…" which she ignored.

"I don't agree. I think we should acknowledge our history." She touched his chest. It was an intimate gesture. "And have a clear understanding that when this business ends favorably…" she turned to Radar and damn near stuck out her tongue, "…on the money tip, then that history ends, too."

Now it was Radar's turn to mock. "What are you, trying to buy him off? Bribe the bogeyman? Honey, you might as well just light our cash on fire."

"Radar, please," said Allie. "It's better this way. Cleaner." She turned back to Ames. "Don't you see it that way?"

Ames stared at her and said levelly, "I do."

Allie came back to Radar and stood by his side. "There, you see, bub? Water under the bridge."

"Fine, whatever," said Radar, seemingly defeated. He nodded to Vic, who handed the vest in his hand to Sarah.

She took it from him and, ignoring the loud lining, began inspecting its pockets. When he was done, she reported, "All here, Adam. Another fifty."

"Good." He turned to Radar and said, with surprising sincerity, "Thank you, Radar."

"What for?"

"For playing this thing straight. I thought you might try some shenanigans with the…'green,' as you call it. That would have put me in a tough spot with Jessup. Tougher than you know." Ames turned to Wellinov. "Now you, sir."

"Well," said Henry, "this will take some doing. I'm afraid it never occurred to me that I would have to disrobe." He removed his ratty velvet vestment, revealing knobby knees, a pair of boxer shorts with Valentine hearts and, over a sleeveless undershirt, a money vest that matched the others, down to the retrofitted black sheath. He tossed it on the table and quickly slipped his wizarding gear back on.

Sarah picked up the vest, surprised by the weight of it. "It's heavy," she said.

"That's what I'm talking about," said Mirplo. "A hundred grand ain't a pack of matches."

Sarah attacked the first pocket with the same kid-on-Christmas glee she'd evinced before. But her face darkened to a scowl as she pulled out its contents. "What are these?"

"Specifically?" asked Wellinov cheerfully. "Bank deposit slips. They fill the pockets nicely, don't you think?"

Ames blinked twice. "Where is your money?"

"Why, in the bank, of course. Where it belongs." He reacted to Ames's gape. "You didn't really think I was going to bring it here, did you? It's a party, for goodness sake. I may go home drunk." He winked at Kadyn. "I might not go home alone."

"Wh—" Ames started. He stopped, then started again, saying in a low, stern voice, "You made a commitment, sir."

"True," said Wellinov. "But then I thought, well, since there'd probably be plenty of cash to go around without mine..." He made a wandy gesture with his chopstick. "I made it disappear."

"Dude, you're a fruitcake," said Vic. "What if we hadn't brought ours?"

Said Wellinov solemnly, "Ah. Well, that would've been a blow to everyone's credibility." He paused, then added, "But you did—good lads—so it all worked out. We'll announce the donations, solicit generous pledges, and then have a wonderful—dare I say magical?—evening." He turned to Kadyn. "My dear, I understand that you are technically Mr. Jessup's escort, but I do hope you'll save me at least a dance. My sambas have been known to seduce."

Kadyn said nothing, but she did place her hand on his forearm.

"You're still planning to donate, aren't you?" asked a visibly shaken Ames.

"But of course. By wire transfer, first thing in the morning." He patted Kadyn's hand and grinned wolfishly. "Perhaps second."

Kadyn smiled prettily, took his hand and held it.

"Oh, for God's sake," muttered Vic.

Kadyn shot daggers at him with her eyes. "Now what?"

"No, I just want to know: Are you going to hit on every old fogey in sight tonight?"

"God," said Kadyn, dropping Henry's hand. "I thought we had this sorted out." She went to Mirplo and stood toe-to-toe with him, a smoky, surly look in her eye. "Look, let's get this straight once and for all. Vic, you're a nice guy and a funny guy but you don't call my shots. Who I choose to be with and how I choose to be with them is my affair, and the next time you try to make it yours I will hurt you some. Do you not think I can?" Vic said nothing. Kadyn repeated, *"Do you not think I can?"*

Sarah gawped and said, "But I thought he was her sweet dummy." Even Ames seemed enthralled by the sudden soap opera.

Which is why neither of them noticed Radar and Henry switching vests.

Vic held Kadyn's gaze for a long moment, then collapsed under it. "Sorry," he said, "I'm sorry. I'm not the boss of you."

"You're damn right you're not." Kadyn shook her head in evident disgust. She turned back to Wellinov. "You know what, Henry?" she said. "Show me that damn samba." Kadyn practically shoved Henry out the door. Affecting a look of great surprise—and no small impish delight—he allowed himself to be led away as he clutched his vest—well, *a* vest—to his chest.

Vic aimed an impotent kick after them as the door slammed shut.

"Wow," said Sarah, breathlessly. "What was all that about?"

"Didn't you hear her?" muttered Vic. "I'm not the boss of her." He slumped against the closed door, seemingly lost in self-pity.

Radar regarded his friend sadly and said without conviction, "She'll get over it." Then he turned to face Ames. "Okay, Adam," he said. "Let's see your green and get this tired gymkhana over with." Adam's face stayed blank long enough and expressively enough for Radar to read it. "Oh, shit," he said.

"What?" asked Allie.

"Ask him," said Radar. "Ask Mr. Water under the Bridge. No, don't bother. I'll tell you: He stiffed us. He doesn't have his share."

"I have it. It's in the building. It's just not on me now. You have to admit, that's just prudent. A layer of protection. In case you decided to...."

"What? Get frisky with your money?"

"It could happen. Admit it, Radar, you're not the most reputable of characters. You could say it's because I respect you that I'm not holding cash."

"You can't imagine how honored that makes me feel. So if it's not here, where is it?"

"Two big men have it. They'll be there when we meet Jessup."

"Two big men," repeated Radar, shaking his head. It was laughable, but he didn't laugh. Instead he said, "What makes you think Jessup will hold up his end?"

"Of course he will. Why wouldn't he?"

"Because he's a con artist and you're his mark."

"Oh, God, Radar, not that old song."

"Yes, that old song. By process of elimination. Either he's scamming you or you're scamming me. Now which is it?"

"For the millionth time, no one is scamming anyone. I don't even know how you can say that. You're the one who arranged to pay Jessup in the first place."

Radar snatched his vest up from the table. "You know, that old man had the right idea, not showing true green. Now he's on the outside looking in, lucky him. But I did. And Vic did. And that makes us chumps." He balled the vest in his fist and shook it angrily at Ames. "But you didn't show true green either, and that means all our deals are off." He said to Allie and Vic, "Come on, guys, we're out of here."

"Wait!" said Adam urgently. "Don't go!"

"Why not?"

"He…" Adam's voice broke, "he's threatened to hurt me."

"What?" gasped Sarah, theatrically shocked. "Who?" It wasn't a bad line reading but it didn't ring close to true.

"Jessup. If I don't have his money tonight. All of it. He put it in no uncertain terms."

"A respected university man?" said Radar dispassionately. "Why would he do that?"

"You know these Texans," said Ames. "They get an idea in their head." He slumped into a conference chair as if unburdening a great weight. "He called me the other day and said he decided he doesn't trust you. Seems he broke your Wellinov's cover."

"Wellinov's yours," said Radar. "You let him into this. I told you he was bogus from the start."

"I know, but what could I do? I had to hope he'd come through just the same." Radar stared at him with a look of venomous contempt, and Adam said plaintively, "I *had* to. Jessup made some promises and advanced some money around, and now he says I'm responsible for the lot."

"Well, good luck with that," said Radar. "Maybe your big boys can run interference, keep Jessup off your ass."

"Radar, please," said Ames. "I'm begging you." He paused, then gave the appearance of playing what he regarded as his trump card. "Look, I don't know if you know it, but Jessup has cash, too. He told me he'd be bringing it."

"Oh, he did, did he?" sneered Radar. "And why in heaven's name would he do that?"

"For the same reason as the rest of us," said Ames. "*Your* reason, Radar: to create a frenzy of giving among the guests."

"How much?" demanded Radar.

"A hundred grand, same as you."

They tried. They really did. But not one of the three could completely stifle their laughs. "What?" insisted Ames.

"It's script, Adam," said Radar, "and it's tired. Frankly, it sounds like something Sarah would say."

"Thanks a lot," Sarah pouted.

"I swear, Radar," said Ames, "it's the truth. Word for word, it's what Jessup told me."

"Even so, so what?"

"Well, look," said Ames eagerly, "we're here to give Cal money. We have to give him yours. Radar, we *have* to. But if the money he brought got somehow lost and made its way back to you, then you wouldn't be out anything at all, would you?"

"Thus, I could do you a solid for free."

"Exactly."

"Just by letting you hold my cash a while."

"That's right."

"If a word of this is true."

Adam said nothing. He just spread his hands, palms up, throwing himself on the mercy of the court.

The moment opened. Ames could see Radar exchanging looks with Allie and Vic, silently soliciting and receiving their approval for whatever he had in mind. At last he said, "It's a shame we let the old man go."

"Why?" asked Ames.

"Because he had a vest full of fake bills, and that could come in handy."

"Handy for what?" asked Sarah.

"Something fun," said Radar with a twinkle in his eye. "Real fun. The ol' switcheroo."

27

The Walkaway

Radar and Adam were alone.

Allie had gone off to finish her "bride stuff." Sarah had declared herself bored with all the money talk and determined not to let a perfectly good party go to waste. Vic, apparently emotionally crippled by Kadyn, could think of nothing better to do than trail along in her wake.

"Okay, here's what's what," said Radar. "We don't do anything until after the wedding."

"Why?" demanded Ames.

Radar smiled. "Because I'm not going to disappoint my betrothed, duh." He let the smile fade from his face, conveying that there would be no further discussion of the subject. "After that we'll move on to the public presentation, flash our cash, get those donations going. You don't have a problem with that, do you?"

Ames was feeling belittled. "Radar," he said, "just because I've put myself in an awkward position, there's no need for you to lord it over me."

"I'm not doing that," said Radar evenly. "If you feel that way, trust me, it's all in your head. Anyway, Jessup will be our surprise guest. We'll bring him up onstage and have him rouse the rabble with a little Lone Star jingoism—'Let's make this brain center the one that kicks all other brain centers' ass,' that sort of thing. Meanwhile we have my cash, Vic's cash, Cal's cash, your cash—you *were* telling the truth about that, right?—all that cash, all in the same place, all at the same time. Throw in some crowd noises, special effects, a misdirectomy or two, and Cal will never know what hit him."

Ames looked skeptical. "Are you telling me that you'll make the…switcheroo right there in front of God and everyone?"

"Front and center, yep."

"I can't believe no one will see."

"Oh, they'll see," said Radar. "It'll look like a magic act. Very entertaining."

"What's my part?"

"You're what we call the beard." Ames gave him a blank look. Even at this late date, Radar didn't know if it was a real blank look or a fake blank look straining to look real. He decided that it didn't matter. How schooled or unschooled a grifter Ames was had become beside the point. He was showing his cracks. All Radar had to do now was drive the appropriate wedges. "The respectable front," explained Radar. "You don't do anything. You just stand there and beard."

"I see," said Ames. Then, suddenly, "Wait, this won't work. If we steal from Jessup, he'll never let the endowment funds be released."

"Oh, you're just figuring that out?" said Radar sardonically, but Ames absolutely didn't react. Radar was a little amazed at the man's capacity for cognitive dissonance.

Ames suddenly snapped his fingers. "I know! I'll blame it on you. I'll kick you out of the foundation and take the grant under a clean slate."

Radar nodded solemnly. "That's a good plan. That will work."

"Are you mocking me?"

"Not at all. See, that's why you're the beard. So you have plausible deniability. Don't worry, Jessup's gonna walk bad paper right out of the building, but he'll be so nicely buttoned up that he won't even mind."

"Buttoned up?"

More grifter slang you don't understand, I suppose, thought Radar. But all he said was, "Taken care of. Feeling good. No doubt, no suspicion. Buttoned up."

"I see," said Ames slowly. "I guess it makes sense. But I have to tell you, Radar, I feel like I'm on dangerous ground."

Radar found himself growing impatient with Adam's innocence act but quickly swallowed his annoyance. It was his job to put Ames on the wobble—not the other way around. He threw a brotherly arm around Adam's shoulders and said, "Life is risk, brother. Which means you have a choice: Short-change Cal Jessup and see how he likes it, or trust me to make sure he gets his reacharound…."

"Reacharound?"

"Oh, don't even." Once again Radar clamped down hard on his anger at Ames's insistent innocence. "Adam, do you or don't you want your grant?"

It was the walkaway moment for Ames, and Radar watched him process it. He thought he saw Ames more clearly now, saw that he was engaged like Radar was engaged, locked into the endgame and committed to winning it. And Radar suddenly thought, *Is that all this is? Grifter mind wars? What if it's nothing more than that?* But instinct told him otherwise. Just as Adam's true grifter nature was straining at the seams of his façade, his darkness was, too. It had to come out sometime, it had been bottled up so long. And this had been Radar's design: putting the long, slow squeeze on the mark. Everything in play tonight—the party, the vests, the proposed switcheroo on Cal, Kadyn and Vic's conflict, even the wedding—Radar had pieced together to give Adam's darkness plenty to stew over. Stew, Radar hoped, to the boiling point, which now lay probably no more than an hour into the future, and which would be tricky and potentially dangerous but necessary if they were to "break him like a thing that breaks" and ease him out of their lives.

And now, if Radar's skills and his script were such as he thought they were, Adam would raise the stakes on himself through the simple act of walking away.

Ames rose slowly to his feet, and the resentful part of him that had earlier uttered *Doctor Mirplo* with such affront now reemerged. "Radar," he said, "your plan makes no sense. This ridiculous switcheroo? It's cartoon stuff. It doesn't happen in real life." In a tone of triumphant disappointment he continued, "Frankly, I thought you were better than that. You certainly represent yourself as better than—well, better than everyone. That's your arrogance, isn't it? Your pride. I'd say it's your tragic flaw. My mistake was engaging you, thinking I could harness your strengths. Well, consider yourself disengaged." He extended a hand for Radar to shake. Radar just looked at it. "No? Okay." Ames went to the door and walked out.

Radar sat completely still, listening to Adam's footsteps fade away down the hall. In the silence that followed, he got up, threw the two remaining vests into Vic's cargo bag, and zipped it shut.

He smiled a wry smile. *Now we're getting somewhere,* he said to himself. *Now to go some batshit crazy.*

Radar returned to the ballroom, where the party was peaking, along with some of its more ecstatically dosed guests. A quick exchange of texts with Mirplo brought him to the *Fool's Rush Inn,* a Gold Rush installation where Vic and Sarah stood over a trough filled with water and soil, trying their hand at panning for gold but panning, largely, for dirt. If they did happen to find color, an assayer and banker stood by, ready to get rich twice, first by buying their pokes for pennies and then by gouging them on food and supplies. Later tonight, an improv troupe would reenact a claim war that, in the nature of these things, would not be fully resolved until the miners banded together to torch the Chinese camp.

It was a fun installation.

But Radar barely seemed to notice. He trotted up to the two of them, looking edgy and nervous, actually on the point of hysteria. Sarah took quick and concerned note, for she'd never witnessed such cracks in his cool. "Radar," she said, "what's the matter?"

He didn't answer. He just clamped a clammy hand on Vic's shoulder and said, "I can't believe what that asshole did."

"What asshole?" asked Sarah, internalizing Radar's agitation and reflecting it back.

"Radar," said Vic softly, eyeing Sarah with some concern, "maybe we should have this conversation in private."

"No, screw that," said Radar. "Who cares?" He turned to Sarah and said, "Your boyfriend bailed on us."

"Bailed?"

"Departed. Retreated. Took his toys and went home."

"Toys? What—?"

Said Radar, exasperated, "It's a metaphor, you nitwit. He called off the deal."

"Off?" asked Vic. "All the way off?" Radar nodded. "Wow," said Vic, visibly stunned. "That's a thing. Maybe a thing and half."

"Yeah, it is," said Radar. He ran his fingers through his hair. "I can't believe it. What a goddamn waste of time."

"I don't understand," said Sarah.

Vic explained impatiently, "Look, we figured Adam for a Texas Twist, a straightforward money hustle. We figured out how to hustle him back, but now he's gone, so… no hustle, no Twist, no payday for anyone." Vic turned back to Radar. "That's weird that he backed out. How'd he wriggle off the hook?"

"I don't know. I mean, I had him on the ropes pretty good, especially after he failed to show true green, but that wouldn't—" Suddenly Radar blurted, "Oh, shitfuck!"

"Radar, what is it?" asked Sarah.

"God, I overplayed my hand. Christ, what a screwup!"

Panic bloomed on his face. "Vic, we have to find Allie. We've got to get out of here now! Where is she? At the chapel?"

"Probably."

Radar tried to push past Sarah, but she blocked his path. "Sarah," hissed Radar, "get out of my way!"

"Not till you tell me what's going on. What did you just think of?"

"It's none of your business."

"Well, Mr. Smartypants, it looks to me like you're afraid. And if you're afraid of Adam—my boyfriend, as you yourself pointed out—then I think it is my business, don't you?"

"God," said Radar to no one in particular, "the scales on this one's eyes." Then he addressed her directly. "Sarah, look, first and foremost, a con game is a game. Practiced at the highest levels, it's an art. Whatever you imagine Adam to be, to me he's a practitioner of a pretty high art. We were playing a game, and he quit. I can't make it make sense that he quit. Not while there's still money on the table."

"But what's the problem? If he quit, you win, right?"

"Not while there's still money on the table," repeated Radar in a nearly feral tone that Sarah had not heard from him before. It seemed to her that Adam had him rattled—like all the way rattled, and that was new, too. It further destabilized her, for who had the power to flap the unflappable Radar Hoverlander?

Vic, meanwhile, seemed to have fully digested Radar's news, and he said in a dread-filled voice, "Radar, if he thinks he can't get what he wants by wits, he'll go to the other thing."

"The other thing?" asked Sarah, her breath bated.

"Violence," said Radar plainly. "He'll have to. There's too

much cash not to."

"I told you we shouldn't show true green," said Vic. "That was a mook move."

"Yeah, yeah," said Radar. "Flog me with that later, okay? Right now, we have to find Allie. We have to shade and fade, like pronto." He turned back to Sarah one last time. "Babe, I still don't know who you are to Adam in this—his moll or his doll or his dupe or his dope—but for the love of God, if you have any affection for me at all, or Vic or Allie—especially Allie—go to Adam and tell him we fold."

"Fold?" asked Sarah.

"Quit. Surrender. While we still can. *If* we can." Radar made no effort to hide his incipient hysteria. "Tell him he can have the money, all of it, no questions asked." Then he said to Vic, "Come on, let's find Allie!"

They skittered off, and Sarah soon lost sight of them in the crush of gold rushers. *Poor Radar,* she thought. She went off to find Ames.

Once outside the Fool's Rush Inn, Radar and Vic came down from their fabricat panic. They worked their way methodically through the teeming installations back to the Midway, which was now so packed that it formed a solid, sluggish, surging two-way human traffic jam, impossible to cross. "Now what?" asked Radar. "Go around?"

"Got a better idea," said Vic. "We'll surf it. Come on." He walked up to the river of flesh, forced an opening with his bindle stick, and wormed his way into the flow. Radar followed, holding the waistband of Vic's *calzon flojos* to keep from getting separated and swept away. They angled across the current, verging slowly but steadily toward the middle.

When they got there, they simply reversed their field and surfed out on the other side, emerging almost directly opposite where they'd gone in. Ahead they saw a skeletal steeple rising to the rafters, topped with a pulsing red neon heart. They moved away quickly, following the neon beacon until they arrived at its base, where stood a cheesy sitcom version of a wedding chapel. At this installation, called *Love Is on the Air!* you and your insignificant other (laugh track!) could take each other to half and to whole (laugh track!) for better or worse—mostly worse (laugh track!) in sickness and in hell (laugh track!) for as long as you both shall last (laugh track!). Camera operators captured the whole scene, recording a digital video that you could take away on a souvenir data chip—of course for a price. A long line of couples stood patiently waiting their turn, laughing and playing grabass. It was romance at its most ersatz, not at all the sort of place that any thoughtful couple would choose to wed.

Yet there sat Allie, alone in a pew, her gorgeous gown splayed out around her. "Hello, lover," she said when she saw Radar. "Took you long enough."

"Traffic was murder," he said. "Come on. We don't want to be here when they arrive." He took her hand and led her away from the tacky TV set. A few strides away they found a cleft of deep darkness made inky black by the back-shadow of strategically placed, impossibly bright halogen flood lamps. Stepping into this installation was like stepping behind a velvet drape. "What's this one called?" asked Radar.

"*Black Hole*," said Vic. "We're functionally invisible in here."

"And none too soon," said Radar. "Here they come."

Peering out of the darkness, they saw Adam walking up to the sitcom set. Sarah was with him, holding his hand—clutching it, Radar thought. Trailing behind were two thick-necked, broad-shouldered goons in bouncer outfits of black suits, kick boots, earpieces, and Ray-Ban sunglasses. Mirplo sneered at this hopelessly clichéd version of nightclub monkey men, saying, "Little on the nose, why don't you?" Allie slapped his hand to shush him.

Ames and Sarah searched the set, carefully inspecting the line of waiting daters, but of course not finding Allie and Radar. Adam circled the set again, then hand-commanded Sarah to stay put as he collected his sidewheels and headed back toward the Midway. Sarah stood there alone for a moment, watching the mock matrimonials before becoming bored and wandering afield. She passed close to the *Black Hole* installation but seemed to be safely moving away until Radar unleashed an ungodly (and wholly artificial) loud sneeze. Sarah's head swiveled to the sound. She shielded her eyes from the floodlights and peered into the gloom. "Radar? Is that you?" She walked into the pool of darkness, where she found Radar sheepishly wiping his nose. "It *is* you!" said Sarah, delighted. "What are you doing in here?" Before anyone could answer, she said, "Hey, look, you guys, you don't have to hide. I talked to Adam and he says everything's cool."

"Everything's cool?" repeated Radar, clearly skeptical.

Sarah smiled and patted his hand. "That's right," she said. "I lobbied for you, mister." She turned to Allie and said reassuringly, "And no, this has nothing to do with old crushes. Just a friend being a friend to her friends." She turned back to Radar. "Honestly? Adam thinks you're a little nutso. He said, and I quote, 'I told him that it's over and it's over. Why is he bent out of shape?'"

"I'll tell you why," Vic chipped in. "Because of the sidewheels."

"Sidewheels?"

"Those beefy monkey men with Adam."

"What, they're just friends of his. Look, you guys, listen: It's all all good. There's nothing to do now but enjoy the party." She turned to Allie and smiled her best best-girlfriend smile. "So before I decide to get all handsy with Radar again, can someone please tell me: When are you two kids getting hitched?"

Allie looked at Radar. Radar looked at Vic. It seemed to Sarah that all three of them let go of their anxiety together. That pleased her. It made her feel all *mission accomplished*. Vic opened his bindle and pulled out his Rabota. He poised his finger over a touch screen button and said to Radar, "Something like now?"

Radar looked at Allie, whose eyes sparkled with anticipation. He looked back at Vic and gave him a nod. "Yeah," he said, "something like now."

28

The Book of Mirplo

Vic touched the button. At first nothing happened. Sarah watched the nothing happen for a moment, looking more perplexed than usual. Then, in ones and twos, members of a uniformed work crew began to drift in. They converged on the sitcom set and quickly struck it, disassembling the modular chapel walls, rolling out the cameras, and hauling off the pews. Vic pressed another button and an intricate play of laser lights sprang to life, creating within the former chapel space a forest of strong and slender birch trees: holograms, and very convincing ones, right down to the peeling papery bark and termite trails on the trunks.

"Wow," said Sarah.

"I know, huh?" said Allie. "I always wanted an outdoor wedding."

The crew continued its alchemy, transmuting the chapel into a bucolic glen. They laid down a lawn of lush, fresh sod, arranged rows of hand-hewn wicker chairs, and erected an arbor twined with lily vines and white roses. Allie inhaled deeply, drawing in the heady scent of fresh grass. "Yeah," she sighed, "that's more like it." The sound of chirping birds could be heard, and the distant *thock-thock* of a woodpecker. From somewhere a gentle breeze rose. Amazing what you can do with soundtracks and fans.

Sarah stared at it all through Barbie-colored eyes. "It's beautiful," she sighed. Unconsciously, she took Allie's hand.

Vic clicked a couple more buttons on the Rabota, then said with satisfaction, "Okay, word is out. The guests will be here soon." He turned to Radar. "Are you ready? Do you know what to do?"

Radar grinned. "Absolutely," he said. "This part is easy."

"Righty-right, then. We rock, we roll." Vic walked off, whistling an air.

Radar turned to Allie. "How about you? Ready to be my bride?"

"Like you said, lover: This part's easy."

They walked together into the birch forest. Though the trees were made only of light, they were careful to keep to the path created by the laser illusion. Sarah trailed behind, saying to no one in particular, "I'm sorry, but this is *so* romantic."

When they reached the glen, Radar came to a halt. Allie kissed his cheek and sailed off across the clearing, moving out of sight beyond the line of trees on the far side. Guests started filtering in, some counterfeits, some random invitees. Henry Wellinov walked in alone, wearing a stoic, stony look. "What's the matter with him?" Sarah asked Radar. Before he could answer, she saw Kadyn walk in on Cal Jessup's arm. How Kadyn had ended up there was not immediately evident, but the blow to Wellinov's dignity was. Despite herself, Sarah felt sorry for the old man. She could practically see his heart breaking from here.

For his costume, Jessup had gone for the General Custer look, fully authentic with vintage fringe buckskins, a wig of golden curls, and a thick blond moustache. Chewing on a piece of licorice root, he seated Kadyn, then walked over to Radar, his shiny black leather riding boots making soft shovel-heads in the living sod. On his head he wore a Union blue felt hat with a broad brim and a low crown.

On his hip he wore a holster.

The long snout of his weapon extended almost to his knee: the blued, tapered hexagonal barrel of an authentic period piece, fully eight inches long with an angled steel loading lever that looked like a pelican's neck.

"Pretty sharp hardware," said Radar.

"A Remington New Model Army," said Jessup, proudly patting its walnut grip. "Of course it's a black-powder gun, so it's really just a heavy, expensive prop, but what the hell. It was Kadyn's idea." He waved a hand to indicate the totality of his outfit. "Most of this was. She's quite a gal."

"Yep," said Radar. "She's a talent, that one."

Jessup suddenly loomed in close, close enough for Radar to see the spirit gum adhering his moustache and smell the licorice on his breath. Sarah watched, rapt, as Jessup muttered with constrained fury, "Ames says you didn't show green."

"I did," said Radar. "He didn't."

"Uh-huh. Well, guess what? I believe him. But you get to prove me wrong." Jessup shot a nod toward the arbor. "As soon as this damn skit is over, it's you, me, and the money. Got it?" He didn't wait for an answer, but gave Sarah a gentlemanly tip of his hat and went to sit down.

"He's not a nice man," said Sarah.

"I thought you said it was all all good."

"That's what Adam told me."

"I'm starting to think he was fibbing," said Radar, manifesting false bravado. He cast a wary eye at Jessup's sidearm. "I wish Cal hadn't brought the gun."

"What? He said it couldn't fire."

"What do you think black powder is?" asked Radar.

"I don't know."

"It's gunpowder, as in cartridge, as in bullet, as in bang, okay? It's a real gun. It can fire."

"I don't know, Radar…."

"Yes, you do, Sarah. Think it through. He and your guy are in business, and tonight their business is me."

"No."

"Yes." He turned to face her, grasping her shoulders in his hands. "Sarah, listen to me: It's not too late to wake up. There's real danger here tonight. Real as in 'real dead.' Just remember that."

"Well, you're wrong, Radar. You've been wrong all along."

"Fine, I'm wrong," said Radar archly. "Enjoy the ceremony. My advice? Don't stick around for the reception."

"Radar?"

But Radar had already walked away.

With an *ouch, my feelings* look, Sarah flounced down into a chair. As Radar stepped to the arbor, he noticed Ames and his sidewheels standing among the trees—within them and across them, carelessly breaking the plane of the laser lights, disrupting the illusion. It lent them the appearance of being there and not there at the same time. Ames wore a tight-lipped expression, but to Radar's practiced eye he seemed to be struggling to stay clamped down. How unraveled was he now?

How much more unraveled would he need to get?

At the arbor, Mirplo stood waiting. He had changed out of his Fool finery and now wore a flowing ochre dhoti, mystic medallions, sandals, and a skullcap, striking the lost chord of some sort of generic holy man. "Hello," he said to Radar. "My name is Sri Mirplo Mirplo, I'll be your religious practitioner tonight. How many in your party?"

"Two."

"Ah, the perfect number." His tapped his Rabota and music swelled to fill the glen, a soothing processional thick with flutes and violins.

Radar leaned in and asked Vic in a low voice, "Do you see Ames?"

"Uh-huh. And his bulky boys," replied Vic without moving his lips. "They look pretty serious."

"It's in the job description."

"So…sally we forth?"

"Sally we forth."

Vic nodded to a spot in the trees. "Then here comes the bride."

Borne on the wings of the processional, Allie shimmered through the trees and strode with regal grace to a place by Radar's side. She stood there, radiant, waiting for the ceremony to start. Her hand strayed to her belly and she felt the bulge. *Finally,* she thought, *something to grab onto there.*

Vic's medallions swirled around his neck as he turned to face the assembled guests. "Friends," he said solemnly, "dear friends, welcome. Welcome into this—" with a sweep of his arm he took in the arbor, the chairs, and the holographic trees "—somewhat sacred place. In just a moment we will join this happy couple in eternal wedded bliss. But first if I may," he said slowly and imperiously, "a few words from the Book of Mirplo." He clicked open his Rabota with great ceremony, held it out before him like a scripture of substance, and began to read. "'And it came to pass,'" Vic read or recited in stentorian tones, "'that in the time of King—' well, his name's not important. 'In the time of this king the rains came not, and the crops grew sere, and the seeds grew riven and died. Neither a tenth part of the people survived, nor a tenth of a tenth, nor a tenth of a tenth of a tenth, and those who lived became wild men, savage and without grace, visiting violence and destruction upon foe and friend alike....'" He read on.

And on.

And on.

Where a spiritual verse or two might have been appropriate, some "to everything there is a season" sort of riff, Vic seemed intent on reading the entire body of a strange testament that no one had ever heard before. As faux scriptures go it went well enough, but *way* too long, with labored accounts of wars, prophecies, and visitations from the Lord on High. And while it had a beautiful, lyrical quality to it, what it had to do with a wedding was anyone's guess.

And, man, did it go on.

Radar and Allie didn't seem to mind. They just stood there with their eyes on each other, blind to the rest of the world. But the guests grew restive, the hired ones because that was part of their script and the randomly invited ones because, really, how long does it take to beat a dead horse?

Sitting alone on the aisle, Sarah was suddenly aware that Adam would never give her a moment like this. He lacked both the imagination and the whimsy, and the thought made her sad—and miffed. Who was she to Adam, after all? She thought about Jessup's confederacy with Ames. She wondered if Radar was right about that.

Was he right about the gun?

A tale emerged from Vic's narrative: the saga of a Chosen people (or Afflicted, depending on how you looked at it) who took all the adversity their God could throw at them and used it to wise up. Who they were, exactly, remained unclear—some lost tribe from somewhere—but as the story unspooled, they seemed over time to become more collaborative, more productive, more accepting, more enlightened. Some would say more hip. Still, it was a dense text, and it made for the sort of soporific sermonizing that puts parishioners to sleep on Sundays.

At a certain point, Ames and Jessup exchanged looks. Jessup's grimly set features made it clear that he regarded this delay as Adam's fault. Adam just looked a little green around the gills. Although Jessup had been his partner and coequal at first, the past few weeks had brought out his bully side. And that Custer getup—a little too militaristic for Adam's taste.

It was during a seemingly endless list of bogus begats that Kadyn started squirming in her seat. Genealogies never make for gripping prose to begin with, but she seemed to find this passage particularly infuriating, as if it were specifically delivered for her benefit or at her expense. She fidgeted, looking pissed, aggressively eyeballing Mirplo, trying by sheer force of will to shut him the hell up. At last she couldn't stand it anymore. She jumped to her feet and clumped in her sensible shoes down the aisle to the arbor, where she stood, truculent, with her hands on her hips. When this brought no reaction, she waved her hand in front of Vic's face, but he looked through her like a pane of cellophane and just kept droning on. She punched his shoulder. Nothing. Flicked his nose with her finger. Still nothing. At last, exasperated beyond patience, Kadyn said, "That'll do, Vic. We get the joke already. Religions are funny, ha-ha."

But Vic stayed right on his text. "…and Jasper begat Malachite and Malachite begat Larimar.…"

"Enough with the names, Vic!" said Kadyn. "Enough with the fricking Book of Mirplo! Just knock it off already, huh?"

"…and Mica begat Ruby and Ruby begat Jade.…"

Kadyn pushed her glasses up her nose. "Vic, we were never going to happen. I told you that but you didn't believe me." Her glasses slipped down. She pushed them up again. "We are not a thing. I don't love you. I don't even like you a lot. I only told you I did to keep you from freaking out completely, but we can all see that that didn't work."

"…and Gypsum begat Feldspar and Feldspar begat—"

"Vic, *basta!* This crypto-churchy bullshit is not going to change anything. So stop being a total douche and finish the wedding." Kadyn's glasses slipped down again. They wouldn't stay. "Ooh," she said, grabbing them off her face and hurling them away in frustration. "Last chance, Vic."

"And lo was born to Onyx and Umber the child Obsidian, also known as Snowflake."

Kadyn snarled, backed off three steps, bent at the waist, rushed Vic, and head-butted him in the gut. He went down and Kadyn jumped on top of him, straddling him and pummeling him with both fists. His tried to block her blows with his tablet, but she grabbed it and beat him with it till it broke. Enraged, he flipped her over, pinned her down... and kissed her hard. "That's sexual assault," she snarled. He kissed her again and her neck veins stood out as she suddenly strained to kiss him back.

This brought Jessup to his feet. "Get off of her!" the big man shouted. He ran up, pulled Vic from Kadyn and roughly tossed him aside.

Ames closed in as well, with his sidewheels right behind. Sarah edged closer, captivated by the tumult—during which tumult Allie slipped away, which is just the sort of thing a tumult is good for.

Mirplo got to his feet, straightening his dhoti and his chains and affecting a look of bruised dignity. Kadyn slumped into a wicker chair, panting, coming down off the surge of her fury. Jessup fronted Radar, his jaw clenched. "You don't think I know what this is? This is bullshit, this is a stall. And now it's over."

"We haven't finished the ceremony."

"Finish it later! Right now, we're goin' someplace quiet and talk money."

"Or what?" asked Radar, "You'll sic Adam's monkey men on me? Careful, I'll sic Kadyn on them." This elicited a wry, knowing smile from Jessup, which prompted Radar to say,

"Oh, shit."

"What?" asked Sarah. "Radar, what?"

"Oh, nothing," said Radar, downcast, "just your garden-variety double-cross."

"That's right," drawled Jessup. "Y'all thought you were puttin' Kadyn with me." He offered her his hand. She got to her feet and took a place by his side. "I saw it comin' a mile away, didn't I, darling? Offered her a better deal." Kadyn said nothing. Mirplo just looked gutshot. Jessup said to Radar, "But none of that matters now. Now we wrap up this ol' business once and for all."

"No," said Radar defiantly. "I'm walking away. Come on, Vic."

Jessup unholstered his gun.

"For the love of God!" shouted Sarah. "Don't shoot!" Jessup and Ames turned briefly to the sound of Sarah's hysteria, and when they looked back, Radar and Vic were running off through the hologram woods.

"What's the matter with you?" Ames yelled at Sarah.

"He could hurt someone. That's a real gun."

Ames gave her a dark glower, then chased after Radar and Vic, followed by Jessup and the sidewheels. After a moment, Sarah shrugged and went after them, her cedar chest tucked under her arm like a football.

All this time, Wellinov remained in his seat, unmoving and unmoved. Kadyn came over and sat down beside him. "Looks like they left us alone, Gramps."

"Do not dare to call me Gramps," he said jovially. But the lightness of his tone belied his inner disquiet.

Woody hoped his son would be all right.

29

Radar Fucking Hoverlander

The party was pulsing now, filled to fire-code trespass and fused by lights and trance music into a single, writhing, organic mass. It wasn't a hard crowd to get lost in, and Radar and Vic proceeded to do exactly this. They ducked into the *Betamax Viewing Room and Eight-Track Tape Exchange* and paused there to catch their breath. "You all right?" Radar asked. "Heart in one piece?"

"Just wish she'd picked up the pace some. I was running out of improv."

"Improv? You made all that up?"

"The whole thing. On the spot."

"Jeez, Vic."

"Don't worry, I taped it. Might be good for something someday. Now that I've finished my book."

"You finished your book?"

"Oh, yeah. Sent it to the publisher today." Off Radar's amazed look, Vic just spread his palms and said, "What? I had some free time."

Radar shook his head. "The Amazing Dr. Mirplo."

"Ever and always."

"Come on, let's go get found before their ire cools."

They moved to an open spot near the Midway and loitered there, looking as much like scared rabbits as two talented grifters intent on looking like scared rabbits can look. It wasn't long before they spotted Ames, Jessup, and the sidewheels moving through the crowd, scanning for them. Jessup wore an expression of implacable fury; Ames seemed to be almost twitching with anxiety.

"He's ticking," said Vic.

"Let's make him go boom."

With that, the two of them suddenly and provocatively panicked and took off running. Of course the motion caught Adam's eye. He and the others gave chase.

"So predictable," said Radar as they ran.

"Candles from babies," agreed Vic.

Vic and Radar raced past an installation called *Tulpenwoede,* a living model of the tulip mania of the Dutch Golden Age, where tonight hundreds of would-be tulip kings would ride its speculative bubble to riches or ruin. They ran on, past the Olestra and New Coke tasting party and the box wine bar. Outside the *I'm OK, You're OK Corral,* they almost trampled a pair of Siamese Trumps, and that's when Radar very convincingly tripped and went down. Vic looked back, and then he stumbled, too. By the time they righted themselves, Jessup and Ames were upon them, along with the sidewheels, who grabbed them and manhandled them out through a service door leading to the back of the house.

The sidewheels pushed Radar and Vic up against a wall. Jessup brought himself close, staring them down. His face was red and puffy from the effort of chasing them. Ames stood by, just watching, his control of the moment overwhelmed by the juggernaut of Jessup's rage. "Can we assume," growled Jessup, "that I am of serious intent? Can we assume that I'm the sort of man who will do what must be done?"

Radar said nothing. Vic squeaked, "We can."

"Okay, then. So now it's just a question of how hurt you want to be, and that's on a scale of none to all. Adam saw your money. He says there's a hundred grand, and that'll do me fine for a clusterfuck like this. So let's take a walk."

They took it: a short walk back to meeting room 23, where Vic pulled out his card key, opened the door, and did his level best to look shocked and amazed at the discovery that his cargo bag was gone.

"Wha—?" he said.

"Where's the money?" demanded Ames. "The vests. Where are they?"

"Well, gone," said Mirplo sadly, and with finality. "Gone with the wind."

"Or more precisely," added Radar, "with Wellinov."

"What do you mean?" asked Jessup.

"Vic gave him a card key."

"He's old," explained Vic. "He needed a place to chill. How was I to know he'd go walkabout?"

"How do we know this wasn't your plan all along?" asked Ames.

Jessup turned to his partner and asked in a cold voice, "And how do I know you ain't in on it?"

"What? Cal, no, that's ridiculous."

Jessup glared at Ames, and Radar saw the smaller man wilt under the Texan's threatening gaze. They saw Jessup's fist go up.

Just then Kadyn walked in. "Ease up, cowboy," she told Cal. "The money ain't gone far." She opened her library book and pulled out her Serengeti. "And who says I can't track it?"

"You GPSed his vest?" asked Radar, seemingly incredulous.

Kadyn hooked her arm in Jessup's. "All part of the service."

Jessup looked pleased. "Ain't she a pip?" He said to Kadyn, "Lead on, little gal." As Kadyn led the little group down the hall to the elevators, Jessup asked her, "How did you know the old guy took the money?"

"Oh, I told him to," she said brightly.

"What?" asked Ames, perplexed. "Why the hell would you do that?"

Jessup grabbed a fistful of Adam's Joker coat. "Y'all don't use that tone of voice, hear?" He released Ames and turned back to Kadyn. "Just the same, honey...."

"The money was in their control." She indicated Radar and Vic. "I thought it'd be better off in ours."

Jessup nodded. "Makes sense. You're a smart young filly."

"I am, ain't I?"

"Modest, too. But full of good ideas."

"Speaking of which," she said, "here's one you're gonna love." She leaned up to whisper in Jessup's ear.

Jessup listened at length and then said, "Yep, indeed I do." He turned to the sidewheels and said, "Come here you boys, I got a job for you."

"Hey," said Adam, "those are my guys."

"And you don't mind lendin' 'em to me, do you?" Jessup's tone dared Ames to cross him, and he backed down. Then Jessup said something to the men in a low voice. They nodded and briskly walked away.

Kadyn, meanwhile, had come to a halt in front of the service elevators. She was looking at her tablet with a perplexed expression. "I don't get it," she said. "According to the GPS, he should be right around here." She contemplated the reading for another moment, then snapped her fingers. "Of course!" she said. "Right place, wrong height." She summoned an elevator, and in a moment they were heading down to the bottom level of the underground parking garage. There they found a utility door propped open. It led to the convention center's engineering space and physical plant. Kadyn glanced at her GPS and said without looking up, "He's in there."

"Well," said Cal, "let's go give 'im a howdy."

They walked the length of an industrial space lined with repair bays and equipment rooms. At its dead end they found a small vestibule surrounded by chain-link cages in which thrummed giant air conditioning compressors. In the middle of the vestibule lay the cargo bag.

With Sarah kneeling beside it, rifling its contents.

She turned at the sound of their footsteps, stood, and said, "God, there you are! I've been looking all over for you!" Then she held her nose and gave the cargo bag a big thumbs down. "That's a waste. There's no money in there."

Said Adam, "But the vests—"

"Oh, the vests are packed with phony baloney. See for yourself."

Adam dropped to his knees and inspected the pockets of both vests, finding nothing but a bounty of banking slips. "But I saw...." He stopped. "Oh." He looked at Radar. "You?"

"Us," acknowledged Radar. "The ol' switcheroo."

"But how?"

"The eyes play tricks," said Vic with a shrug. "So do reversible vests."

Ames stood up. "Well, that's that, Cal. There's no money."

"Is that right?" said Jessup. He pushed his cavalry hat back on his head, evidently not buying anything he was being sold. He asked Sarah, "Darlin', how did you get down here?"

"Well, after you guys ditched me," she said petulantly, "I wandered out. I thought maybe you were having another meeting in that meeting room. So I went looking. That's when I saw what's-his-name wheeling the bag down the hall. He went down in the elevator and came in here. I was chicken to go in after him, so I waited. After a minute he came out without the bag."

"Where did he go?"

"How should I know? I didn't follow him, duh. It looked like he stashed the cash in here so he could come back for it later." She kicked the cargo bag. "But like I said, phony baloney. It was like a, what, a decoy like."

"A GPS wild goose," muttered Kadyn. "Okay, that's one for you, old man."

Ames picked up one of the vests and shook it at Radar. "Where is the money?"

"You mean the money we showed you twice and then romanced out the building?"

"That was a bad mistake," said Ames. "You shouldn't have done that."

"Oh, here's a thought," said Radar calmly. "Why don't we just say 'good game' and all go home? You tried to play us and it didn't work out, so, 'good game,' all go home. Hell, I'll even eat the cost of the shindig."

Jessup said, "Nah, buddy, I know horseshit when I smell it, and I'm smellin' a powerful load of Flicka's finest right now." His eyes narrowed. He said to Radar, "I want the damn money."

"Will you settle for sixty seconds of straight talk?"

Jessup considered this. Finally, he said, "No promises. Speak your peace."

"Okay." Radar sighed. "Here's what I think. At some point in the past, Adam Ames somehow got on Allie's and my trail. Maybe just Allie's, maybe just mine, I don't know, but whatever, he took it into his head to take us down. It wouldn't be hard to figure we had cash. So he set up a Texas Twist, with a bogus allocation board as its centerpiece and you as his beard. Only problem is, Adam picked the wrong partner: a hard guy who'd insist on getting paid whether the play panned out or not. Then he was stuck, because you could squeeze him but he couldn't squeeze me. So all he could do was roll through the Twist and hope for the best, but he's not very good and he gummed it up. And now here we are, stuck in the fantasy world grifters live in, where a half-billion-dollar promise puts a few hundred grand in play. Only it's not a few hundred, it's only fifty." Radar picked up one of the vests and idly peeled back the black sheath, showing the harlequin camouflage. "I made it look like twice as much, but that was just to get under Adam's skin." He looked at Ames. "Sorry, dude, I like getting under skin." He turned back to Jessup. "The point is, are we going to fight over fifty grand? When we've already dropped the get from the lofty heights of half a billion? Could we be that desperate for a score? I'm not, but I didn't know about you. So instead of fifty grand, I dialed it all the way down to zero. Wellinov's gone. The money is gone. We're sensible men, yeah? We don't fight over zero."

Jessup looked Radar up and down. "You think you're pretty swift, don't you?"

"I have my moments."

"Maybe you do at that." He turned to Ames and said with a contemptuous half laugh, "Shithead. You bought the same damn money twice." He turned back to Radar. "What'd you call me? A hard guy? I guess I am. I guess I do aim to get paid no matter what. And let me tell you something about little ol' Austin. It ain't as friendly as it sells itself to be. Kind of a locals-only place, when all's said and done." He hooked a thumb at Ames. "This Yankee asshat screwed up, coming into my town, thinking he could make a score. But guess what, son? You made the same mistake."

"I'm no threat to you, Cal," said Radar. "I work out of state."

"Maybe so, but even so," and now the threat in his voice was clear, "fellow comes onto my turf, he pays to get off."

"Blood from a stone," said Radar. "There's no money here for you."

Jessup contemplated this for a moment, then seemed to

take the conversation in a different direction. "About y'all's wedding," he said. "I'm real sorry that got interrupted." He eyed Kadyn narrowly. "And, darling, you and me's gonna have a long conversation later about why that happened."

"Cal—"

"No, you be quiet now." He turned back to Radar. "Thing is, I never got to see the ring. I heard it was a real beaut. Suppose I take a look at it now."

"No need for that," said Radar. "It's paste, pure dime store. Part of the playact. I'll get Allie a real one later."

Jessup put up his hands in mock surrender. "Fine," he said. "I'll believe it's a fake if that's what you want. But we both know it's not, don't we? Oh, it's not the crown jewel you made it out to be—Savransky cut, whatever the hell that is—but it's easily worth that fifty grand you think I won't fight over." Jessup fired off another denigrating grin at Ames. "This one here," he said, "he bought that it was a fake. I wanted to see if you would, too, and if you did would you tell him. When you didn't, that told me how to play you. Now give me back my ring."

"You're blowing smoke, Cal. Adam's going to end up disrespecting you. We all know that ring's a fake, but it kind of has sentimental value now. If I let you have it, the little woman will have my hide."

"It's okay, Radar," said a voice nearby. "The little woman says okay."

It was Allie.

Radar turned to see her standing at the head of the vestibule, with the sidewheels blocking the exit behind her. Adam and Sarah exchanged looks; they hadn't seen this coming. As for Allie, she just smiled a wan smile and said to Radar, "You're totally not hurt, aren't you, bub?"

"Of course I'm not hurt. Why would I be?"

Radar turned to Jessup, his eyes flashing with anger. "You sent them to kidnap her, you son of a bitch. That doesn't work for me. Not here, not anywhere."

Radar balled his fists and took a step toward Jessup, but Jessup just laughed. "Nobody kidnapped anyone," he said. "They told her a story is all. Ain't my fault if she bought it. Now give me the ring."

"No way."

"Radar," said Allie, "come on, be smart. It's time to cut losses."

Vic chimed in, "She's right, Radar. It's just a thing. Since when do you care about things?"

Radar seemed to be parsing his thoughts. After a moment's inner struggle, he shrugged and said, "What the hell." He pulled the ring out of his pocket and tossed it to Jessup, who snatched it out of the air and stashed it in his buckskins.

"All right," said Jessup, "that's that with that." He turned to Ames. "Now there's just you."

"Just me what?"

"You need a ticket out of town, carpetbagger. And that's gonna cost you."

Reverting to his true-believer stance, Adam said slowly, "Look, I don't quite understand what's going on around here, apart from…clearly I've trusted the wrong people."

"That's how you're gonna play it?" asked Jessup. "Really? Dickweed, that candy-ass Boy Scout image might work for them but it sure as shit don't work for me."

"It's the truth," said Ames plaintively. "I thought I could do some good around here, but I see I'm in over my head. You say I've violated some 'locals-only' code, I apologize. But I can't buy my way out. I don't have any money. I never did."

Sarah started, "You have that—"

Adam cut her off, "That's not your department." His eyes darted from face to face. He looked like he could feel walls closing in around him. He suddenly turned to his sidewheels and ordered, "You two: Take care of this."

But they just stood there.

"Oh, what've we got here?" drawled Jessup. "Looks like your ol' boys don't hop to for you no more. Seems maybe they ain't yours after all."

"But I hired them," Ames protested.

"Guess I hired 'em more," said Jessup.

"And there goes your leverage," said Radar.

"Not all of it," said Ames. He slipped his hand inside his Joker coat and pulled out a gun. Radar recognized it instantly as a Walther P22.

Sarah let out a little "eek" and sagged back against the chain-link enclosure.

But Radar just calmly moved forward and stood in front of Ames.

"Radar," said Ames fiercely, "don't make me shoot."

"Shoot if you want to," said Radar. "You might hurt my ears but that's all. I know what kind of gun that is. I know where you got it. I know the day you bought it."

"How—?" The penny dropped. Adam's shoulders sagged. "Kadyn."

"Yes, Kadyn," she said brightly. "Kadyn playing kissyface with Wellinov. Kadyn giving Cal here such good advice. And Kadyn getting shirty with Vic—all part of the stall." She turned to Jessup. "We can have whatever conversation you like, Cal." She took Vic's hand. "But my part of the chat starts and ends right here."

"So let's have the toy," said Radar to Ames, who was now so rattled by all the reversals and revelations that he made no effort to stop Radar taking it away. Radar examined it carefully. "Not gaffed," he said. "Guess you didn't know how to do that. Though why a supposedly upright citizen like you should need a gun, even a fake one, is a bit of a mystery to me. I don't suppose you'd care to shed a light on that. Or explain why you have those pictures of us on your tablet. And before you ask again, yes, Kadyn. Again."

"I don't know what pictures you're talking about," said Ames. "I don't know who or what you think I am, but clearly you're all just delusional."

Blam! The report of Jessup's vintage revolver assaulted their ears as he fired through the chain-link fence and down alongside one of the AC units. "Tired of this crap," said Cal. The gun barrel smoked, and the acrid scent of combusted black powder filled the air. "Nothing but crap since the moment I met you." He leveled the gun at Ames. "Tell the man what he wants to know."

"Why should I?"

"Because I'm curious, too," said Jessup. "Curious and ornery." He cocked the gun. "Talk!" Sarah screamed and covered her head. Adam dropped to his knees. "Okay, okay! Shit! Christ! Allie!" He looked up and looked around for her.

She met his eyes and found them hard. "It's your fault. All yours."

"What, because I shot you down at some show?"

"That wasn't all of it. You know it wasn't. There was the bus. The…other thing. You humiliated me. In fact, you did it every chance you got."

"What?"

Ames stood up. "I watched you work, you know. I followed your career. I knew you were good. I wanted to be with you. I wanted to be your friend. But you kept me away. Every time I came around, you turned on your force field and drove me away."

"I did that to everyone! What the hell is the matter with you?"

"I was in love with you. I could have been good for you. I knew I just needed a chance. So I kept my eye on you."

"For how long?"

"Off and on all along."

The creepiness factor of this hit Allie like a fist. "Oh, God," she said. She almost fainted and fell, but Kadyn held her up.

Adam's eyes flashed. "Then you started running with this one, Radar Fucking Hoverlander, king of all cons, and now you two go around proving over and over again how smart and clever you are. Along with the Marvelous Mirplo, who has his head shoved so far up his own ass that he can't see what a fool he is."

Mirplo didn't respond. He knew exactly what a fool he was, but he didn't want to distract Ames. The valve was open. The truth was coming out.

"I watched. Yes, I watched. I thought about the payback you deserved. Then I ran into Sarah, running her pathetic sick-kid scam."

Sarah was affronted "Pathetic? Hey, Jason and I had a good thing going."

"Don't you mean Jonah?" asked Radar.

"Jason, Jonah, same difference. His real name is Bobby. I borrow him from a friend." She looked at Ames and harrumphed. "And we were doing just fine until you came along. How I ever let you talk me into your twisted little revenge trip, I do not know. And why? Because Radar got the girl you wanted? You want to know who's pathetic? You, that's who."

"Okay," Radar told Ames. "It's done. You're done. Whatever you were aiming for, you missed. So now you disappear and you are never heard from again. If you can fix your obsession, that'll be great. If you can't, you'd better teach it to keep its distance. Because if I ever see it again, I will end you."

Adam spat his contempt. "Oh, you could do that, Radar—"

"*Yes,* Radar Fucking Hoverlander can do that. Try him and find out." Radar turned to leave. "Come on," he said to the others. "Let's go." To his manifest surprise, the sidewheels did not step aside for him. He looked back and saw Jessup's gun.

Now it was pointing at him.

30

Curiosity

Radar Fucking Hoverlander," said Ames. "This is just great." He stood with his hands in the air. They all did, at Jessup's demand. "You double-crossed us both right into the shitter."

Radar shook his head sadly. "See, this is just where I didn't want to be. I hate it when the guns come out."

"Makes you rethink your stand on that fifty K, don't it?" said Jessup. Radar just nodded. "Well, I'll collect that in due time. Meanwhile…" he poked the gun barrel in Adam's chest, "your time for making good choices is about run out. Now where's your money?"

"I don't have any money."

Jessup cocked the gun.

"Don't!" cried Sarah, fumbling with her Pandora's box. "It's at the coat check! Come on, he's pathetic, but don't make a mess of him!" With trembling hands, Sarah unlocked the chest and withdrew a numbered plastic disc. She handed it to Jessup. As he flipped it like a coin, he nodded to a side-wheel, who nodded back—and kicked Adam's legs out from under him.

Then did the same thing to Radar.

Jessup stood over them and said, "From my point of view you're both punks, and that's because neither of you has the stones to do what needs to be done. Radar, you might—defending your brood and whatnot. But you, Ames, you're a cartoon. I had to keep from laughing all along. So I come out of this half-respecting Radar, and that means you keep clear of him. Because I come out of this not respecting you at all, and if Radar won't end you, trust me, I will." He turned to Radar. "Fifty grand in my hands by tomorrow, or I come lookin'. Do we have an understanding?"

"We do."

"Good. I reckon it's a small enough price to pay." He addressed his men. "Hold 'em a while, then let 'em go." He looked at Kadyn. "You sure had me going, sugar belle," he said, seemingly smiling at his own vanity. "Still, all's fair, I guess." He tipped his hat to her, then turned back to Radar and Adam one last time. "Remember, boys: 'Round these parts, locals only. Oh, and by the way...."

Blam!

He fired the gun again, right at them, point blank. They screamed and fell back. Jessup chuckled. "That's how you sell a gun that shoots blanks." Jessup stepped between the sidewheels, who closed in behind him to form a fourth wall.

Allie ran to Radar and held him. Kadyn buried herself in Vic's arms. Ames shook uncontrollably.

"Shit," said Radar, staggering to his feet. "Holy shit, shit!

I just got not shot!" He looked at Ames, wide-eyed. "You just did, too! Man! Dude! How do you feel about that?"

"I don't know."

"Me personally, I feel pretty damn shocked."

"A gun in the face sheds a certain light," observed Mirplo.

"That it does," said Radar. "Wow." He looked at Ames. "Makes you think about fights not worth fighting." He seemed to be sorting out a thought, deciding whether to voice it. Finally, he said, "So: New light, clean slate, arm's length, yeah?"

Ames blinked. He blinked again. "Yeah," he said, slackjawed.

Radar helped Adam to his feet. "And that's a meeting of the minds. Get your shit straight, Ames, and get the hell out of Dodge." He turned to Sarah. "You should go with."

"I don't know," said Sarah. "I didn't end up with any money at all. Or rings or anything. And he used me, *and* he called me pathetic. I think I should be really mad at him."

"Rethink that," said Radar. "You called him pathetic, too. Could be you're birds of a feather. No need to hold a grudge, right?"

Sarah contemplated this. "I guess," she said. She looked at Ames. "I mean if you guess, too."

Adam nodded numbly. In his current state of mind he'd go along with anything.

"Okay, then." Radar turned to the sidewheels. "You understand what's going on here. We're going to leave now and they're going to leave later. Everything's cool, as you see." The big dogs exchanged looks, then let Radar, Allie, Vic, and Kadyn pass by. Radar didn't look back. He never saw Adam or Sarah again.

Later Radar would say that his detente with Adam had nothing to do with a gun in his face and everything to do with locking Ames into a new reality where no thoughts of Radar or Allie need ever more trouble his mind. Reality, he knew, was contagious. That's why he'd made Jessup's gun real to Sarah: so that she, in turn and in the critical moment, would make it real to Ames. When the gun went off, Adam broke, and this was Radar's design all along, the application of sufficient pressure to deliver the two things he needed: understanding of why Ames had attacked them; expectation that it wouldn't happen again.

And that's called buttoning up the mark.

It would have been a much different story without Cal Jessup—Radar's ace in the hole.

He'd known from the start that Jessup was on the razzle. How could he not be? That allocation board was always the phoniest of phony baloney, a manifest transparency that Adam, Radar, and Jessup each went along with for reasons of their own.

And when it turned out that Jessup knew Woody....

They'd recognized each other instantly, back at their first encounter in Adam's office. Each had been slick enough to keep that fact to himself; however, Woody remembered Jessup warmly from a con he'd once run that had required the tools of a tough Texan, and Jessup recalled Woody as good folks and fine company. He eagerly teamed up with Hoverlander *père et fils*, and from that point forward it was game over for Ames.

Just the same, a gun in the face, even a scripted one

shooting blanks, will shift a man's outlook, even Radar's, and even when he'd scripted it and knew it was coming. When that gun went off, his life changed forever. You could say that he buttoned himself up. In that instant, he left the game for good. It wasn't a matter of keeping his family out of harm's way. Harm, Radar knew, had a way of finding its own way. It was just knowing that he'd outgrown the grift. It was time to do better than that. With the others' blessing, he even donated to a legitimate charity the legitimate get from the fest. Between admission fees, Midway gaffs, auction items, food, drink, and diversions (plus some scams that the guests wouldn't really figure out until later) it was plenty. And giving it away felt great.

Not that there wasn't a payday, for Adam proved a mook after all. Uncertain how the money-go-round would play out, he had in fact shown up on the night with substantial true green, two hundred grand in a FedEx box left at coat check. Split six ways it wasn't a huge take for anyone, but no one complained, for they all got other value. Kadyn won the experience she craved, a blitz introduction to a new career in which her manifest gifts could grow. That she'd also bagged a Mirplo was just a bonus for them both. Allie would always cherish the snuke as the one that saw her off into parenthood and very different adventures. And for Woody it had been a chance to run one last script with his son. Now he looked forward to playing the grandfather card.

For Radar Hoverlander, money was a burden no more. It could bankroll a straight play or maybe a baby's college fund, but it meant nothing in and of itself. It was just how you kept score, and there's no need to keep score in a game that you've already won.

On a stunningly sunny August afternoon, in forested hills above Puget Sound, Allie got her woodsy wedding at last. She stood radiantly blimpy beneath an arbor of lily vines and white roses and accepted the Savransky-cut true diamond ring that Radar had given to Jessup to give to Ames but really all along planned to give her. Woody gave the bride away and Boy was best dog. Vic officiated, but he left the Book of Mirplo at home, for the world, he'd decided, was not yet prepared. He ratified the couple's union, congratulated them on their good judgment in choosing each other, and blessed their journey into the future they'd share.

He would not be sharing it with them. Mirplo was hitting the road, off to see all the Perus and Katmandus he'd never seen so far. Kadyn was hitting it with him. How they would make their living remained to be seen, but Radar had a hunch that work permits and tax returns would not figure in.

Afterward, at the reception, Mirplo marveled at Allie's belly out to here, and wondered if she and Radar were still playing the name game.

"No, we've settled that," she said. "If it's a boy, Woody. If it's a girl—"

"—when it's a girl," said Radar.

"*If* it's a girl," Allie repeated, "Curiosity."

"I knew it!" cried Vic. "It's what I predicted all along!"

"Oh, did you?"

"You'll see. You'll see when my book comes out. Anyway, great choice, awesome choice. Curiosity Hoverlander. Sounds like the name of a detective."

"It does, now doesn't it?" said Radar.

And his eyes went to a faraway place.

THE END

Next: Radar and Curiosity Hoverlander team up as father-daughter detectives in The Seattle Straddle.

Afterword

Off the Snuke

People ask me all the time, "JV, are you a con artist?" By which they usually mean, *'Cause if you're not, you sure know a lot about that world.* Okay, let me state for the record that I, personally, am not a con artist. I know that's exactly what you'd expect a con artist to say, and there's not much I can do about that, by the logic of *Only a witch would deny being a witch.* But what can I tell you? The cons I've invented—the ones I hold dear to my heart, like the Doolally shorthair terrier scam or the Visine gag—are ones I *wish* I had the balls to pull off. No, dear friends, I exist in the world of my imagining. I find that it's safer that way.

But come on, admit it—you're fascinated, too. I mean, duh—I know you are because here you are at the end of a book about cons. But it goes deeper than that. When you read a story about just some audacious scam—your *Hitler*

Diaries, your *Catch Me if You Can*—don't you think, *Who would get into that line of work?* You know that you wouldn't. You'd be too scared. And maybe too moral.

Others share not your compunctions.

Just today I get a phone call from a teenage stranger who tells me in a hoarse voice that he's "my oldest grandson" who's been sick, so that's why he doesn't sound like him. Can you guess where he's going with this? Seems last night he was out driving with some friends—*You know those crazy friends of mine, Grandpa*—and got into a teeny tiny accident. Well, he'd been drinking a little, so now he's in jail, hoping "Grandpa Duffy" can throw some cash at the owner of the other car and make this whole thing go away.

Of course "Grandpa Duffy" was a dead giveaway, because that's my wife's surname, not mine, but who wouldn't see through this from the start? You would, right? I think most people would. Yet there must be enough profit in this scheme to keep people trying it. I strung the guy along for five or ten minutes before he realized I was messing with him and clicked off. Most of the time he just gets hung up on, I'm sure. Every now and then he gets a nibble, but can he land the fish? That has to be a victim clueless enough to buy the caller's fake panic, yet together enough to, you know, have cash. Do people like that abound? They can't *abound.*

The thing I think about most attempted cons is they're just colossal wastes of time. But let's take somebody who cooks up one of these grand scams—a multi-million-dollar pyramid, let's say. That's a job that takes time, effort, planning, organization, infrastructure, collaboration, *seed money,* and sales—tons and tons of sales. It's a *business,* muthafucka, and

I just have to ask, if you have what it takes to launch and run a successful scam, couldn't you apply those same tools to something legit?

Maybe the part I don't get—the part I can only comprehend in the world of my imagining—is that it's not about the money for these guys. It's about *getting over* on their fellow man. They take joy in ripping people off, satisfaction in proving they're better than you. In my book, that's called *sociopath*. Okay, so that's what they are, and that's what I'm not.

At least I *think* I'm not. Here I am, cooking up these cruelties to inflict on innocent people, things I know I'd never do in the real world. *Steal* from someone? Strip-mine some senior's savings account? I can't even imagine it. Except that I *can* imagine it, and I'm lucky enough to do just that for a living. Which begs the question: If JV's not a con artist, yet he represents himself as an authority on con artists, doesn't that make him something of a...con artist?

Oops, yeah, kind of it does.

So here's where we get to the intersection of invention and morality. I mean, like all novelists, I lie for a living. So do con artists. What's the difference between us? We do it to entertain; they do it to steal.

Which is why I used this novel to get Radar off the snuke. I invented him to entertain; I could no longer stand that he'd steal. Sure, he tries to justify it, with phrases like *metaphorical reacharound* and *verbal prostate massage*, and he rationalizes that crossing paths with him isn't the worst thing that could happen to a mook. But I don't buy it. Never have, really. If you want to be moral, be moral, Radar. Quit screwing around and get right with the world.

You might be thinking, *Hang on, now, JV. I've read all the Radar novels (or at least this one) and he seems to be doing things for a worthy cause. Self-defense, if nothing else. What's wrong with self-defense?* Nothing, friend, nothing at all. But you don't know Radar like I know Radar. You only see his stories—stories designed by me to protect him from your disapproval.

But he's never escaped mine.

Isn't that a weird thing? And what a discovery to make after already having lived with the guy for a quarter of a million words. Don't get me wrong: I like and love Radar Hoverlander. I admire that he can "read lips, pick pockets, pick locks, run a six-minute mile, and build a car or disable its engine." I just never liked what he stood for. And he never liked it, either. In a sense, he's been fighting against his nature since page one of book one. And trying to explain it away. So his inner conflict is my inner conflict. He's as fascinated by the world of cons as I am. He's always wondered if he was as good as the game, and always wanted to prove that he was. Even while knowing that the game itself was no good.

It took me three novels to get Radar off the snuke, but now that he's out, he's out for keeps. He recognizes that his talents, cleverness, and bent perspective are "powerful tools that can only be used for good or for evil." He's determined to use them for good. Up next, then, *The Seattle Struddle,* in which Radar becomes a detective. Working with his daughter, no less. I'm very excited by that. Now he can use his massive mental dexterity for good works *and* good parenting. No moral ambiguity there.

I wonder if that will be a problem. Maybe a Radar Hoverlander without inner tension just falls apart, or isn't worth looking at. Nah. That won't be a problem. He'll have a little girl for a partner. That'll keep his hands full.

Honestly, I have no idea what the next novel will be about. I want to advance Curiosity's age to the point where she can be an effective girl detective. But what age is that? If she's a Hoverlander, she's bound to be precocious; I feel I can start her as early as I like. That said, though, if I advance her timeline even a few years, I'll get out ahead of the present day, and have to start thinking of my tales in some *world of the future* context, maybe even a sci-fi one. Or, no, probably I won't. Radar is witty enough to manipulate his reality; I'm half-witty enough to manipulate mine.

For the record, I always make this shit up as I go along. Some writers don't. The smart writers, I'd say, map their moves out way in advance. That never worked for me; if I know too much about where the story's going, I lose my desire to follow. So I'm forever treating my novels as puzzles where I'm simultaneously creating the pieces and trying to make them fit. It's not an efficient process. No more efficient than trolling for senile grandparents by phone. I guess I do it because it gets me off, and I guess at the end of the day that's why the con guys do what they do, too. So join me in *The Seattle Straddle,* and we'll discover together what Radar and Curiosity are up to next.

Thank you for reading this book. Sincerely. With your support I can continue to live in the world of my imagining, creating devious traps for Radar to stumble into and think his way out of (now with the help of his clever and cunning little girl!). While meanwhile the real world stays safely out of range of my nature's dark side. It's for the best. I know it is. Otherwise, heck, I might have to be a con artist for real.

—Southern California
February 2013

About the Author

JOHN VORHAUS first introduced the charming con man Radar Hoverlander in the novel *The California Roll,* followed by *The Albuquerque Turkey.* When not spinning such yarns, he travels the world teaching and training writers—twenty-nine countries on five continents at last count. His many non-fiction works include the *Killer Poker* series and the best-selling comedy writing text *The Comic Toolbox: How to Be Funny Even if You're Not.*